OPERATION: RUNNING BROOK

A SAM BARRETT THRILLER

THE SAM BARRETT OPS
BOOK 1

KA BIGGERSTAFF

By

KA Biggerstaff

OPERATION: Running Brook (2nd Edition), KA Biggerstaff. Copyright © 2026

This book first published in 2022

kab@kabiggerstaff.com

www.kabiggerstaff.com

Cover art by

Ivan Zanchetta & Bookcoversart.com

Ebook ISBN: 979-8-9900297-8-1

Paperback ISBN: 979-8-9900297-7-4

KAB-BAK Co.

❀ Formatted with Vellum

1

———————

Her eyelids fluttered open to a blinding light. As she put her hand up to block the light, the sounds became clearer.

"Welcome back." The voice came from in front of her. "How do you feel?"

She tried to sit up, but as she rose, her head began to throb.

"Easy does it." He nodded to another person in the room, the lights dimmed some, and the man continued speaking. "You have quite a bump on your head and a slight concussion. I'm Dr. Thomas. Can you tell me your name?"

Trying to focus and think, it took her a minute to answer. "Um, it's... uh... Jaime. Where am I?" she said, saying the first name that came to her mind—but that wasn't her name. It was Sam, but she didn't want him to know that. At least not until she knew where she was and what happened to her.

"City Memorial Hospital. Jaime, can you tell me what day it is?" Dr. Thomas said.

Again, she took her time in answering. "Tuesday?" she guessed because she had no idea.

"Actually, it's Wednesday. Do you know what city?"

"Uh." She placed a hand to her forehead. "No," she admitted.

"It's okay. You are in Austin, Texas. Do you know what happened? What brought you here?"

Sam thought for a few moments and replied that she didn't. She was suddenly aware that her left foot was in a walking cast.

"What's wrong with my foot?" she asked.

"You have a distal fibula fracture and some strained ligaments. Luckily, it doesn't require any surgery, just that walking cast for about four to eight weeks. I want you to stay off it for three days or so. We'll give you a set of crutches. Elevate it when possible for the first few days. How's the pain, on a scale of one to ten, ten being the worst?" the doctor asked.

"About a seven," she replied.

Dr. Thomas turned to the nurse and began speaking to her. Sam looked around the room. *I'm in a hospital, but how did I get here?*

"Where were you born?"

"Italy."

The doctor smiled. "Good. What's your favorite food?"

"Pizza."

"What's your full name?"

"What's with all the questions?" she asked.

"I'm determining how your memory has been affected by the bump on your head. What's your full name?"

"Jaime Sommers."

He crossed his arms and shifted his weight. "I watched television too."

He didn't seem to believe her but continued. "Where did you go to high school?"

She hesitated and narrowed her eyes at him.

"Do you remember where you went to high school, Jaime?" he asked again.

"Yes." *I just don't like talking about my past. It's nobody's business.*

"Would you tell me, please? Everything you tell me is confidential."

"Aviano Air Base," she said.

"So, were your parents military?"

Sam was getting tired of these questions. She'd put her childhood behind her years ago and didn't want to talk about it. "Not necessarily, and you don't need to know that. Just give me some pain pills and I'll be on my way." A sudden bout of nausea came over her, and she hopped off the exam table and opened the lid of the silver can she saw near the wall. Dr. Thomas and the nurse grabbed her arms to support her as she retched in the can.

Dr. Thomas said, "Since you have a concussion with some memory loss and nausea, I'd like to keep you here overnight for observation. Your memory loss is most likely temporary. Retrograde amnesia. You remember your past, but not the accident or trauma that caused your amnesia. Also, the police are on their way since you may have been mugged. You'll have to give them your real name. You have some abrasions on your hands and face, but you'll be fine."

"Is it really necessary for me to stay?" Sam asked as the nurse gave her a cup of water and a paper towel from a nearby sink.

"Well, do you have someone you can stay with? I'd like for someone to keep an eye on you in case you develop any more symptoms, like more nausea, dizziness—or if your memory doesn't get any better."

"Yes, I can call a friend," she lied.

"You remember a friend you can call? What's the friend's name?"

"Christine Chapel."

At first he looked like he believed her. Then his face changed. "You don't have to lie to me. Are those your favorite television shows? That's the nurse's name from *Star Trek*, and Jaime Sommers is the Bionic Woman. You're quick with your answers, I'll give you that. Is anything you told me the truth?"

"Yes. I was born in Italy and went to school there."

"What's the last thing you remember?"

Sam thought and searched for something to tell him. "Running. I remember running."

"Running away from someone?"

"No. Not like that. It was... an obstacle course. I was running an obstacle course."

"Where was the course? Why were you running it?"

More about her past. *Some college, but I didn't have permission to be on the course.* "I'm done answering questions. Will my memory return?"

"Most likely. You need to stay here and rest. The police will help you figure out what happened. They'll probably run your fingerprints and maybe put your picture in the paper."

Sam immediately glared at him. *No photos. I can't have my photo taken.*

"*No!*" she said in a raised voice. "I'm sorry, Doc. I just don't like hospitals. A relative..." She didn't finish the sentence. "Just let me leave. I'll be fine."

"Where will you go?" Dr. Thomas asked. "We can call social services."

"Hell, no! I live at 432 North Starlight Drive," she said quickly. Taking a deep breath she calmed down and said, "See I remember that. I can take care of myself." *I've been taking care of myself since I was sixteen.* Sam had no idea if the address was real or not. She didn't think it was but wasn't about to go to a shelter or wherever they'd send her.

"All right, but I'd like to consult with a neurologist, and you need to wait for the police. The nurse will bring anti-nausea meds. Take them as needed. Take acetaminophen, like Tylenol, for the pain in your ankle. There's also some paper-work to fill out. Do the best you can with it. Again, if your pain persists, you have any more dizziness, nausea, or more memory problems, come back or see your personal physician. Since you insist on leaving, there's a discharge form for leaving against medical advice. Please wait here, okay?"

"Yes, thank you very much," she said.

As Dr. Thomas left, the nurse continued typing on the computer attached to a rolling cart. After a moment, she looked at Sam and said she'd be back.

Sam acknowledged her and began taking inventory of herself and the room she was in. She was wearing a navy-blue polo shirt, which was slightly wrinkled, tactical cargo pants, and... *Where are my shoes?* A chair was in the corner, and underneath it was a pair of black boots. Not fashion boots, but the kind law enforcement or military would wear. They were six inches and zipped on the side. Her clothes and boots had some dirt on them, as if she had fallen. *Was I mugged?* For some reason, that didn't seem quite right. *But I was running. No, being chased? From what or who?* Something was nagging at her. She just couldn't remember.

The nurse returned with a pair of crutches and placed the anti-nausea meds and a pain pill on the tray next to the bed. A cup and a container of water were already there.

"As Dr. Thomas said, take one pill as needed for the nausea." She handed her a piece of paper with instructions for postconcussive care. "You may want to wear sunglasses because of light sensitivity. You can use these for now." She gave her some flimsy dark glasses like an ophthalmologist would hand out. "Do you have any questions?" the nurse asked her.

Yes, a bunch, but you can't answer them. "No. Yes. How long have I been here, and did I have any personal items when I came in?" Sam asked her.

"At least a couple of hours. Your phone is in that bag, along with anything else you had. Here's the paperwork we need you to fill out for your discharge." She handed Sam a clipboard with multiple papers on it and a black pen. "Take your time. I'll be back to check on you in a little while."

I need to get out of here. I do not like hospitals—that much I know. As the nurse turned and left the room, Sam leaned over and reached for the large clear bag on the small table next to her exam bed. Inside was a phone, but it wasn't what she'd expected. It was an old-school flip phone. Besides the phone, she found a zip ID case. Inside was a ten-dollar bill but no identification, credit cards, or anything else. *If it was a mugging, why didn't they take the cash? Maybe they were interrupted before they could grab it. Or maybe it was in a pocket and not in the case.* She began searching all her pockets, but the results were nil.

Sam grabbed the ID case and the phone and stuffed them in her cargo pockets. Nothing else was in the room or the bag. She slid off the exam table and carefully made her way across the room to the chair. The walking cast was going to take some getting used to. Sitting in the chair, she looked underneath at the boots and found a pair of black socks. Quickly, Sam put on the right sock and boot. Even though the boot zipped on the side, it still had laces, and she tied them. She grabbed the other boot and sock and placed them in the plastic bag. Looking around the room, she saw a wardrobe for clothes that was empty except for a few hangers. Nothing else of importance. She remembered the pills and shoved the bottle into her front pocket. "I'm going to need a backpack," Sam said to herself as she grabbed the crutches.

With one last look around, she opened the door and peered out into the hall. No sign of the nurse, but she saw the doctor talking to some cops further down the hall. *Time to beat feet.* Taking a deep breath, she left the room and followed an exit sign toward an elevator. Once Sam had hobbled over, she pushed the down button. After what seemed like an eternity, a bell rang, and the elevator door opened.

As she got into the elevator, a man asked, "What floor?"

"One, please," replied Sam.

The elevator stopped once more then finally arrived on the first floor. She left the elevator—once again, she looked for the exit and made her way down the hall toward it. The floor was busy with doctors, nurses, and patients, making it easy to just limp out the main door and onto the street.

The question now was which way to go. Sam looked around and saw a coffee shop across the street, about fifty yards to the left. *Looks like a good place to sit and figure out what to do next.* After about twenty yards, she realized how much her head and ankle hurt. She paused for a moment then continued to the coffee shop. Once she arrived, she quickly scanned the room and saw a corner table that had recently been vacated. She immediately headed toward it and sat down facing the entrance to the shop, with her back to the wall. This way, she could see everything and everyone. She scanned the room, noting exits, hallways, cameras, and reinforced wall. Realizing what she was doing, she considered why she would do that. A memory flashed into mind. She was scanning other rooms the same way. All the scenes of when she scanned a room came to mind. *I'm protecting myself. Why? Am I a cop? But why didn't I want to talk to them?*

One of the baristas came over to wipe the table and pick up the cup that had been left behind by the previous customer. Noticing the crutches leaning against the nearby wall, the barista asked Sam if she could bring over her order.

"No, thank you."

"Are you sure? Really, I don't mind."

"Uh, well, how about a sweetened green tea, if it's not too much trouble," Sam finally said.

"No problem." The girl smiled at her.

Sam started to feel slightly nauseated and lightheaded, but it passed quickly. *I hope the pills kick in soon.*

The barista returned with her tea. "Are you okay?"

"Yes, thanks." She tried to give the girl some money, but she refused, saying she would take care of it.

"You look like you've had a tough day."

Sam managed to smile and thanked her again. She retrieved the pills from her pocket and read the label. *Maybe I should wait before taking another one.* She shoved them back in her cargo pocket.

Taking the phone out of her back pocket, she flipped it open and began to look for phone numbers or names she recognized. All of the numbers and contacts had been deleted.

"Great," Sam mumbled to herself. *Back to square one.* Sitting back, she ran her hand through her short brown hair. She took a deep breath and thought about the past few hours. She had plenty of questions.

How did I get to the hospital? What happened to my head and ankle? Why don't I have any identification or credit cards? Was I mugged and they were stolen?

Again, for some reason, she didn't think she was mugged, but something had happened. She still had ten dollars and an inexpensive Timex field watch on her wrist. No rings on her fingers. Other than her broken ankle, she seemed to be in decent shape. *What kind of work do I do?* The boots suggested something like law enforcement or military. *Maybe I'm an undercover cop?* No gun or holster—maybe not. Though they could have been stolen as well. That wouldn't be good.

Sam went to rub her neck and felt a chain. *A necklace? Dog tags?* She pulled it out of her shirt and saw that it was a key. That seemed promising. The key was small with a round head. Turning it over, she saw a letter and numbers. *A389. I need to find out what this opens. A hardware store or a place that cuts keys.*

The girl came back and asked if she needed anything else.

"Yes, I need a hardware store or someplace that cuts keys. Do you happen to know of one?"

"Yeah, there's a place near Highway 290 and Mopac."

"Great, thanks." *Now to figure out how to get there.* She needed to get to that store and see what the key opened. A smartphone sure would be helpful right now. But how would she get one? She only had ten dollars. It could wait—for now.

Catching the eye of the girl behind the counter, Sam gestured her over.

"I was wondering if I could bother you for one more thing. Could you call me a cab or rideshare?" Sam asked.

"If you can wait fifteen minutes, I can give you a ride."

"You don't need to do that," Sam protested.

"Really, I don't mind. It'll be my good deed for the day." She smiled. "By the way, I'm Lisa."

"Lisa, you're a lifesaver. I'm Jaime." *Might as well stick with the ruse.*

While Lisa finished her shift, Sam took the last sip of her tea, got up, and made her way to the ladies' room. She took the opportunity to give her body a once-over. No tattoos or visible scars. Only a few bruises that looked recent.

Okay, go over it again. I'm wearing a polo, tactical cargo pants, and law enforcement-style boots. I have small heart-shaped earrings with a bit of western flair. Cute. No rings and an inexpensive watch... I got nothing.

She glanced up at the mirror and saw the earrings again. A scene popped in her head of a boy handing her a box. She opened it and saw the earrings. *"Happy birthday, Sam. You said you might get your ears pierced, so I thought I'd give you your first set of earrings."* Jimmy. *Her younger brother had given her those earrings on her fifteenth birthday.* Her eyes began to glisten and she swallowed to keep her emotions in check. *Focus, Sam.*

Other than the memory, it was another dead end. Sam left the ladies' room just as Lisa was gathering her belongings from an office down the hall.

"Ready?" Lisa asked.

Sam nodded, and they headed toward a back door. On

the drive to the store, Sam managed to learn a bit about Lisa. She was a student at the local community college, working at the coffee shop part-time. She was saving money by living at home with her parents. She had one brother, three years younger than herself. Lisa didn't ask too many questions about Sam, which was fine. Not that she could give her any answers.

When they arrived at the store, Sam thanked Lisa and told her she might be a while, so there was no need to wait.

"Are you sure? Where are you going next?"

Where ever that key leads me. "It's okay, really. You've done enough."

"If you're just having key made, I can wait. I'll drop you off where you're going, and that'll be it."

Sam needed the free ride. "Are you sure?"

"Yeah. Come on. Leave your stuff here. I'll go with you."

Sam agreed, and they went inside the home improvement store. They found the area where keys were made and waited for someone to come assist them.

"How can I help you today?"

"I have this key and can't remember what it goes to. Can you tell me by the code on it?" Sam handed him the key.

He looked it over and said, "Oh yeah. This goes to a padlock. Just a regular one you can buy anywhere."

Sam frowned. "A padlock. No telling where that padlock is located."

"Sorry." He handed the key back to her.

"Thanks anyway," Sam said turning to Lisa. "I'm ready."

On the way to the car, Sam saw a sign for a fitness center. Flashes of placing a metal box in a locker came to mind. *Fitness center.* She closed her eyes and then smiled.

"Jaime? Hey, are you okay?"

"What? Yeah. Can you take me one more place?"

"Sure. Name the place."

"Frogman Fitness. You may need to look up the address."

She pulled out her phone and looked it up. "Found it. 2463 Boxer Street."

"I CAN GET a ride from here, Lisa. I really appreciate your kindness." She said she had a friend at the fitness center who would give her a ride. Another lie. Perhaps she'd see her at the shop again.

When Sam was heading toward the gym door, Lisa suddenly yelled through the window for her to wait. She emptied her books onto the passenger seat and leaned over, holding her backpack through the window. "I just bought a new one, and this is better than that plastic bag you have," Lisa said. "Please, take it." She reached to the back of the vehicle and pulled a new backpack out of a bag. "See? I just haven't switched over yet."

"Uh, well, if you're sure. Thanks so much. I really appreciate it." Sam smiled and took the backpack.

After saying goodbye, Sam went into the gym and was greeted by a young man behind the reception desk.

"Welcome back. Haven't seen you in a while. Now I know why," he said, noticing the crutches and walking boot. "Don't forget to sign in," he said when Sam began to walk by.

She saw someone else place their finger on a small pad, so she did the same. Too bad she couldn't see her information on the computer screen. "Yeah, I just need to check my locker." She assumed the key was for a locker. *What else could it be for?*

Sam walked farther into the gym and saw a sign for the women's locker room. Making her way toward it, she rounded the corner and looked around. Not all the lockers had locks, and some had combination locks. She didn't see anyone else in the room. Then she noticed a locker with a key lock on it—she tried it, with no luck. Just then, a woman came in. Sam smiled at her and went toward the bathroom stalls.

After a few minutes, she came out and washed her hands. Again, looking around, she didn't see anyone and looked for another lock. She found another and tried it. It opened.

Inside was a lockbox with a biometric lock. It opened with her thumb. She hesitated before placing her thumb in the proper position. This could be the answer to everything. The answer to who she is and a life she couldn't remember. A sense of trepidation washed over her, and a million questions crept into her mind. What if she didn't like her life? What if she wasn't happy with the recent choices she'd made? Did she have a job she hated? Friends? Colleagues? Sam took a step back and sat on the bench behind her. Try as she might, she couldn't remember. *Do I have a family? A husband waiting for me somewhere? Surely he would be looking for me. Children? Do I have any? Maybe a boyfriend? A girlfriend? Wait, what?*

Maybe this box didn't hold any answers at all. It could be empty. *Well, only one way to find out.*

2

Placing her thumb on the reader, she heard the click then opened the lid on the box. The stack of cash was the first thing she saw. Looking around to ensure she was alone, she quickly counted it. Two thousand dollars would come in handy, at least for a little bit. *If I can find a cheap motel that averages a hundred dollars a day, that would be twenty days. But I need other stuff like food. Okay, half for cheap motel and the rest for necessities. That gives me ten days, give or take.*

She replaced the cash and picked up a key. Nothing special and no unusual markings. There was a piece of paper with an address written on it.

Sam placed everything inside her backpack and headed out of the gym. She stopped at the desk to ask the young man if he could look up the number for a cab company. He gave her the number, and she used her flip phone to call one.

She waited outside then gave the driver the address on the note. They pulled up to a storage unit. She paid the driver in cash and told him he could leave.

She punched in the code that was under the address and hobbled to the storage unit. Using the key that she'd found in the box, Sam unlocked and lifted the garage-style door. *Wow! Sweet rides!* Inside were a newer-model Harley-Davidson motorcycle and a 1965 Ford Mustang convertible, both with keys in the ignition.

Nice! The motorcycle was not an option with her ankle, so she took time to look the Mustang over then hopped in. Suddenly, scenes of her looking at a classic 1963 Alfa Romeo Giulia Spider popped into her head and learning to drive that same car. *"Easy on the clutch, Samantha."* The glove box contained a handgun and holster, but nothing else. No insurance or any paperwork. *Crap. An address would be nice. Why is there a gun here? Is it mine?* She reached for the weapon then stopped and decided to leave it for the moment.

Glancing around the unit, she was curious about the contents. Perhaps she could find answers if she went through some things.

She didn't find much. Other than the bike and the car, she noticed a few boxes and a footlocker. She placed her hand on the car door but froze when a truck drove by slowly. Suddenly on edge, she changed her mind about sticking around.

Maybe I should get out of here and come back later.

Sam backed the car out, closed and locked the unit, and drove around until she found a cheap motel.

AFTER SETTLING IN, Sam decided to find a store and get a smartphone. She stopped by the motel's front desk and asked where the nearest big-box store was. After driving to it, she bought a pay-as-you-go smartphone, the cheapest laptop she could find, a couple of T-shirts, underwear, and toiletries. Her stomach was rumbling, so she grabbed some power bars and beef jerky. She also thought it might be a good idea to load some cash onto a prepaid debit card. All of that didn't leave her with much cash left. Before she left the store, a headache came on, so she picked up some Tylenol as well. When she returned to the motel, Sam charged the phone and laptop, took some Tylenol, and fell asleep.

Tired of sitting in the motel room, Sam was back at the coffee shop the next day. She ordered her iced tea and sat at the same table she had when she first hobbled into the shop. This time when she sat down, she spent her time furiously typing on her new laptop—scanning the web for missing persons or anything that might give her a lead to who she was or what had happened to her. Something like a car accident that she'd wandered away from. But she didn't have any luck.

Sam returned to the coffee shop every morning around ten and stayed until about two in the afternoon. Lisa would come over and talk to her sometimes when she had breaks or if it was slow.

Sam started to recognize the regular customers. Sometimes, they would sit at a nearby table and start small talk. Occasionally, they'd ask how she broke her ankle. Rather than get into the story about how she didn't know, she just said she'd stepped into a hole while out on her daily run. Being a keen observer, Sam would watch the customers' habits and try to guess their occupations and family status. Occasionally, Lisa would join in and let Sam know if she was right about the customers Lisa knew. They got along well, and Sam enjoyed talking with her. She also appreciated the fact that Lisa never pried and didn't ask many personal questions. That way, she didn't have to lie—since she still didn't remember anything yet.

One day, Lisa invited Sam out with some of her friends from school.

"Friday night, a couple of my friends and I are going to a club. Would you like to come with us?" Lisa said.

"Uh, I don't know. It's not like I can dance with this thing on my foot."

"Come on. I don't know what you do when you're not here, but maybe a night out would be a nice change of scenery. Something different."

Sam thought about it and decided that maybe a night out wouldn't be so bad. They agreed to meet back at the shop at nine on Friday night.

⁓

So on Friday night, Sam met Lisa and two of her friends, Amy and Michelle, back at the shop.

"No crutches?" Lisa asked.

"Too much trouble. I'll just hobble along on this walking boot," JaimeSam explained. "Besides, the doctor said I could put weight on it after three days, and it's been that."

They all hopped into a Lyft and went to Club Diablo. As they stood in line to enter, Sam tapped Lisa on the shoulder and said, "Hey, I don't know if I can get in—I lost my ID."

"You look old enough. What are you, about twenty-five, twenty-six?"

I have no idea. She remembered her first name and some things about her childhood, but she still had gaps. As far as recalling anything past running the obstacle course was concerned, that was a big fat no. "Yeah, about that." Sam decided that was a good guess.

Lisa poked her head out of line to see who was checking the IDs. "It's okay. The guy checking cards is in one of my classes. That's why we started coming here. He gave it a good recommendation."

As they inched closer, Sam became anxious. She took a deep breath and let it out. *No big deal. I'll just go home if they don't let me in.*

"Hey, Jordan." Lisa flashed a smile at him.

"Lisa, you ready for that test next week?"

"You bet. Let me know if you want to get together and study."

"Yeah, I might take you up on that." He gave Sam a once-over.

"This is Jaime. She lost her ID, but I promise she's okay. She's twenty-six," Lisa told him quietly.

"Uh, yeah. Go ahead," Jordan said. Then he called Lisa back over after he waved them in and whispered in her ear.

Sam was curious and didn't want to get Lisa or Jordan in trouble. "Hey, I can go if he's going to get in trouble for letting me in."

Lisa smiled and said, "No, that wasn't it. He wants me to get your phone number, if you're single."

Sam was taken aback. "Oh, uh, I'll think about it. I don't know."

"He's a nice guy, if you are interested. Let me know."

Once inside, the girls pushed their way toward the bar. One seat was suddenly vacated, and Michelle grabbed it and told Sam to sit down. Grateful for the chance to sit, Sam took the seat and offered to buy the first round. Since the girls had no problem getting into the club, she assumed they all were at least twenty-one years old, but for some reason, she still felt the need to ask. Lisa and Amy were twenty-one, and Michelle had just turned twenty-two. So she ordered a round of drinks for all of them. Not sure what she liked, she ordered a beer for herself. Turns out it was a good choice.

Michelle and Amy went out onto the dance floor, which was starting to get crowded, and Sam lost sight of them. Lisa stayed at the bar until Sam finally told her to go have some fun. She'd guard their drinks. After a couple of songs, the girls made their way back to Sam. Every so often, someone would say something, but the music was so loud, they practically had to yell in each other's ears. Mostly, they just drank and pointed at cute guys.

As the night went on, the girls started dancing with some of the men. The club played the top Billboard hits. Occasionally, they'd throw in a slow song or some retro tune. Sam didn't mind sitting at the bar alone. The girls checked on her every so often, and the bartender kept the drinks coming, although Sam ordered water to keep her wits about her.

Even though it was crowded, people gave Sam some space and were careful not to bump her foot. The large walking boot was hard to miss. Sam was wearing a conservative dress she'd picked up earlier in the day and what would be a pair of flats if she was wearing both shoes.

Suddenly, a woman bumped Sam's arm after someone had run into her.

"Sorry about that—it's crowded in here." She leaned in close so she could hear her.

"It's okay," Sam said.

The woman smiled at her and said, "Hi."

"Hello," Sam replied.

"First time here?"

"As far as you know." Sam smiled.

She smiled and dropped her head for a second. Sam thought she had a nice smile. *Wait, what am I doing? Am I flirting with a woman? Am I a lesbian?* She remembered a conversation she had many years ago. *"Dad? Is it okay if I go to the movies with Jenny, Rich...and Pete?"*

"No. You can't date until you're sixteen."

"I'll be with Jenny and Rich. It's a group." She'd talked her father into letting her go, but there was a chaperone who tagged along. Sam was shy, and Pete didn't get any farther than holding her hand.

Another scene came to mind. *"He wants to date you. He's a nice kid. Smart and a good leader."*

"I don't have time to...date."

"You might if you joined us. An ROTC scholarship—"

"Sir. I have my plan, and I'm doing fine."

"Very well. You need to stay off this course." That was it. The obstacle course she remembered. It was college.

"Excuse me, are you all right?" the woman asked.

Sam smiled and said, "Yes." She was a pretty woman with long hair that was darker than hers. Appearing to be close to her age—or a few years older—the woman stood about five foot ten in her two-inch heels and looked fit, in her jeans and sleeveless blouse. Sam caught herself staring at her toned arms. Fit but still feminine.

"Can I get you a drink? I'd ask you to dance, but I think that cast might hinder you some."

"Sure. Thank you." Sam smiled.

She ordered a beer for her, and they ended up talking as best they could through the loud music. When she found out her name was Leia, Sam had to make a Star Wars reference, and they both laughed. Sam knew it wasn't the first time she'd heard a joke about her name, but it was nice of her to play along. The music was loud, and Sam could feel the thumping bass of the song in her stomach. She didn't care for the song but was glad they didn't have to make as much small talk. They exchanged glances, and Sam knew Leia was flirting with her. She was a bit surprised she stayed next to her for as long as she did. Eventually, she told her she could go dance—if she wanted.

"No, I'm having fun right here."

When the girls came back to check on her at about midnight, Sam decided she should call it a night. She hadn't been out since... Well, she didn't know.

Michelle and Amy decided to stay for a bit longer, but Lisa said she was ready to go as well. Just as Sam got out of her seat, a slow song started playing.

"Would you mind dancing this one song?" Leia asked.

Sam looked down at her cast and shrugged. Throughout the evening, she'd seen a few lesbian couples dancing. Leia said it would be okay and told her to follow her. She obliged. The crowd had thinned a little, which made it easier for Sam to get out onto the floor. She picked a spot near where Leia had stopped. Looking at each other for what felt like forever to Sam, Leia flashed a smile and placed her hands gently on Sam's waist. As the music played, Leia started swaying a little bit. Sam just stood there for a few seconds and then placed both hands on her shoulders. As she became more comfortable, she began to sway slightly. This seemed new to her. Not dancing, but dancing with a woman. She started to get lost in Leia's deep brown eyes, then she realized the song was over.

"I really should be going," Sam said, quickly moving her hands.

Leia removed her hands from her waist and thanked her for the dance. She asked if she could see her again. Sam said she wasn't sure. Leia said she'd be at the club next Friday and hoped she'd be there too.

They found Lisa, and Leia walked with the women outside.

"Jaime, do you want to share a ride?" Lisa asked.

"Thanks, but I already ordered one," Sam said. "I had a wonderful time and really appreciate you inviting me."

Lisa's ride came up and stopped nearby. "That's my ride. See you later."

"Bye," Sam said, and Leia waved.

Leia and Sam stood for a moment in silence. Just as she started to say something, Sam's ride appeared. Leia helped her into the back seat, leaned in, and briefly touched her on the arm.

"Good night, Jaime."

"Um, good night."

In the moment Leia's hand touched her arm, she felt a wave of emotion. Her heart was suddenly racing, and she felt the thumping like the music inside the club. She wasn't sure what it was, but it felt familiar and... good. Leia closed the door, and the driver took off. Sam glanced behind her and saw Leia watching her drive away. *Wow, what just happened?*

THE NEXT MORNING, Sam woke up thinking about Leia and smiled to herself. Although it had been difficult to have a conversation with the music being so loud, Sam enjoyed Leia's company. The dance wasn't so bad either. Leia was an attractive woman, and she found herself wondering more about her, but she also needed to find out more about herself.

SAM LOOKED at her favorite seat in the coffee shop, but it was taken, so she hobbled to the next best choice. It was Saturday, and Lisa wasn't there. Maybe she didn't work weekends. Sam had her laptop with her and again was scanning for anything that might help her figure out more about herself. Memories were returning, but not fast enough.

Why don't you just go to the police?

Because it just doesn't feel right.

Three hours later, she was interrupted by a person standing over her. "Hey, mind if I sit?" Lisa said.

"Not at all. Are you working today?"

Lisa sat down in the seat across from her. "Yeah. I took a later shift since I knew I'd be going out. So..."

"What?" Sam asked when Lisa didn't finish her sentence.

"I know we don't know each other well. In fact, I think you know me better than I know you. I respect that. Your privacy, I mean."

"I'm just not a big talker."

"That's fine, but... what do you do for a living? Work from home?"

"Oh, I'm on a medical leave right now."

"Of course, your foot. That didn't stop you from dancing with someone last night." Lisa grinned.

Now we're getting to what she really wants. Sam leaned back in her chair and crossed her arms. "You want to gossip?" Sam asked directly.

Lisa's face flushed a light pink. "I'm sorry. It's none of my business."

Sam relaxed and laughed. "It's okay, but I'm afraid you'll be disappointed."

"What's her name?"

"Leia."

"What's she do?"

"I don't know. I couldn't hear a dang thing in there."

"Are you going to see her again?"

"I don't know." Sam really wasn't used to having a friend to talk to. At least not that she remembered. "What about you? Did you meet anyone?"

"No. I ran into a couple of guys from school, but I wouldn't date them."

"What about girls?"

Lisa became uncomfortable and shifted in her seat. "Oh, uh, I'm not... I mean it's fine. I know another..."

Sam decided to save Lisa from herself. "Relax. I'm messing with you."

Lisa let out a breath. "Sorry. This is Austin, and I'm used to it, I just didn't get that vibe from you."

"You didn't?"

"No. I thought you were straight. In fact, can I be honest?"

"Why not?"

"When you came in the other day on crutches and the way your clothes were wrinkled and dirty, I thought maybe you'd been in an accident. Then my imagination went wild. I thought what if she was running away from an abusive husband or boyfriend? I've heard you tell others you stepped in a hole. But why would you be running in those pants and polo shirt?"

Sam stared at her. "What are you studying?"

"English literature. I'd like to be an author someday or maybe teach and write on the side."

"Taking a creative writing class?"

"Yeah," Lisa admitted.

Sam felt she needed to clarify and hated to lie but wasn't

ready to share that much. "I was trying to keep a dog from getting hit by cars and took a tumble."

"Aww. That's sweet. Why don't you tell others that?"

"Lisa! You working or what?" one of the barista's came over and said.

"Yes, Ronny." Lisa rolled her eyes. "I'll see you later."

"Bye." *Wow, I'm good at coming up with lies and telling them.*

The computer screen had gone dark, and Sam saw her reflection in it. One of her earrings was twisted. She reached up and touched it to straighten it. Then the other one.

A memory flashed of her next to a woman holding a baby.

"Oh my god." She closed the laptop and gathered her things, rushing out the door.

It took all her strength to not drive recklessly back to the motel. She parked and grabbed her things, then she unlocked the door and dropped everything on the bed. Taking a breath, she looked at the drawer under the TV. Swallowing, she walked over and pulled it open, staring at the empty ID case. She picked it up then backed up to the bed and sat down. The reason for the sudden memory was unknown to her. She turned it over in her hands. Unzipping it, Sam felt around inside. It was empty, but she felt something between the fabric and the outer edge.

Sam had picked up a small pocketknife at a store and removed it from her key ring.

She cut the threads inside the case and pulled out a folded photo. Inhaling deeply, she unfolded it as her hands began to shake. She ran her thumb over the old photo of a woman, the baby in her arms, and herself. *Mom, Jimmy, and me.* She blinked, and the tears ran down her cheek. Looking at her mother, Marie, she realized how much she resembled her. It was her mother who had been in that reflection, and there was no denying it was Marie's eyes staring back at her. Even with the short hair Sam now sported, she was still the spitting image of the woman holding the baby. It would be less than a year later Marie would lose her fight with cancer. Sam knew she was four when her mother passed. Then when she was fifteen, tragedy would strike again, and Jimmy would be gone. That was the turning point in her relationship with her father. Things between them were never the same, and a year after Jimmy's death, Sam left home, never to return or speak to her father again. It hadn't been easy leaving her home in Italy at sixteen, but her father had taught her how to survive. Everything she'd done since then had been on her own. Without his help or influence right up through... college. *What happened after that?* She still couldn't remember anything past the obstacle course.

Wiping the wetness away, Sam stood and paced the room as she remembered her

mother and brother. Her father had taken the photo because he wasn't in it. Thinking about her father made her angry. He blamed her and pushed her away after Jimmy died. After a year of guilt, Sam finally packed a rucksack and left the only home she'd known.

SAM SPENT the next few days in her motel room, processing the memories that had come with the photo. She hadn't done anything on the internet for three days.

On Thursday, she went back to the coffee shop. "Jaime! It's good to see you. I was beginning to think you ditched me," Lisa said.

"No, something came up."

"Well, I'm going back to the club tomorrow night. Would you go with me? Michelle and Amy have a project they have to finish and have procrastinated on, so they're staying in."

"Uh, I don't know."

"Come on. Maybe your friend will be there."

"She'll be there. She said she would." Sam thought about it. The past few days had been depressing, and she was still feeling it. Maybe a night out would lift her spirits. "Okay."

"Great!"

~

ON FRIDAY, Sam went with Lisa back to the club. Again, she hobbled up to the bar, but this time, no seats were available. The bartender saw her and walked over with a drink. He pointed to a woman at the other end of the bar—Leia.

The bartender said, "She's been sitting there in that seat, waiting for you."

Sam and Lisa walked over to Leia. Leia stood to let Sam sit down. Lisa said she saw a guy from one of her classes and was going to dance.

"Hello again," Leia said.

"Thanks for the drink. And the seat."

Leia smiled. "It's good to see you."

Sam smiled back and took a sip of her drink. Again, the noise and music made conversation difficult, but they managed to engage in some small talk. Leia finally asked how she broke her ankle, and she told the same "white lie" she'd told everyone else about stepping in a hole while out on a run. Whenever she asked a question about her life or work, Sam managed to redirect her or steer the conversation in another direction. She was kind of glad it was loud—she was able to pretend she couldn't hear her when she didn't want to answer a question. Sam wasn't trying to be difficult or play games with her. It just seemed easier this way. She hadn't remembered anything about herself before her amnesia and hadn't gone back to the storage unit yet. She was very curious but had some apprehension about returning. Her gut told her to wait before going back.

Sam had some ideas about what line of work she was in but went ahead and asked.

"So, what do you do when you're not out saving the galaxy from the Dark Side?"

After a smirk, Leia said, "Right now, I'm teaching a class at the university. Cybercrime."

That means she most likely has a degree in cybersecurity, computer science, or maybe law enforcement training. She'd wondered if she had a military-slash-law enforcement background. Military and police personnel carried themselves in a certain way, and she could see something in Leia that reminded her of that. Sam really was good at observing people. For some reason, she was drawn to Leia, but at the same time, she felt like she needed to be careful. She didn't think she was dangerous—just the opposite. She seemed the type of person who would protect or help you, no questions asked. But something in her gut told her to keep being careful.

Before she knew it, it was one in the morning. When she looked at her watch, Leia asked if she needed to go. It was late—Sam felt it was time.

Leia walked her out after she let Lisa know she was leaving. They headed outside to request their rides. On a Friday night, plenty of cabs and rideshares were available near the club, even at this hour.

"Would you like to get a cup of coffee or a drink somewhere else?" Leia asked Sam.

After mulling it over, she smiled at her. "Yes."

"Great. I know of a couple of places that are still open."

"Uh, do you live nearby?" Sam asked.

"Not far."

"Would you mind if we went there and had a drink? I'd like to get away from the crowds."

"Oh, okay," she said with surprise. "No, I don't mind at all. I'll get us a ride."

"You sound surprised. Can't I trust you?" she asked.

Leia took her hand and looked into her brown eyes. "Yes, you can."

They didn't have to wait long. She was right—it only took about seven minutes to get to her apartment. The complex seemed new, and she lived on the second floor. She asked if Sam wanted to take the elevator, but she said no. The stairs were close.

When Sam stepped onto the first landing, she had to stop. She felt a little lightheaded.

"Are you okay?" Leia asked.

She nodded. "Yeah. I'm fine." Sam continued toward the next landing, holding the handrail.

"Wait a second. Hold onto the rail and put your arm around me." Leia placed her arm around Sam's waist and carefully helped her up the stairs.

"Chivalry is not dead," Sam said as she held onto her. "Thank you."

"It's no problem."

"Just don't try and carry me over the threshold," Sam said, grinning.

They laughed, and continued up the stairs. Once they

reached the landing, Leia began to let go of her but Sam held on. "Still a little lightheaded."

Leia smiled, and they walked down the hall to the last door on the left. They glanced at each other as Leia unlocked the door. She let her go inside first.

The apartment was very modern, with wooden floors, stainless steel appliances, and granite countertops. Leia said she'd only been there about a year. She led her over to the theater-style leather sofa. The two seats on the end of the sofa reclined to make it comfortable for watching television or a movie on the big-screen TV mounted on the wall. The end seats sported cup holders and buttons on the insides of the armrests to position the chairs.

"Please, have a seat, and I'll get you some water," Leia said.

Sam sat on the sofa, and Leia went to the kitchen. The apartment had an open floor plan, so Sam could see her as she grabbed a glass from the cabinet. She put it under the spout in the refrigerator door. As she came back, Sam glanced around the room.

"Is this your she-cave?" Sam asked.

Leia handed her the glass of water, and Sam took a sip. Now that she was sitting down, she felt better.

"I can see why you might think that. Big-screen TV and the sofa. Not very feminine?"

Suddenly Sam was embarrassed. *Crap.* "No, that's not what I meant. I like it. Sorry. I didn't mean to offend you."

"You didn't. Working on a computer screen for most of the day can cause eye strain. Hence, the big screen. As for the sofa, why not be comfortable?"

"I agree," Sam said.

"Do you get dizzy often?"

"No, I'm just not used to staying out this late, and I might be a little dehydrated. Thanks for the water."

Leia got herself a glass of water, came back, and sat down a couple of feet from her on the sofa. Sam noticed some books on the shelf and a few pictures. She walked over to get a closer look and noticed one picture of Leia receiving her Second Lieutenant bars.

"You're military?" Sam asked.

"Yes. I'm in a reserve unit out of Fort Sam Houston."

"That's in San Antonio, right?"

"Yes. I'm in a military intelligence battalion."

Military Intelligence. Why does that seem familiar? She's Army, though. Why would I care which branch she's in?

"Jaime?"

"Is that a Turkish rug?" Sam asked, changing the subject.

"Yes. I got it and that chest over there when I was on temporary duty in the Middle East." Leia pointed to a small wooden chest with gold inlay, tucked in a corner of the room.

Taking in the entire area, Sam realized it wasn't feminine or masculine. The apartment gave off more of a neutral vibe. There were a few trinkets, probably picked up from her travels, and the photos.

"What were you doing over there?" Sam was very curious about this.

Leia said she was still in the Army Reserves, had spent six months in Saudi Arabia, and had deployed to Iraq twice and to Afghanistan, but she didn't say more than that.

Afghanistan. When she mentioned Afghanistan, Sam became uncomfortable. Her stomach swirled as if something bad had happened there, but she couldn't remember.

"Jaime?"

Needing a moment to think, Sam asked, "Could I use your bathroom, please?"

Pointing down the hall, Leia stood to show her. "It's the first door on the right."

Making her way down the hall, Sam saw a picture of a man and woman in desert combat gear. The woman was Leia—she wondered about the man. Once in the bathroom, Sam looked in the mirror. *Why did military intelligence seem familiar? Afghanistan too. She couldn't remember. Other memories had come, but not these. Why not?*

Am I a veteran? The military felt familiar for some reason, but not the Army. Perhaps another branch. *Did I know someone else who was? A civilian contractor?* More questions. *Why can't I remember?*

Sam relaxed a little as she took a deep breath then slowly let it out. When she started back toward the living room, she noticed more pictures on the walls. One was of Leia with a girl in her late twenties and a young man in his mid-twenties.

"That's my brother and sister. I'm the oldest. These are our parents over here." Leia met her in the hall. She approached slowly and stood close to her. As Sam looked up at her, Leia leaned over and kissed her. She was wearing those two-inch heels again, which put her about an inch taller than Sam.

There was that feeling again—a warmth that came over her entire body. *God, she's so sexy in those jeans and blouse.* The blouse had been teasing a peek of her breasts. Sam opened her eyes as their lips separated. They looked at each other and began to kiss again.

Leia placed her hands on Sam's waist. Sam wanted to throw her arms around her neck, but she wasn't sure she was ready to make that bold of a move. So she stood there, but then Leia pulled away and stared at her. Her deep brown eyes looked into Sam's. She suddenly felt safe and reached up, putting her arms around Leia.

"Would you like to go to another room?" she asked.

Wanting to continue, Sam answered with a single word. "Yes."

Leia took her hand and led her to her bedroom. She gently pushed her on the bed and began kissing her again.

Sam untucked Leia's shirt and pulled it over her head. As she set it on the bed, Leia got up and dimmed the lights. Sam watched her as she came back to her. She could see the outline of her toned and fit body in the dimly lit room.

What am I doing? I barely know this woman.

She lay beside her and closed the gap, but then she stopped.

"Jaime? Are you okay? Is this too fast?"

"Uh, what if I said yes?"

"Then I'd stop and ask if I could take you to dinner some time."

Good answer. But something inside her told her Leia was a good person, and she wanted this. It was more than just sex. It was a need to feel close to someone. Leia felt familiar. *Why?* It wasn't her, personally. They didn't know each other. It must be her military background or maybe it was the way she looked. *Maybe she reminds me of someone. A colleague or a girlfriend? A girlfriend didn't feel right. Nor did a boyfriend. Maybe I'm single. Stop overthinking it. Just go with it. Do what feels right.*

She reached a hand behind Leia's neck and gently pulled her closer until she was hovering just above her lips.

Then as Leia's lips met hers, the woman moved her hand from Sam's waist, down her hip to her thigh. Sam's dress gave her easy access, and she slowly moved her hand up the outside of her right thigh under the fabric of her dress.

Sam lifted her head so she could kiss her neck. She felt Leia's hand on her cheek, her thumb wiping away the tear.

"Jaime? What's wrong? Do you want to stop?"

She hadn't even realized the tears were slowly falling. Leia increased the distance between them.

"It's okay," she said rolling on to her back.

With the palm of her hand, Sam swept away the moisture on her cheeks. She was quiet as she took in a few deep breaths. Leia began to sit up, but she grabbed her arm.

"Please. Just give me a minute," she said quietly.

She gave her the minute and more, but Sam remained silent.

"I think I should take you home or arrange a ride, Jaime."

"My name's not Jaime," she whispered.

Leia turned her head toward her. "Well, whatever it is... Mrs. Smith, maybe you should go."

"You think I'm married?"

"Aren't you?"

Staring at the ceiling, she tried to search for memories, but they wouldn't come.

"I'll take your silence as confirmation."

"I can't remember," she blurted out as Leia sat up. "I don't think so."

She sighed. "What does that mean?"

Sam decided to confide in her. "I woke up in a hospital, with this broken ankle and no memory of who I am. Some things have been coming back, but it's been slow."

"Didn't you go to the police?"

"No, I can't." She paused for a second and then said, "I can't tell anyone. I shouldn't be telling you."

"Why are you?" Leia asked.

She sat up and ran her hands along her arms and then gave her a gentle kiss on the nape of her neck. "You asked if I trusted you. I do. I'm asking you to trust me. I'm not betraying anyone."

"If you have amnesia, how can you be sure?"

"It's a feeling. Hard to explain but I know I'm not. No ring, no tan line. No evidence to suggest otherwise."

Leia turned and narrowed her eyes. "You sound like a cop. You really can't remember?"

"No." *A cop? Maybe I was.*

"Maybe you—"

Sam placed a finger over Leia's mouth. "As much as I want to know who I am, it can wait." Placing her hands on Leia's shoulders, she gently massaged them and pecked at her back, giving her butterfly kisses.

"I don't want to take advantage of your situation," Leia told her.

"I don't have a situation. Right now, in this moment, I want you. I need you. Can't we just have tonight?"

"Then what?"

Sam sighed. "I don't know. What I do know is that you got me all hot and bothered, and we're talking too much. *You're* talking too much, and I don't like a lot of talk."

Leia seemed to be considering everything she said. Assuming the moment had long since passed, Sam dropped her hands and swung her legs over the side of the bed. She felt Leia's hand on hers, and she turned to meet her eyes. What she saw in them made her lean close and touch her forehead to her.

Leia's hand caressed her cheek. She met her lips and leaned her back as her legs came up beside her. Leia sat up and carefully took the boot off her foot. What she did next surprised Sam more than anything else. Sliding her left arm under her and rolling her onto her side, she snuggled close and spooned her. Her right hand trailed down her right arm, and she intertwined her fingers in hers.

"Let me just hold you for now," Leia said softly.

Sam suddenly realized this is what she really needed. She felt safe in her arms and relaxed. Taking in a deep breath, closing her eyes, she slowly exhaled. The stress of the past ten days disappeared, and all her problems melted away as Leia held her and she drifted off to sleep.

SAM LAY in Leia's arms and saw a clock that read three in the morning. She could tell from Leia's breathing that she was still asleep. Feeling a sense of happiness, she closed her eyes and snuggled closer to her.

When she next looked at the clock, it was five thirty. Leia was still sound asleep. Slowly and carefully, Sam extricated herself from her arms and the bed. Standing next to the bed, she looked at Leia. A flash appeared of a blond-haired woman in this exact position. It took Sam by surprise, and she almost gasped. Closing her eyes, she tried to picture the woman, but her hair was obscuring her face. *Come on. Who are you?*

Sam quietly sighed and opened her eyes. Leia was still in her jeans and bra. Just as she had been when Sam had fallen asleep in her arms. She was glad that Leia had recognized what Sam needed. *Maybe I should wake her and say goodbye. No, let her sleep. She looks content and... beautiful. I need to go.* After placing the boot back on her foot, she made her way down the hall. In the living room, she looked in her purse for a piece of paper and pen. She wrote a note:

"Thank you." She placed a coffee cup on the paper in the center of the kitchen island, grabbed her purse, and headed out. She stopped before reaching the door and went back to the note and added her phone number to it.

On the cab ride home, she went over the previous night's events in her head. She'd had a good time and had felt something she wasn't sure she had felt in a while. She really liked Leia. Some of the things she learned about her seemed familiar to her—like the military and Afghanistan. She smiled to herself and hoped that she'd see her again. But in the back of her mind she was wondering who the blonde was.

3

The following morning, Sam went back the coffee shop and treated herself to a breakfast quiche and a chocolate mocha. She was able to extend her stay in the motel by carefully rationing what she had left.

"Wow. I've never seen you eat anything, and you usually only have a plain coffee," Lisa said, sitting down. She feigned a gasp. "You got lucky."

"No, no I did not." Sam was sure to set the record straight. "But we did have a nice evening together." She couldn't help but smile. Sam was happy. For the first time since she woke up in the hospital, she was content and joyful.

"That's great. Well, I better get to it. Need anything else?" Lisa asked.

"No, thanks."

Lisa smiled and went to start her shift.

Sam's phone buzzed, and she looked at it. Her smile could have lit the room up. Catching herself, she shifted and wiped the smile from her face.

LEIA

Good morning.

Sam began her text.
Good morning. Thank you for last night.
Is that too much? She deleted the last sentence. *Keep it simple.*

SAM

Good morning.

Send.
She stared at the three dots.

LEIA

I enjoyed last night. May I take you to dinner one evening?

Dinner? Yeah, I'd love to go to dinner. Her thumbs hovered over the screen. Suddenly Sam didn't know what to do. *Should I really start something? I still have so many questions and gaps about my life.*
The phone buzzed.
Dang it, I waited too long.

LEIA

It's ok.

The dots disappeared. *Shoot.* Sam liked Leia but just wasn't sure about anything until her memory returned. *It's just dinner. I have to eat.*

SAM

Yes, I'd like to have dinner with you.

LEIA

No pressure. I'll text you.

SAM

Looking forward to it.

SAM CONTINUED her search but was getting nowhere. She'd even expanded her search to the outskirts of the Austin area. *If someone was looking for me, wouldn't they have gone to the police or posted a missing persons ad? I should just go to the police.* But Sam's gut told her not to. What reasons would there be to not go to the police? The thought had crossed her mind once or twice. *A fugitive? Am I a criminal? No. I can't believe I am. Think, Sam.* Getting frustrated, Sam decided to go back to her motel room.

THE NEXT MORNING her phone buzzed. "Hello?"

"I'm sorry, did I wake you?" Leia asked.

"No, I just... It's fine."

"Are you available Tuesday evening for dinner?"

"Oh, uh, yes."

"Great. Tuesday at seven? We'll go to Carve. Are you familiar with it?

"No."

"They serve American food. Let's go casual. I'll pick you up at seven."

Pick me up? Sam sat up and looked around the dank motel room. "No, uh, can I meet you?"

"Of course. I'll see you at seven?"

"Yes," Sam said before hanging up.

Tuesday approached, and Sam was chickening out about the date. She needed to focus on finding out what happened to her, so she texted Leia.

SAM

I'm sorry. I have to cancel.

Then she turned her phone off. But it didn't last, and the next day, she turned it back on while sitting at her favorite table in the coffee shop. Multiple texts and missed call messages appeared from Leia. Sam felt like crap, but couldn't deal with a relationship right now. She also couldn't help herself and listened to the last voicemail.

"Jaime, you didn't tell me your real name, so I'll have to call you that. You trusted me with telling me your situation. I can help you. No strings. No dates. Just one person helping another. I've made friends in my career. I want to help you. You have my number. I won't bother you anymore."

I'm such a jerk. Maybe I can't do this alone. She heard a voice in her head say, *"You can't be a lone wolf. They don't like that. We're here to learn to be leaders, right?"* The voice sounded familiar, but she couldn't see his face. A feeling of defeat came over her. She sighed. Sam took the photo out of the ID case and looked at it.

"Sorry, Mom. I failed. I can't complete this mission."

Mission. She had a mission to complete. Why was that familiar? She ran a finger over the photo. *I've been dragging my feet on this. Okay, I'll give it one last shot, Mom.*

Sam put the photo away, went out to her car, and drove back to her motel room.

The boxes in the storage unit didn't yield any help. They were mostly filled with trinkets and souvenirs from Europe. Sam assumed she'd traveled in the past. The footlocker was locked, and she wasn't ready to break into it—yet. She was almost afraid of what she might find, so she decided it could wait.

No, it can't wait. She looked over at the motorcycle and searched inside the saddlebags. She hadn't been back to the storage unit since she'd found it, but now she hoped to find some answers. She found a Walther PPQ 9-mm handgun. *Now, this is interesting.* In the glove box of the Mustang, she had found a Smith & Wesson Bodyguard .380 with a laser. She'd been carrying the .380 with her ever since. Obviously, she was familiar with handguns and felt very comfortable with them.

Sam needed to know just how good she was with these handguns. Inside the other saddlebag, she found a business card for an indoor range—Three Dogs Guns and Ammo. Digging deeper, she found an envelope containing three twenty-dollar bills. *Jackpot.* She stuffed the bills into her pocket then gathered the two guns, one small range bag, and some ammunition. The range bag and ammo had been in the trunk of the Mustang, along with a large gear bag. She had brought them into her room to check them out a few days before. Sam would love to drive the motorcycle, but couldn't with the boot. It was a chore just to drive the Mustang with its clutch. So she loaded the small range bag and ammo into the car and headed to the gun range, which wasn't very far.

It was early afternoon on Wednesday, and the range was a little busy. The sign outside advertised half-price lanes for women on Wednesdays. Sam collected her belongings and headed inside.

As she approached the counter, the man behind it smiled and said, "Hey, Sam. How've you been?"

He knows my name. My real name.

"Sam?"

Quickly, she said, "Hi. Sorry, I was miles away."

"We haven't seen you in a while. Work keeping you busy?"

"Something like that."

"Are you limping? What happened to your foot?"

"Stepped in a hole while running. Another couple of weeks and I can see about taking this off." She started to pick up the clipboard with the range safety instructions on it and realized she needed to initial as "Sam Watson." Her given name was Samantha Watson. *But that just doesn't seem right.*

He stopped her and said, "You don't need to sign that. Remember? Last time you were in, I mentioned we were computerizing all that."

"Oh, right. Well, it has been a while."

He pulled up her info on his computer and then turned the screen toward her. He said that since it was her first time signing in on the computer, to make sure all her info was correct. As she was looking it over, trying to memorize her info, a lady asked him if she could look at one of the rental guns.

"Be right back," he said.

She took out her phone and quickly snapped a picture of the screen. She managed to put the phone back into her pocket just before he returned.

"Everything look okay?"

"Yeah, great." According to his information, her name was Samantha E. Barrett. She already knew her name was Sam. *Barrett. Mom's maiden name. I changed my name when I ran away from home.* It was no wonder she couldn't find anything on Samantha Watson. She'd been searching the wrong name. Gaps in her memory still existed.

The man told her to sign her name on the small digital

pad in front of her. This was just to acknowledge that the information was correct. She hoped the signature was close enough to pass. It must have been, because she had to sign twice more for the safety rules and for the shooting lane he gave her. *I guess my signature wouldn't change.* The computer was able to keep track of the dates and times people came to shoot. It also tracked whether they rented any weapons and, if so, which ones. All this info was privacy protected.

Hearing protection already in place, she took a paper target the man gave her, went to her assigned lane, and prepared her weapons. It all seemed natural. Like she'd done it many times before. She stapled the target to the board and sent it back to the seven-yard mark. Eye protection was already in her bag, so she put the glasses on. The magazines were loaded and ready to go. She pulled out the Walther first, inserted a magazine, racked the slide, and fired two shots. The gun felt extremely comfortable in her hand. She looked at the target and saw two holes dead center. She took aim again and emptied the magazine. Fifteen rounds dead center made quite a hole.

"Okay, let's send it back," she said to herself and sent the target back to fifteen yards.

Sam reloaded and double-tapped her way through half the magazine. Same result—headshots. She sent the target back to twenty-five yards and aimed at the small silhouette in the upper-left corner. After how well she had done previously, she wasn't surprised to see the target's appearance.

Wow, I'm a really good shot.

Another memory appeared. She was shooting, but not a pistol. It was an air rifle. *"Keep shooting like that and you'll have no trouble making the Olympic team, Samantha. Or the rifle team at the Air Force Academy."* The voice was her father's. She was so young, barely a teenager. He was so proud of her back then and she loved to please him. But that was before Jimmy died. Before her world turned upside down. *How could things have gone so wrong?*

A shot from another lane snapped her out of her memory.

Sam put up a clean target and switched to the .380. The gun was smaller, but that didn't matter. Her results were almost identical.

When Sam had used all the ammo she'd brought, she went out to pay her bill in cash. Her cash was getting low as time wore on. Lisa had offered to recommend her for a part-time job at the coffee shop if she needed it.

The man at the counter handed her a receipt, and she saw his name on it—Tom. She also noticed that he'd given her a veteran's discount. *So I am a veteran. But I don't think I went to the Air Force Academy.*

"How'd it go, Sam?" he asked.

"Good, Tom. Thanks."

They said their goodbyes, and Sam headed back to the motel room. Before she cleaned her weapons, she took out her phone and looked at the photo she had snapped earlier. It showed her name, address, and email. She knew she should check out the address but decided to wait until it was dark. The email address didn't really help unless she could figure out the password or hack into it. Leia might be able to help her with that since she had cybercrime experience. She did offer to help her, but Sam wasn't ready for that, yet.

I might find a password or something that jogs my memory at that address.

❧

Sam finished cleaning the two pistols and put the gear away. She made herself a peanut butter and jelly sandwich and turned on the TV, waiting for the right time. Then she had a thought. Opening the laptop, she googled Samantha Barrett. A few came up.

As soon as it was dark, Sam changed into dark jeans and a dark shirt. She retrieved the .380 and replaced it into its holster, tucked on the inside left side of her waistband. Sam thought about what else she might need. If it was her house or apartment, she'd have keys. But she had no idea where they'd be. So she'd have to break in or pick the lock. *Can I even pick a lock?*

Then she remembered one of the saddlebags on the bike had contained a pocketknife, a boot knife, and a small case. She had placed those items in the large duffel bag in the trunk of the car. She walked back to the car and retrieved the items.

Back in her room, she strapped the boot knife to her leg and opened the small case. It looked like a small tool kit. All the tools were similar except for the ends. She also noticed something that looked sort of like a gun, but it had a metal piece sticking out. As she picked it up, she realized it was a lockpick gun and set. *This will come in handy. I guess I can pick locks.*

All the items were placed in her backpack. She needed a flashlight and remembered seeing a couple in a large gear bag. After checking that one worked, she tossed it into the backpack. Sam took a mental inventory of the items, double-checked her weapon and magazine, and decided she was ready.

Why do I have all this stuff? Maybe I'm a private investigator. That thought hadn't even occurred to her until this moment. *No, I don't think I'd like spying on spouses to catch them in an affair. I think I'd want to do more than that. More for... others. Investigating crimes seems interesting.*

Sam pulled up the address on her phone, grabbed the backpack, and headed out. It took her fifteen minutes to find the place—an apartment complex. She double-checked the picture of the address she had taken... Building 3, number 3A.

The complex was gated. She could either try to find a place to jump the fence or wait for someone to come in and follow behind. Jumping the fence with this boot on her foot was out of the question.

After finding a place to park, she adjusted the ball cap she was wearing and went to the pedestrian gate. Luckily, it was unlocked. Walking around, Sam found building 3 and took the stairs to the third floor. It was quiet.

Approaching apartment 3A, she listened for a moment then knocked on the door. No answer. Sam looked around. No one in sight. She could hear a little bit of activity out by the pool. It would probably pick up as the evening went on since it was Saturday night.

She reached for the backpack and pulled out a pair of black latex gloves. Sam grabbed the lockpick gun out of her duffel. She found it easy to use, and in less than a minute, she was inside.

Taking a moment to let her eyes adjust to the darkness, Sam glanced around. From what she could see, the apartment was nice and reminded her of Leia's. She took the flashlight out of the backpack and attached a red lens to it. The red lens wouldn't attract as much attention as the bright white light. She turned it on and looked around. The apartment looked like it was lived in, but was relatively neat in appearance.

She made her way through the living area, down the hall

on the right to a bedroom. It must have been the guest bedroom because it contained only bed and a dresser. Across the hall was a bathroom. Neat and clean—not much there. Making her way back down the hall, she stopped in the kitchen and decided to check the refrigerator. A six-pack of craft beer, some deli meat and cheese, eggs, and milk that was now past its expiration date. *Well, I have been gone a few weeks.* She closed the door and went through the living room to the opposite side of the apartment. She came upon the master bedroom, which held a queen-size bed, a dresser, night table, a chair, and an ottoman.

Sam went to the dresser and opened the drawers. There were bras, underwear, socks—all the usual stuff. On top of the dresser was a jewelry box. Inside, she found a gold class ring and another ring that would probably fit on her pinkie. She also found some simple earrings and a gold necklace with an alligator pendant on it. No... not just an alligator, a Florida Gator. The University of Florida. It seemed familiar.

But I didn't go to school there. This was a gift from...Grrr. Why can't I remember? She looked at the class ring. Inside, a name was inscribed— "Samantha E. Barrett." On one side was "BS" and on the other side was the graduation year, 2005. The ring was from Sam Houston State University.

That's where that obstacle course was! Army ROTC. Sam rolled her eyes. *Ugh, Army. I would never join the Army. Of that, I can be sure.*

At the very back of the box was a small black velvet pouch. She opened it and poured out another ring—a wedding ring. Sam Barrett was married. But that didn't make sense. Why wasn't she wearing it? How could she forget her husband? She looked for an inscription inside the ring. "S Love Always R." She held it in her palm. Closing her eyes, she tried to remember. She wanted to remember, but nothing came. A feeling of disappointment came over her—a feeling of failure, like a pit in her stomach—and she didn't like it. *Why didn't this ring jog a memory? You would think it would. Who was R? Ron, Ray, Rich. I got nothing.*

She opened her eyes and put the ring back. Maybe she just wasn't ready to remember yet. Sam sighed. It had been a few weeks, and she was beginning to wonder if she'd ever recover those memories.

Walking over to a door, Sam opened it to find a walk-in closet. A few dresses, dress shirts, khakis, T-shirts, polos, a dark pantsuit with a matching skirt, some jeans, and a few pairs of different-colored tactical pants were hanging up. On a wall was a hook with two purses dangling from it. She took one off then searched inside, but it was empty.

The second purse reaped better luck. The small wallet had a military identification card in it. She pulled it out and looked at it. The name was "Samantha E. Barrett." The picture... It was her. It had her rank as a captain, pay grade was O-3. Air Force.

Of course it was Air Force. "Fly, fight, win," she said quietly as a feeling of pride came over her. *But I'm in Austin. That's a long commute to San Antonio. What am I doing here, and why didn't I have this on me? Am I on leave? Was I visiting someone? No, this seems to be my apartment. But there really isn't a lot of stuff here. Maybe I'm on terminal leave setting up my place for when I get out of the service. Okay, I'm a captain, so I've been in for at least four years.*

She looked at the date of birth on the ID card. *Figuring I graduated college at twenty-one or twenty-two, add four years to make captain, and my DOB tells me I'm twenty-six with a birthday coming up. That means it's too early to make major with time in grade and time in service requirements. Why would I get out?* More questions.

Replacing the ID card, she also found a credit card with the same name. *Yes! Cash. Five twenty-dollar bills. This is one more day in the motel. I may need a job. Am I stealing from myself? No. This is my stuff. My money.*

Continuing her search in the purse, she found a business card holder. The cards were printed with Sam's name on them, and underneath were the words "Independent Firearms Instructor and Armorer." It also had Sam's email and a cell phone number.

Okay, my name is Samantha Barrett, and I have an active duty Air Force ID card but also these business cards. Do I run this business on the side? Again, what am I doing in Austin? San Antonio had the closest Air Force bases. What the heck am I doing?

She put everything back. She was feeling overwhelmed with questions and no answers, and her head started throbbing. The headaches had gone away until now. This was all too much. As she closed the closet door, she saw a picture frame on the nightstand next to the bed. Walking over, she saw herself standing next to a man of about the same age.

We're wearing US Air Force service dress uniforms. No... those are mess dress uniforms. It looked like a formal party—a military dining in, probably. Her uniform was that of a first lieutenant, and so was his. They looked happy.

Sam picked up the frame. *Nice-looking guy. What was my Air Force Specialty Code? Why can I remember crap like that but not other stuff?*

Sam looked for any identifying badges, but she couldn't see anything on the uniform—nothing on the right side of the uniform, and the left wasn't visible because of the way she was turned. The guy who was standing on her left had a medal and an occupational badge, but Sam couldn't tell what it was because it was too small. Taking her phone out,

Sam took a picture of the photo. Trying to zoom in on the badge didn't help. It was too fuzzy.

Then a thought occurred to her. *Where's my uniform and military stuff? Packed away? If I recently resigned my commission, I wouldn't have that ID card.* She sighed. Nothing was making sense.

Wait a minute. Where's his stuff? If I'm married, where's his stuff? She went back to the closet and didn't see any clothes or anything that looked like it belonged to a guy. *The bathroom. Maybe an extra toothbrush.*

She walked into the bathroom and opened the cabinet drawer. Toothpaste, hairbrush, the usual things. No extra toothbrush. *Maybe I'm divorced or separated.* Birth control pills. *That's good to know. Maybe I should take them.* No. This was a fact-finding mission, that's all. She still had questions. She noticed a bottle of aspirin and took a couple of pills.

With her head still throbbing, she decided she'd seen enough for now. She had one more look around and then went to the front door. Pausing, Sam changed her mind and went back to the bedroom closet. Finding a duffel bag, she grabbed some clothes and placed them inside. Heading back to the front door, she turned off her flashlight and put it in the backpack. Sam peered through the peephole to see if anyone was in the hall. It looked clear, so she opened the door and left.

She passed a couple of guys on the stairs who were already "three sheets to the wind." They whistled at her and yelled some catcalls. But they kept going, and so did she— right back home to her crappy motel room.

Sam's head didn't feel any better. She stopped and picked up some more aspirin and a six-pack of the same craft beer that had been in her apartment. Her mind was racing. She wasn't thrilled about walking into this room after being in Sam's apartment. All she had was a room with a kitchenette, in a less-than-desirable neighborhood, which she had paid for by the week. But this was all she could manage with the cash she had, and that was getting low. She'd been living on water, protein bars, and beef jerky. It might be time to look for a job or something. She could save some money by going back to Sam's place, but she didn't feel comfortable doing that just yet.

Sam sat down and popped a couple of aspirin with a gulp of beer. She had found out quite a bit but needed to know more. *How should I proceed?* She sat and thought a while. Three beers later, she gave up and went to bed.

4

S am rose the next morning, and after getting dressed, she pulled out the photo. *I'm closer, Mom. There's still some things I need to figure out, but I feel like I'm headed in the right direction. I know this path may not be the easy one, but I feel like it's the right one.*

It would have been simple to go to the police. They could fingerprint her and see what came up. She didn't need that now. She knew who she was. Captain Samantha Barrett, United States Air Force. What was still a mystery was what she was doing in Austin right now. *Thanks, Mom. I know I can figure this out. I just need time.*

Returning the photo to its spot in the ID case, Sam felt like she was finally making some progress. A good night's sleep had done her good. She felt refreshed and ready to go. The way she saw it, she had two choices. She could just reinsert herself into Sam's life and hope her memory returned, or she could be cautious and try to find out more information. She opted for the latter. Sam was trusting her gut and instincts. She needed as much information as possible so she decided to stake out her apartment. Her hope was that someone would come looking for her. Maybe a friend or coworker. Someone had to be missing her. Depending on who it was, it might lead her to some answers.

There was one thing she wanted to do first. Picking up her phone, she called Leia, but it went to voicemail, so she left a message. "Hey, it's... Jaime. I wanted to apologize. You're probably in class, so maybe we can meet for coffee or something. Oh, but I may be busy the next few days, so I'm not sure when I'll be available. I just hope you'll give me another chance. Bye."

She packed her bag with everything she thought she'd need for a stakeout. Water and snacks mostly. She pulled into a drugstore just in front of the apartment—a great place to park and keep an eye out for anyone entering the complex. That was the easy part. The hard part was that she had no idea who she was looking for and didn't know if she would recognize anyone. So she sat and waited.

After eight hours, she went into the drugstore and bought water. She got back in the car and watched. Her phone buzzed, and she checked the text. It was from Leia.

LEIA

Yes, coffee or something sounds fine. Just let me know.

SAM

I'll be in touch.

Every couple of hours, she went around the block and parked in a different spot so she wouldn't draw too much attention. The drugstore was a twenty-four-hour one, so she could go inside at any time. Sam purchased a book but didn't want to get to wrapped up in it and miss something. So she only read a few paragraphs at a time.

By the fourth day, she was ready to quit—but then she

saw something. She thought she recognized a man going into the apartment complex. She waited for him to come out, and sure enough, it was Tom, the guy from the gun range.

What are you doing here? Are we friendly enough that you'd come visit me?

She followed him—from a safe distance—to a house. He parked and went inside. This must be where he lived. Sam decided to call it a night and went back home. It was getting late anyway, but she wanted to send a text first, so she pulled over a few houses down.

SAM

Hey, I haven't forgotten about you.

LEIA

I haven't forgotten about you, either. You're unforgettable. 

Sam grinned and drove back to the motel.

~

SAM RETURNED to Tom's house early the next morning. She'd been thinking about what kind of relationship she'd had with Tom and decided to investigate further. She saw a woman leave the house at seven, and at seven thirty, she saw Tom come out with a little boy about six years old. They waited near the curb, and soon, a school bus rolled up. She noticed a handicapped sticker on the bus. The boy wore a backpack, and his stance was staggered as he rocked back and forth. Sam watched the little boy flap his hands as they waited for the door to open. *Is he autistic?* Tom said something to the boy, gave him a high five, helped him onto the bus, and waved goodbye as the bus pulled away. Then he went back to the house.

At eight thirty, Tom left the house, and Sam followed him to the range. Thinking he was just going to work, she turned around and went back to the apartment. Sam thought about what she'd seen. It appeared that Tom had a family—a wife and son. *Why did he go to Sam's apartment complex? Were we having an affair? It didn't seem that way when she was at the range. Were they friends? Maybe she knew his wife and they all hung out together. Should I confront Tom or not?* Tom might be able to give her the answers she needed.

No, an affair didn't feel right. There had been a picture of Sam and someone else in the apartment. They appeared happy. But she wasn't wearing her wedding ring and had seen no signs of a man in the apartment. Being separated or divorced made sense.

Sam was getting frustrated. She could probably end this nightmare by going to the police. *But why haven't I done that already? I know why.* Something was holding her back. *I may not know exactly why I don't want to go to the police, but I do know going to the police is not the right call.* That's why she'd fled the hospital the way she did. *If not the police, what about the air force? I could call the Military Personnel Center at Randolph Air Force Base. What would I say? This is Captain Samantha Barrett. Could you tell me where I'm stationed? They'd think she was crazy. Wander up to the gate and tell the gate guard the same thing? Again, they'd think she was crazy.*

Taking the lockpick, she entered the apartment and turned on a light. This was her place, so no need to worry about not belonging here. She went back to the closet in her bedroom. Retrieving the ID and credit card that was in the purse, she also found another twenty-dollar bill in a shoebox. Sam took that, as well as two business cards.

She sighed as she looked at her surroundings. *Maybe I should just stay here. But what if something happened here? What if Tom did something to me here? It doesn't look like it. No signs of a struggle.*

She didn't feel comfortable staying there, but the ID and credit cards seemed okay to use. She knew the credit cards could be traced, so she would wait to use them—in case something nefarious was going on.

One more week. If I don't get any more answers or leads, I'll come back here and go to the police or Randolph.

Feeling a need to relive some stress, Sam decided to find another gun range. She located one on the outskirts of town, loaded up, and drove there. The woman checking her in asked for identification, so she was glad she had retrieved it.

"You're all set. Pick a lane."

"Thanks." Placing her hearing protection on, she went through two doors and settled into a lane. The more rounds she fired, the more at peace she felt. Toward the end of her hour, she was having fun, and she finished her session by making a smiley face on the silhouette. Just as she was getting ready to leave, a woman approached her.

"Excuse me. I was wondering if I could ask you a question?" she asked.

"Yes."

"I saw you through the observation window and noticed that you're a pretty good shot."

"Thank you," Sam said hesitantly.

"I want to learn to shoot, and I think I'd be more comfortable with a female instructor. Do you teach?"

Sam wavered for a moment but decided it might be good

for her. And she could use the money. She asked the woman a few questions about what kind of experience she had with guns and why she wanted to learn. They discussed prices for the lessons, and then Sam arranged to meet her back at the range on Tuesday at ten thirty in the morning. The woman's name was Sara Caldwell. Sam went ahead and told her that her name was Sam. *Might as well start using my real name.*

After Sara left, Sam looked at the rental guns offered at the range. She had an idea of what she thought Sara should start with. On her way back to the motel, she stopped at a sporting goods store and picked up some more ammunition, including enough for Sara to use. For the rest of the day, Sam put together a lesson plan for Sara. It was a nice distraction.

Hmm. Would this be such a bad life? Teaching others firearms safety and how to shoot? But Sam wasn't sure it would be quite fulfilling enough for her.

That night, Sam went back to the "nice" apartment. She searched for a phone. No luck. *Where would I hide a laptop?* She went to the bed and lifted the mattress. *Bingo.*

She pulled it out and turned it on. Of course, it was password protected. She closed it and took a deep breath. She knew Leia could help her. Maybe it was time to start trusting someone. She had to think about it some more.

No, not yet.

She came up with another plan. She'd go to a few cell phone stores and try to figure out which carrier she had used. Then she'd tell them she lost her phone and ask if they could "ping" it for her.

But first, it was time for that apology. Sam phoned Leia.

"Hello."

Sam smiled at the sound of her voice. "Hi. I was

wondering if I could take you to dinner tonight. I know it's short notice, but are you available?"

"Yes."

"Good. I'll pick you up at seven, if that's okay?" Sam said.

"I'll be ready."

"Oh, text me your address."

"Okay. Is this casual or dressy?"

"Casual or business casual. Your choice."

"See you at seven."

Sam disconnected the call and searched for a place to eat dinner. She decided on a place and then looked at her clothes. Nothing she had would do. Not here anyway. She drove back to her apartment and looked in the closet. She found a pair of dress slacks, a blouse, and heels. No, no heels. She found a pair of dressy oxfords.

She looked around for some makeup and found some. She checked her watch. It had taken her so much time deciding where to go, that she was better off getting ready at the apartment. So Sam showered and changed to get ready for the date.

Date. I'm going on a date. From what she remembered, she hadn't dated much. But she didn't know what had happened in college and up to waking in the hospital. That was a long time, six or seven years, give or take.

SAM SWALLOWED as she rang the doorbell. *Why am I nervous? I don't think I've dated much. Okay, I can do this. Just relax.*

The door opened, and Leia smiled at her. She had also opted for business casual and wore dress pants and a blouse with one-inch heels. That put them at the same height. "Hi. You look great."

"Thank you. You do too. Let me grab my purse."

Sam waited, and when Leia returned, she stepped aside to let her lock her door. She followed Leia downstairs until she stopped walking.

"Did you forget something?"

"No. I don't know where you parked."

"Oh, right. It's the Mustang over there." Sam led her to the car and opened the door.

"Thank you. This is a nice car. What year is it?"

"It's a sixty-five." Sam closed the door and went to the driver's side. She drove to the restaurant and they went inside.

"Barrett," she said to the hostess.

Leia raised a brow, but Sam didn't say anything. Once they sat down at the table Sam began to explain. "My name is Samantha Barrett. Call me Sam."

"I take it your memory came back."

"Some of it. I had a lead and followed it, which helped me learn some things about myself. I still don't know what happened to land me in the hospital." Sam was almost excited as she told her. It was the search. As stressful as it had been, it had been fun in a way. Like solving a puzzle.

"Well, I'm glad you're making progress." Leia smiled. "Sam. I like it. So what line of work is Sam Barrett in?"

"It gets a little complicated there." Sam wasn't sure how much to reveal about herself. Was she Captain Samantha Barrett or Sam Barrett the firearms instructor? Or both?

"Sam?"

"Is it important that you know?"

"Are you a criminal?"

"No. At least I don't think so."

"I have friends, and we can run your name," Leia offered.

"No. Please don't. I'm trusting you as an Army officer."

Again her brow raised. "All right. I won't do that. Did you google yourself?"

"Yes. No luck. Can we talk about you?"

"What would you like to know?"

"Did you grow up here?"

The conversation turned to Leia, and Sam became more relaxed.

"I grew up in Round Rock. Not far from here. I earned a soccer scholarship to the University of North Carolina at Chapel Hill, but broke my leg and lost my ride."

"UNC. You must have been a great player," Sam said. "They're a powerhouse in women's soccer."

Leia looked at her with surprise. "Were you a player?"

"Yes, a little. I loved watching the World Cup. The US Women's team was great. I also read Mia Hamm's autobiography. But my best sport was shooting air rifles." Sam laughed a little. "I've remembered a few more things about myself. What happened after you got hurt?"

"It wasn't so much the leg as it was the concussion. As much as I loved the sport, I didn't want to take a chance on another one. I'd taken other hard knocks in high school. Anyway, I came back home and joined the Army Reserves. Used the GI Bill to let them pay for college. Got my degree and put in for a commission." Leia took a sip of her wine and said, "Now tell me about you."

Sam hesitated. "There's not much to tell. I still can't remember some things."

"Sam, please."

Her voice was comforting so Sam obliged. "My parents were Americans, but we lived in Italy. I came to America to attend college." Sam looked down at the class ring she was now wearing. "I graduated from Sam Houston State University, according to my ring. I can't remember anything past that." The ring. She had a bachelor of science, but in what? Maybe the symbols on the side could tell her and that would give her more answers.

"Sam?"

"Sorry, I thought of another way to get some answers."

"If you need any help, the offer will always be on the table." Leia reached for Sam's hand and gave it a gentle squeeze.

"Thank you."

SAM HAD GONE AHEAD and paid for dinner with her credit card. She decided to live Sam's life as she knew it, but still search for answers on her own.

As they were driving back to Leia's place, Sam took a different route. Leia noticed a few right-hand turns, like she was checking for something.

"Sam, is something wrong?"

"Probably not," she said quietly. "I'm sure it's nothing. Me, just being paranoid." But Sam's instincts were telling her to be aware. If she were a dog, her hackles would be up. Instead, the hair on the back of her neck was up. She wasn't sure but thought someone might be following her.

Sam kept her eyes on the rearview mirror for the rest of the way back to Leia's but didn't see anything suspicious. She parked and walked Leia back to her apartment.

"Would you like to come in for a drink?" Leia asked as she unlocked her door.

Sam stepped close and pushed some strands of Leia's hair away from her eye. Then she leaned in for a kiss. Their lips barely brushed before Sam pulled away slightly. She whispered, "I would love to come in for a drink, but I'd like to wait." Sam felt more confident and didn't want to rush into anything. She stepped back. "Thank you. I'll call you."

On the way back to her motel room, Sam's head was on a swivel. She took the scenic route and doubled back to ensure no one was following her. It was dark, and Austin was a busy city. It was difficult to spot a vehicle in this traffic. But hopefully that meant it made it difficult for someone to follow her. Although a 1965 classic Mustang did stand out.

Satisfied for the time being, she finally pulled into her motel parking lot. Grabbing her purse, something she wasn't always comfortable with, she reached inside and gripped the handle of the Smith & Wesson. *From now on, you will stay on my hip. No matter what.*

SAM STAYED in her room working on her laptop for the next few days. She continued to scour the internet for any leads on her situation. One day, Sam finally decided to check her ankle. It had been four weeks since this ordeal began, and it was time. She carefully took off the walking boot. The doctor had said four to eight weeks, so this was the earliest she could take it off. After unwrapping the Ace bandage from her ankle, she looked it over. Other than some stiffness, her ankle felt pretty good. She flexed it in all directions and rubbed it. She then stood on it and walked around. Her ankle was still a little sore, but it felt good to have the cast off.

Sam made herself another small cup of coffee, and she sat down at her laptop to read the latest headlines.

Thirty minutes later, Sam decided to take a shower and get dressed. Afterward, she returned to the kitchenette area.

Suddenly, a headache came on. She took some aspirin and went to lie down. *I wonder if I get headaches often? Eye strain? Maybe I'm spending too much time on the computer. Or perhaps it's lingering effects from the concussion.* Sam settled on the bed and closed her eyes. It didn't take long, and she was out like a light.

When Sam awoke, she felt reenergized, and the headache was gone. Making a mental note to take more breaks or not put so much time on the computer, she decided to try out her ankle by going for a short, easy run. Before she left the room, she took the Ace bandage and wrapped the .380 and its holster tight and close to her body. Jumping up and down, she tested the security of the holster and weapon.

This will work for now. She'd need to buy a belly band if she was going to start running.

When she walked outside, she decided it would definitely be a short run in this heat. It was late morning but already in the mid-eighties. Starting out with a quick walk, she felt good. About a minute later, she stepped it up to a light jog. Still good. She could tell she hadn't been running for a while. It didn't take long for her to get a little winded, and she was breathing hard. Sam stayed with a light jog, but after a few minutes, she had to slow down and walk. Her ankle started to bother her. She turned around and headed back. Her muscles and tendons were tight, especially in her ankle.

She took another shower and decided to go for a drive. She had been waiting to get the cast off so she could take the bike for a ride. Now she could. She assumed she knew how to ride, and once she was on the bike, everything felt comfortable. She strapped on the helmet then started the bike and took off.

Riding the bike out of town was a pleasant change of scenery. The farther she rode, the more the landscape changed. Rolling hills and farmland were more prevalent. It was no wonder they called this the hill country. It was beautiful. The feeling of the wind and sun on her face felt good. Her mind started to empty of all her troubles and questions. Eventually, she decided she had gone far enough and turned around. The ride had cleared her head and she felt a little better.

So, shooting and a bike ride can be therapeutic for me. I'll have to try and keep that in mind.

When she returned to the motel room, she decided to stay in this relaxed mode and flipped on the TV to watch a movie or show. As she was getting involved in a police drama she'd found, her phone chimed.

LEIA

Hi.

SAM

Hey. I'm sorry. It's been a few days, hasn't it?

LEIA

It's okay, just thinking about you.

Sam smiled. *How does she do that?* Leia could elicit a smile from Sam with ease.

LEIA

I just wanted to tell you again that I really had a great time the other night. Care to do it again? On me, this time?

Again with the wink emoji. *Oh boy. I'm in a relationship. I just need to go slow. How do I respond to that text?* Sam wasn't sure about this emoji thing.

Sam stared at the thumbs-up she sent. *Crap. That was stupid.* The three dots disappeared. *I'm no good at this.* Sam didn't want to worry about that right now. She had more important things to consider.

∽

THE FOLLOWING DAY, Sam hopped on her motorcycle to begin her task. She went to a Sprint store first, but they didn't have her on file. Next was a Verizon store. She explained she'd lost her phone and asked if they could help her locate it. She was pleased when they told her they had Samantha Barrett in their system. She showed her ID, and they asked if she had the Find My iPhone app. She said yes, assuming that was correct. It had been more than four weeks since her accident, so chances were that the phone was dead. But even though it wasn't on, they were able to pull up its last known location when it had been on. That was all Sam needed for now. She got the address and drove to it.

The location was a park. *Where to start?* She began walking around. This park felt familiar for some reason. As she was walking, she saw a bench underneath a large oak tree with some brush surrounding it. She suddenly had a memory flash of herself sitting on that bench. She walked over and sat down. She looked around then got up from the bench and decided to check in the nearby bushes.

Around the back of the tree, deep in the brush, she saw it. She couldn't believe her luck. After all, it had been at least four weeks.

Just as she picked up the phone and stood, she felt something fly by her ear and into the tree.

That was too fast to be a bug.

The hair on her neck stood up. She looked at the tree, and seeing the metal lodged inside, she confirmed it was a bullet. Her training kicked in, and she jumped over the bench just as another round hit the tree and sent a little bark flying. Someone was using a suppressor—there'd been no sound of a gunshot.

Sam squatted low as she positioned herself between the bush and tree for cover. She placed the phone in her pocket. Staying low, she looked all around for the glint of glass from a scope or anything suspicious. Feeling a surge of adrenaline and a small sense of familiarity, she waited. Hide and seek.

Paintball. She had a flash of herself hiding then a paintball splattering on her shoulder. A boy called from behind her. *Gotcha, Sammy!*

A toddler squealing from across the park snapped her back to reality. Sam took in her surroundings. Looking up at the two rounds in the tree, she surmised the shots had come from directly in front of where she'd been standing. Straining to see what was in front of her, she looked across the park. On the other side of the street was an apartment complex with cars and trucks parked in front of the buildings. *I'm a sitting duck. I need to make my move before they do.* Her motorcycle was in a parking lot near the park, on the other side of the tennis court. It was about a fifty-yard sprint to the fenced-in court. She'd have to run around it to get to the motorcycle. There wasn't much cover, but she needed to move. She also wanted to avoid the two mothers and toddlers playing in the small area about twenty yards in front of the tennis court to the left.

Run right. Zigzag. She glanced at her ankle, glad that she had wrapped it for additional support.

After taking a deep breath, Sam darted toward the right of the court, zigzagging until she ran along the fence line and straight to her bike. She hopped on, started it, and took off.

She drove out of the parking lot on the far side then turned to the left and headed up the street. She continued past the street between the park and the apartments and took a left on the next street, then another to enter the other side of the apartment complex.

After parking the bike, she carefully and slowly made her way to where she thought the shots had been taken. Not seeing anyone, Sam took up a position as if she were taking the shot from a vehicle, the most likely scenario. They were gone. *I wouldn't shoot from here.* She looked over at the tree in the park and then back at the apartment complex. Smirking, she thought, *I'd get on the roof or into one of those apartments. That one, and set up looking out that window. A sniper's position. But that would mean a rifle.* She eyed the closed window. They didn't have time to close the window and get out before she got here. This was Texas, and it was hot. All windows were closed on that side of the complex to keep the air-conditioning in.

How do I know all this stuff? Were those shots just a warning? Did they want to kill me or just scare me? Sam had so many questions.

Figuring it was probably safe, she returned to her bike and drove back to the park. Maintaining a sense of awareness, she parked on the street closest to the tree, checked the saddle bags, and pulled out a small knife. She went over to the tree and dug out what was left of the two rounds, pocketed them, and got back on the bike.

After driving around for twenty minutes to make sure she wasn't being followed, she headed to her motel. Her heart was racing, but not from fear.

That was exhilarating. She smiled slightly as she went into her room.

What is going on? Who shot at me, and why? She was extremely lucky she hadn't gotten hit—if they were trying to kill her. Even with the suppressor, it was a bold move in the daytime. She removed the two bullets from her pocket and studied them. Small in diameter compared to a shotgun. She took some photos with her phone and zoomed in to see if she could see any rifling from the barrel. There was definite rifling.

Yep. They used a handgun. The maximum effective range of most handguns is fifty yards. Easy for me to get a bullet on target, but most shooters aren't me. It wasn't bragging. It was true. Sam was a really good shot.

"The Olympics are in your future, Samantha. Rifle, handgun, or both. I look forward to you representing your country and bringing home gold." No pressure there, Dad. At fourteen, Sam tried to make a joke and said, *"Which country? The USA or*

Italy?" Her father did not find it amusing, so Sam clarified her position. *"I'm kidding, Dad. There's only one country I'd ever fight for or represent. The good old US of A."*

Her little brother had to chime in. *"Yeah, you do that and I'll be learning to fly jets for the United States Navy, right, Dad?"*

"You both are on your own paths. Yes, son. A Navy pilot, then maybe a senator, and President of the United States. You are destined for great things. But first, you need to beat your sister's time on that course."

Sam squeezed the bullets in her hand so tight that sharp pieces of the rounds made small cuts in her palm.

That damn obstacle course in the woods at home. A year later Jimmy would be dead due to that course.

Sam opened her eyes, swallowing back the tears. She set the spent rounds on the small table and looked at her palm. The three cuts were small, but she should still wash them to prevent infection.

After cleaning her hands, Sam grabbed a beer from the minifridge and took three big gulps. She began pacing back and forth. She stopped and took a deep breath. After slowly exhaling, she took another sip of beer. One more deep breath in and slowly out. Sam set what was left of the beer on the counter and pulled the phone out of her pocket. The device was dirty and had more than likely been rained on. It had a case on it, so maybe there wouldn't be much water damage. She needed to charge it. She looked at the port and realized the charger she had wouldn't work. A quick trip up the road to a convenience store was warranted.

Upon returning to her room, she plugged the phone in then thought it might have Face ID. If so, she would be able to open it. Instead of watching the phone charge, she decided to get her gear ready for Sara's lesson the next day.

After a while, she looked back at the phone. It had

powered on. She held it in front of her face, but a message came up saying the passcode was required when the phone restarted.

"What the..." *Wait, maybe they can unlock it at the phone store.*

~

SURE ENOUGH, after identifying herself again, they unlocked the phone for her, and she raced back home.

Besides the standard apps, she found apps for music, shopping, fitness, social media, travel, and movies. She opened the phone app that contained contacts. There weren't very many, and she didn't recognize them. She opened the text messages and began reading. Most seemed to be from clients about shooting lessons—canceling or rescheduling appointments. She did find one interesting set of messages from someone named Katrina, but they were a couple of years old.

The texts had been exchanged over the course of a week. There weren't many of them, but they mentioned some homework and meeting others at a bar. Sam inferred that she and Katrina had become friends. The last few texts were the most interesting.

KATRINA

Thank you for a wonderful evening and have a safe flight.

SAM

I had a great time. Be safe, and good luck.

Why weren't there any more messages from Katrina? It seemed like one of them had flown out of town. Sam was getting fed up with all these dead ends. She needed answers. One way to get some was to contact Tom. She decided to wait and contact him on Wednesday. No need to rush into anything. The last thing Sam needed to do was be careless, especially since someone had just taken a shot at her. Was it the same person that she thought had been following her?

5

On Tuesday at ten thirty in the morning, Sam met Sara at the Alpha Gun Range. This range had a few small rooms that customers could rent. Sam arranged to have one room for an hour. They went over some basic safety rules first, followed by breathing and sight picture. It all felt like second nature to Sam. She had a flash of a memory of someone teaching her. *Squeeze the trigger, don't pull it.*

The memory was gone as quickly as it had come. Sam didn't dwell on it and showed Sara the handgun they would use that day—a Sig Sauer P320 9mm. Sara learned the basic operations of the handgun. They practiced loading the weapon, breaking it down, cleaning it, and putting it back together. After the hour was up, Sam took Sara to one of the lanes she'd rented. Everything they went over in the classroom, they now put into practice.

Sam put a target up and sent it back to the three-yard mark. She had Sara load a few magazines and insert one magazine into the pistol. After reminding Sara about basic range safety, she told her to fire two rounds, center of mass.

Sara squeezed off one round and then the second. She jumped a little after the first round went off, so the second round was a little farther off-center than the first.

"Don't anticipate. Just squeeze the trigger and let it happen." Sam had her fire off some more rounds.

"Would you show me please?" Sara set her weapon down and stepped back.

The lane consisted of metal walls covered in a material that minimized the ricochet of the empty cartridge. A horizontal shelf spanned the walls and was at a height for most adults to set their weapons and ammunition on. On the left wall was a light switch that lit a spotlight down onto the shelf. The other switch allowed a person to manipulate the target return. The target could be brought all the way forward to place the paper target on the cardboard behind it, which stayed in place. Then by moving the switch the opposite way, one could send it to any distance up to fifteen yards.

Sam stepped up to the horizontal shelf that Sara had set the weapon on. Not only was it a place to rest the weapon, but it kept a person from walking down the lane toward the target. Picking up the weapon, Sam took up a stance that she didn't always use, but was teaching Sara.

Feet slightly wider than shoulder width apart, she moved the weapon forward, aimed, steadied her breathing, and squeezed off one shot at a time five times. "Take your time. There's no hurry."

"Okay." Sara picked up the nine millimeter handgun and tried again. She did better this time, landing in the seven, eight, and nine rings.

After she felt Sara was comfortable, she moved the target back to the seven-yard mark.

After their hour was up, they cleaned up, gathered their belongings, and walked to the common area.

"Wait here and I'll settle up," Sam told Sara. She walked over to the counter and turned in Sara's handgun that Sam had rented for her. She settled the payment with the range and retrieved their identification. Sam was careful not to let anyone see her military ID. She just didn't want to answer any questions, but it was what she needed for identification since she didn't have a driver's license.

As she handed Sara her ID, Sam said, "You did good for a beginner."

Sara smiled and said, "Thank you. I enjoyed the lessons."

The range had a special room where they could clean their weapons on-site. Sara asked if Sam was going to clean her weapon now or not.

"No, I'll wait until I get home." *That would be the crappy motel room I'm still in.*

Sara paid her in cash for the lessons as they had arranged. As they walked out to their vehicles, Sara again thanked Sam for the lessons. Sam told her to contact her if she had any questions or wanted more lessons. She reminded her it was important to practice.

Sara then asked her if she would like to join her for a late lunch. Sam thanked her but declined. She had some things she needed to take care of—like figuring out how to approach Tom.

6

Sam decided it was time to trust Tom. She would take precautions because, as far as she knew, he could have been the one who took a shot at her. If it had been him, they were warning shots. He most likely would not have missed. But she had a gut feeling that he wasn't the one.

She went back to his range and asked if he had time to talk. He said no but told her the ammo she ordered had arrived. Reaching under the desk, he pulled out a bag with six boxes of ammunition in it. Confused, she took it, thanked him, and left.

When she reached her car, she looked in the bag and pulled out one of the boxes. Nothing special: just a box of 9-mm Hydra-Shok. Her gut told her to open each box. Inside the third box was a small piece of paper. Written on it was "8 p.m. River Place." She searched for River Place on the map of her phone. It was a park. She'd have to wait until tonight to get more answers.

～

AT SEVEN FORTY-FIVE, Sam arrived at the park. It was a small park, with a covered picnic area not far from the parking lot. She wasn't sure whether she was supposed to wait in her car or go to the covered area up ahead. She stayed in her car for about ten minutes, keeping vigilant.

Maybe this was a bad idea. No, I need answers.

It might be safer outside, so she got out and walked to the covered area. While she was looking around, a car pulled into the lot, and Tom got out. Seeing she wasn't in her car, he looked for her and then walked over. He sat down, facing out, at one of the picnic tables.

"Are you going to stand there or have a seat?" he asked.

Sam cautiously approached and sat on his left side with distance between them. She had a lightweight jacket covering her left hand and, without warning, revealed her pistol as she pointed it at Tom.

"Start talking," Sam said.

"Whoa, settle down," Tom said as he showed his hands, palms up. "Sam, what are you doing? You don't need that with me. And why didn't you stay in your car?"

"I didn't want to get blood all over such a nice car in case things didn't work out," she told him.

"What are you talking about? I'm your handler. You can trust me," he said.

Sam kept her eyes and the weapon on him. "Handler?" After a few seconds, her instincts told her to come clean but keep her guard up. "Okay, listen. I had some sort of accident over a month ago and can't remember anything. Now you can start filling in the blanks, or we can talk about other options."

"You have amnesia?" His eyes narrowed. "Seriously?"

"No, I've really enjoyed wandering around this city,

trying to figure out who I am and what the hell I'm doing. It's been a great game." Sam's face screwed up in anger. She needed answers, and he was going to tell her what he knew.

"Okay, I'm sorry. You were acting kind of weird at the range. I thought maybe it was part of your cover." He paused and then said, "Maybe I should call my boss and let him know."

"Before doing that, why don't you tell me what I should already know," Sam said.

"Is that how you hurt your ankle? Did you really step in a hole?"

"I don't know. I can't remember anything before the accident. Just tell me what you know. Now!"

"Calm down. Why are you so angry?"

She took a breath. "I'm sorry. I'm frustrated because I don't know what happened to me. I really need some answers, and sometimes I feel like I don't know what the hell I'm doing." Her face softened, and she quietly said, "Can you help me?"

He stared at the gun, and Sam finally relaxed by setting the weapon on her leg, but she loosened her grip slightly as she still held it.

"How much do you remember?"

"Most of my life up until college. It starts to get sketchy from there. But I found my apartment, and I know I'm an air force officer. Or I was. I'm also a firearms instructor. I don't know why I'm in Austin."

"Okay, I'll read you in." As Tom spoke, the memories returned.

~

The mission before her memory loss...

Sam was attached to the Air Force Office of Special Investigations (OSI) for a special assignment. The Bureau of Alcohol, Tobacco, Firearms and Explosives (ATF) through the Pentagon and Department of Defense suspected one of their defense contractors of providing "poorly made ammunition, firearms, and/or equipment or using suppliers banned by the State Department" to the United States Armed Forces. OSI was asked to help with the investigation.

Sam was chosen due to her background and was given some additional training before going undercover. The suspected contractor, William McKenzie, had a daughter who traveled with him and was learning about the company so she could take over someday. Intelligence suggested she probably wasn't aware of any illegal activity, but it was decided that the daughter, Brooke, was Sam's way into the company. A way to get close to those at the top. The plan was to "arrange" a kidnapping attempt of Brooke. Sam, who happened to be on vacation, would step in and save Brooke from the "kidnapping." Hopefully, that would lead to a friendship or maybe even a job at the company.

KenzieCorp, William's company, was based in Austin, Texas. They had a contract to provide body armor to the military. William was a multimillionaire, so a kidnapping for ransom or bribery wouldn't seem too farfetched. To keep the ATF, OSI, and all the other three-letter agencies as far from suspicion as possible, the "kidnapping" would take place in Europe. McKenzie did a lot of business overseas, so they would have plenty of chances to stage the attempt. If things went as planned, William would hire Sam as a bodyguard for Brooke, and Sam would have access to gather as much intel as possible for all agencies involved.

Sam's background was scrubbed and cleaned so that when William ran a background check, it wouldn't raise any questions. Sam's cover reflected that she was born in Italy to American parents who had passed away. She came to America to go to college in Texas, joined the Air Force, then resigned her commission. She was a firearms instructor, trying to build up her own business. The operation was to take place in Venice, Italy, and to make it more believable, Sam's passport and hotel information would show that she had been in Italy for a month. The longer she was there, the more likely she might cross paths with the McKenzies.

Being a firearms instructor and enthusiast, Sam was going to visit the Beretta Firearms Museum, which was about two hours from Venice. Brooke loved Venice and made many trips there. Sam would be staying at a hotel near Brooke's.

Everything had gone according to plan.

Sam was walking by Brooke's hotel as two men tried to force her into an SUV. Sam thwarted the attack by fighting off the two aggressors. She was a skilled fighter, having trained in Krav Maga and other areas of self-defense. The men gave up, got in the SUV, and drove off.

"Are you all right?" Sam asked Brooke as she assisted her up off the ground.

"Me? I'm fine. I should ask you the same question. That was amazing!"

Brooke was so grateful and asked if there was anything she could do to repay her. Sam declined, but Brooke asked if she could at least buy her a drink. So they went back into Brooke's hotel and had a drink at the bar.

"I'm Brooke McKenzie."

"Sam Barrett."

"You're American. So am I," Brooke said. "I'm from Texas. Austin."

"Wow. I just moved back to the Austin area. Small world, huh?"

"Yes. May I ask what brings you to Venice?"

"The canals. I love looking at them and all the bridges. I was born not far from here. Pordenone. But I'm traveling using Venice as my base. I also wanted to visit the Beretta Firearms Museum."

"Venice is a beautiful city. Firearms museum? I guess that shouldn't surprise me. So, where did you learn to fight like that?"

"I took self-defense classes, and I'm a firearms instructor."

"Well, I'm impressed."

After an hour of talking about Italy and Austin, they exchanged numbers and said their goodbyes.

The next day, someone from McKenzie's office contacted Sam, asking her to meet with Mr. McKenzie at a local restaurant. Sam accepted. The restaurant was exclusive and hard to get into. Sam figured she'd need to dress up. She'd have to go shopping since she hadn't brought anything appropriate. As she was leaving her hotel, the door attendant stopped her and said she had a package at the front desk. She picked up the package and took it back to her room. Upon opening it, she discovered a beautiful dress and a pair of heels. A note read,

Just in case you didn't have anything. No strings attached. I'll send a car.
-WM

William McKenzie. Very impressive. Sam tried on the dress and heels. They couldn't fit any better. She looked at herself in the mirror and turned around. *Very nice.* She'd worn her mess dress—the equivalent to evening wear—but had never had the occasion to wear an evening gown. It clung to her body and showed just enough cleavage to remain tasteful. The slit up the side was also sexy but left plenty to the imagination. Only one thing was missing, and she'd have to go shopping for it—a special holster.

AT SEVEN FORTY-FIVE in the evening, Sam was ready to go to the restaurant. McKenzie had sent the car, and it was waiting out front for her. When she arrived, she was shown to a private dining room. A few men turned and watched as she walked by. She did feel stunning in the long black evening gown. William was sitting at a table waiting for her, with Brooke sitting on his left. William stood as she approached.

"Miss Barrett, I'm William McKenzie, and you know my daughter, Brooke."

Sam shook his hand and told him what a pleasure it was to meet him. He was a tall man, about six foot three. When he spoke, his Texas accent was very apparent. He displayed his manners as a gentleman by holding Sam's chair as she sat down on his right.

After some pleasantries and a drink order, William

began, "I just had to meet the woman who saved my daughter's life and say thank you. She was extremely impressed by you."

"Thank you, Mr. McKenzie. I'm just glad I happened to be there. I'm sure Brooke is quite capable of taking care of herself," Sam said as Brooke smiled at her.

"Yes, that's true. She is a strong and capable young woman. I'm very proud of her. Miss Barrett, what do you do for a living?"

Sam paused for a moment. "Mr. McKenzie, anyone who has the resources to get a woman's dress and shoe size has surely already run a background check on her."

Brooke looked at her father, but William smiled and started to laugh. "Very good. You are correct. I hope that doesn't offend you."

"No, sir." As Sam smiled and took a sip of wine, she noticed one of William's men move slightly. "With all due respect, Mr. McKenzie, if this is a test, I'd hate to break a heel on these new shoes. You have a man by every door, one in the kitchen, and one in the back alley. All of them are carrying a firearm, as am I. Thank you, sir, but I think I had better go. Nice to see you again, Brooke."

Brooke smiled at her and then tucked a bit of hair behind her ear. Sam was very good at reading people and knew it to be an unspoken signal between Brooke and her father.

As Sam stood, so did William. "Wait, Miss Barrett, I apologize. You must understand—after what happened to Brooke, I need to be extremely careful. Please stay. I didn't mean to offend you."

Sam sat back down.

"I'd like to offer you a job. I would like for you to give

Brooke self-defense and firearms training, as well as be her bodyguard."

"Thank you, but I don't—"

"Ms. Barrett. At the same time you were saving Brooke, I received a ransom note. If you hadn't intervened, my daughter would have most likely been kidnapped. I need your help. Look, how about a month trial. If you aren't happy, walk away, no problem."

Sam thought for a moment and took a bite of the sea bass. She didn't want to appear too eager. "Brooke, you've been very quiet. Does your father do all your talking?"

"Not at all. He will hire someone anyway. I wanted to have a say in the matter, and I want you."

"Why?"

"I saw you in action. I believe I could learn a lot from you about self-defense and taking care of myself. Again, I want you."

Sam smiled and said, "Do you need a bodyguard or a babysitter?" Brooke made no comment or emotion, so not wanting to lose the opportunity, Sam apologized. "I'm sorry. I didn't mean to offend you." Then Sam said, "Tell me something your father taught you about negotiating."

"Firmly state your intentions, and never beg."

Brooke had done exactly that. She told Sam she wanted her, and she didn't beg for her to stay when she nearly left, twice. They were in a negotiation.

Sam extended her right hand. "All right, Mr. McKenzie, you have a deal. One month trial, and I can walk away anytime I choose. Oh—two more conditions. Number one, I work for Brooke and not you."

"Fair enough. The second condition?"

While shaking his hand, Sam pulled him closer and whispered in his ear. He smiled and nodded in agreement.

Sam thanked her hosts, said good night, turned, and walked away.

"What did she say, Dad?"

"To stop tailing her and you. You've chosen wisely, my dear. Oh, Miss Barrett," he exclaimed as she was walking away. "Where's the weapon?"

Sam grinned from ear to ear and walked out the door without saying a word.

7

After Tom got Sam all caught up, she stood and said, "I think I need a drink. Why should I believe you? Show me some proof."

"Proof?" He almost laughed. "You're undercover, and so am I. I'm your handler, your contact. How do you expect me to prove it? Besides, why would I make any of this up?"

Fair point, Sam thought. *I'm working undercover. This explains a lot. No wonder I didn't want to go to the police. It might have compromised my cover. It definitely would have if they plastered my face all over the place.* After taking a deep breath, she let it out slowly. He was right. "You have a wife and son. Is he autistic?"

Tom stepped back in shock. "My personal life is none of your business and has nothing to do with this case."

"Answer me or I will hurt you." She raised the weapon, again.

"Yes, he has autism. How did you know about my son? I never told you that."

"I followed you after you left my apartment complex. Came back the next day and saw your wife leave and you put your son on the bus. That must be difficult. I apologize for asking about your personal life. But it tells me something about you."

"What does it tell you?"

"That you have something to lose, and I don't think you'd jeopardize that." Then she wondered about Italy. That was probably her first trip back since she was a teenager. Venice wasn't that far from Pordenone. "Do you know if I went anywhere besides Venice?"

Tom gave her a confused look. "I don't know. Why?"

Sam wanted to know if she went home. To her family home in Pordenone. Would she have taken a side trip to see her estranged father? There was only one person she would have been interested in seeing and that was the woman who'd taken care of her after her mother passed away. Her nanny, Mrs. Rossi.

No, I doubt I went home.

Lowering the weapon, she said, "Forget I asked. Okay, how long was I working for Brooke?"

"So you trust me?"

"Call it a gut feeling." He had a family. Why would he lie or put them at risk?

Tom answered her question. "You worked for Brooke for three months. You checked in with me once a week or so. When you were in town, that is. When you traveled, it was about every two weeks. You were given a long leash."

"Was I making any progress?" Sam asked.

"Slowly, but yes," Tom told her. "From what you told me, you had gained her trust and access to her office. Last I knew, you said you were close and would have some information soon. Then you went dark. Missed a check-in. Then another." He looked around to make sure they were alone. "I was worried you had been caught or..."

"Or what?"

"Gone rogue or been paid off."

Sam was offended. Although she had memory gaps she knew she was a proud American and would never betray her country or her own integrity. She raised the gun again and angrily said, "Listen up, spy boy. I would never compromise my values or betray my country. I may have forgotten this mission, but I could have easily gone to the police and found out who I was. But I didn't. My gut told me not to. So I'm still in this."

"I didn't mean to offend you. I didn't know what to think. Look, you're young and inexperienced. Someone wanted to give you a chance or you know someone that got you this assignment."

Sam was thoroughly pissed now and let him know. "Are you trying to piss me off and get shot?"

"No. It's just that we have plenty of more experienced women who could have done this job."

"So you think I slept my way into this job?"

"I didn't say that. I just questioned the decision until I was told otherwise."

"Told by who?" Sam was curious as to who would go to bat for her.

"He never identified himself. I got the feeling he was a spook. Do you remember our briefing at the Pentagon?"

"No."

Tom sighed. "There were representatives of all the different agencies at the briefing for this assignment. You were there. I wasn't the only one who voiced my concerns over you taking this on. After the briefing, you were told to leave, and we stayed. A man came in and like I said, he didn't identify himself. He told us you were more than capable of completing this assignment. That you were practically born into the life of a spy. You had training from a young age. You speak multiple languages and are an expert marksman. You have self-defense training and have already been on one successful classified mission."

It took her a few beats before she spoke. "I'm not a spy," Sam said practically in shock from what he had just told her. "What did the man look like?"

"Tall, about six foot two, with sandy-blond hair, military cut, medium complexion, about a hundred and seventy-five pounds and very fit. He was about fifty or so. Sound familiar?"

Not Dad. Unless his hair has lightened over the years. I doubt it was him. Could he have sent someone? Possibly.

"No. I've no idea. What classified mission?"

"He didn't say. Just said to trust the decision and give you a chance. You were the right person for this job. Then he left."

Sam couldn't believe her ears. She'd already been on a mission. "Did you look up this mission? The one I already did?"

"I tried. It was heavily redacted. I couldn't make heads or tails of it. Do you remember it?"

"No. I told you I can't remember anything before I hit my head. I remember an obstacle course in college and then waking up in the hospital. Now that you told me about McKenzie, I remember most of that." She glared at him. "I did not sleep my way into this job."

"I know that. You've done a great job up until now."

"What does that mean?"

"Well. You were out of contact for over three weeks. When you came in last week, you still didn't know me, right?"

Sam shook her head.

"It's been nearly five weeks now. What do you think Brooke would say if you suddenly showed up?" Tom asked.

"I don't know. I don't remember her. I don't..." Sam was pacing but stopped abruptly. She was an Air Force officer and was on an undercover mission.

Tom stood up and walked near her, but Sam raised the handgun. "Sam, relax. I think I need to call this in. You can't do this. They're just going to have to figure something else out." Tom slowly took his phone out.

Sam reached over and stopped him. "No." After being told about the joint mission and when Tom had mentioned the USAF OSI, Sam felt something. A need to learn more. A desire to join that career field. *OSI. This case is my chance to get in. To prove myself.* "You said I was attached to OSI for this assignment. What's my job in the Air Force?"

"You're security forces. Assigned to a squadron overseas."

"A military cop." *Good entry into law enforcement.* "I want to do this. Continue the mission. I can do this, Tom. We could play it the way you suggested. Tell the truth, and say I was in an accident and have amnesia. But how would I explain remembering Brooke?"

Tom thought for a moment and asked if she had her phone.

"It took some time, but I found it in a park."

"How?"

"I went to cell phone companies and gave them my name and had them ping it. It was dead but the last location was the park."

"Smart." They looked for Brooke's contact information, and sure enough, it was there. Although Tom was very reluctant, they decided Sam would go to Brooke's and tell her that she thought she had some sort of accident and had amnesia. She found Brooke's name in her phone, and it felt familiar, so she decided to look her up. Hopefully, something would jog Sam's memory, and everything would come back to her.

After Tom gave her more information about the mission and how they would stay in contact, Sam thanked him and began to leave.

He grabbed her arm and stopped her. When Sam growled and gave him a look like she would hurt him, he let go. "Sam, I'm giving you the benefit of the doubt here. Trusting that you can pull this off. Both our careers are on the line. If you have any doubts or problems, you get out and contact me. We don't know what happened to you. Unless you haven't told me the truth."

"I don't know what happened. I woke up in a hospital with a cast on my foot and a slight concussion. No memory of anything, including my name. Current last name, that is."

Tom stared at her. "Current last name? What does that mean? Did you change your name? All your records are under Barrett."

The last thing Sam wanted to do was tell him her birth name. She did not want to be linked to that man. If Tom was in the intelligence field, there was a possibility he might recognize the name and ask her about it. Or go digging on his own. It might bring back those doubts he had about her capability. The point of changing her name was to make sure she didn't ride his coattails. To make sure no one even thought about nepotism. It was important to Sam that she earn her own way.

"It doesn't matter."

Tom was curious about the comment but dropped it. It wasn't important right now. "You managed to find your way to me. How did you do that?"

Sam smiled and said, "I guess I do have skills as an investigator."

Tom smiled back and made a sound. "Pfft. Yeah, I guess they were right about you."

"Who? Besides that mysterious man."

"My boss. By the way, what have you been calling yourself?"

"Jaime."

He grinned. "What's so funny?"

"You wanted to use an alias instead of your real name. Jaime Sommers. From the TV show?"

"Oh." Sam narrowed her glare at him. "You said you're my handler but never said which agency you were with on this joint mission."

The smile grew a little wider and all he said was, "No, I didn't. Stay in contact, and good luck, Sam." With that, Tom left.

BEFORE SHE CONTACTED BROOKE, Sam wanted to take care of something. Knowing her purpose and mission, she needed to concentrate on that. She had a life in the Air Force, and after this mission, she most likely would be sent back to her base overseas. That meant she had some goodbyes to make.

She drove to the coffee shop and asked Lisa if she had a minute to talk. She told Lisa she had taken a new job and probably wouldn't be back. She wanted Lisa to know how much her friendship and help meant to her.

"I couldn't leave without saying goodbye," Sam said.

"Thank you. I'm really glad you came to say goodbye in person. Take care of yourself. If you can keep in touch, I'd like that." They hugged, and she left.

Sam had one more goodbye to say and this one would be more difficult. She called Leia and asked if she could meet her. She had a break in between her classes, so she drove to her office on campus. As she walked into her office, Leia stood up, and Sam's heart skipped a beat. She really looked good in her khakis and button-down shirt.

"Hello, professor," Sam said softly.

"Hi. I've been meaning to contact you." Leia motioned to the chair on the other side of his desk.

Sam sat down, and Leia leaned on the edge of her desk. Uncomfortable for a moment, Sam looked down and then back up into her eyes. "You've come to say goodbye," Leia said sadly.

"Yes. I have a new job, and it's going to keep me busy. It also will require me to travel."

"I see. What about your memory?"

Sam reached out and touched her hand. "I've learned more about myself," she said.

Leia turned her hand over and squeezed Sam's. Softly, she replied, "I wish we could have had more time. I'd really like to get to know you better."

This was harder than Sam thought it would be. She needed to get out of there. She stood and pulled her hand away from Leia's. Her knees started to feel weak, and it took all her strength to not fall back into the chair.

Leia stood and placed a hand on the side of Sam's neck, her fingers running through her short hair. She pulled her close and gently brushed her lips against Sam's.

"Are you sure I can't delay your departure?"

The blinds were already closed, so all they'd have to do was lock the office door. Sam didn't say anything. She knew she should go, but she also wanted to stay and hold Leia in her arms. She imagined her taking her right there on the desk—hot, passionate office sex. She blushed just thinking about it.

"Sam? Are you okay?" Leia asked.

Sam thought about revealing a little more. "Don't take this the wrong way, but can you show me your identification? The military one."

Leia dropped her hands and stared at her.

Crap.

"You don't believe I'm in the Army Reserves?"

"I do, but it's just precaution."

"Precaution? Who are you, Sam?"

"I have a job to do."

"Am I under investigation?"

Leia's demeanor had changed, and Sam knew she'd made a mistake. "No. I want to tell you something, but I just need to be sure."

"Sure about what? That you can trust me? I held you in my arms after you told me you lost your memory. I didn't ask or push you. As much as I wanted to, I did not google you." She shook her head in disbelief. "Maybe you should just go."

"Yeah. Thanks for confirming something else."

"What's that?" Leia asked as she crossed her arms.

"I'm terrible at relationships. I'm sorry. Goodbye." Sam walked over to the door.

"Sam, wait," Leia said.

Sam turned and watched her as she went around to her desk and unlocked a drawer. Pulling out a leather satchel she dug inside and retrieved a wallet and some papers. Walking over to Sam she pulled out her military ID card and showed it to her. Then she showed her the papers. They were her orders activating her to active duty status for a temporary duty assignment to Kuwait. She'd only returned two months ago from a ten-month deployment. She was assigned to the 377th MI Battalion. Just as she said.

Sam felt relieved but also like crap for asking her to prove her identity.

"I showed you mine, now you show me yours."

"My what?"

"Your ID."

She reached in her cargo pocket and pulled out the small ID case. She only had the one credit card. For security she'd left her military ID in the apartment. "I couldn't find a driver's license and my other form of identification is tucked safely away." She showed her the credit card and a business card.

Leia's face softened. "Firearms instructor. You're undercover. Are you a police officer, Detective?"

"No, but you're on the right track." Sam smiled and teased her by saying, "Not bad for a grunt."

"Grunt? How dare you..." Then the realization hit her. "Oh, you're military. In light of the insult, you must be a different branch."

"Air Force and I outrank you, First Lieutenant Leia Coventry."

"I told you I was prior enlisted." Studying Sam, she said, "I probably have more time in service than you. I'm also due for a promotion."

"Congratulations." Sam was feeling a bit smug, and it showed.

"I'm not dating a zoomie," Leia said and walked back over to her desk.

Sam chuckled and followed her. After Leia replaced her wallet and the paperwork, Sam turned her and planted a very passionate kiss on her lips.

Leia gasped when Sam released her. "That didn't feel like goodbye," she said breathlessly.

"Maybe I changed my mind. But I still have a job to do, and it's classified. Army is not included." *Not directly as far as I'm concerned.*

Leia narrowed her eyes. "Undercover zoomie." She whispered the next question. "Are you OSI?"

"I can't confirm or deny that," Sam whispered back.

Leia's right hand came up and touched Sam's left waist. She felt the bulge under the shirt. "Should you have that on campus?"

Sam sighed. "Have you ever heard the saying 'I'd rather be tried by twelve than carried by six'?"

"Yes."

Sam wasn't sure what to make of Leia's reaction to the fact that she was carrying her concealed weapon on campus. "What bothers you more? The fact that I'm carrying on this liberal campus or that I'm carrying at all?"

Leia moved her hand above the weapon. "You're over twenty-one, I believe. You can do what you want. It was in my way. That's what bothered me," she said in a sultry voice. "You seem more confident than you did those two nights in the club."

"Do I?" Sam said as she nuzzled Leia's neck. "When I want something, I can get extremely focused."

"What is it you want, Sam Barrett?"

Sam grinned and pressed herself closer. "You're in intelligence, you tell me. By the way, I already locked the door."

"What happened to taking this slow?"

"I am going slow."

"You came to say goodbye and you suddenly change your mind? Why?"

"Seeing you in person made me change my mind. I'd

like to try this." She backed off slightly. "Unless you don't want to. I'll walk away, and you'll never see me again."

This time Leia leaned closer and placed her arms around Sam's neck. "I want to," she whispered in Sam's ear.

A sudden knock on the door startled them. Sam ignored it and nuzzled Leia's neck. Leia looked at her watch. "Damn, office hours. Sam, you have to go."

"Hmm?"

Leia pulled away and looked at herself. "You have to go. I have office hours now, and that's probably a student." She walked toward the door and unlocked it.

Sam sighed but turned and met her. She grinned like the Cheshire cat, and Leia gave her a quizzical look.

"The schoolteacher and the student. I may have to take a class." She gave her a quick kiss and opened the door to a waiting student. "The professor is in."

8

———

The next day, Sam drove to the address listed in her phone for Brooke. The two-story house was in an affluent neighborhood of Barton Creek in Austin. The walls were partially constructed of limestone, and the manicured lawn was as green as the putting greens at Augusta National Golf Club. Taking a big breath, she got out of the car and walked up the path and the three steps to the covered porch. To her left were two outdoor chairs on a rug and a few plants. Seeing the camera doorbell, Sam took another deep breath and pressed the button. After a long minute, Brooke opened the door. She looked at Sam with disbelief.

"What are you doing here? No, never mind. I don't care. Please leave." Brooke began to close the door, but Sam threw her hand on it to stop it.

"Can you give me five minutes?" Sam asked.

"Why should I? After three months, you didn't even have the decency to give me an explanation. Why are you here?"

Sam could tell that Brooke was hurt and angry. "You're

right. I'm really sorry. I owe you an explanation. May I come in? Please?"

Brooke gave it a couple of heartbeats then opened the door and stepped to the side so Sam could enter. Not remembering where to go, she waited and followed Brooke into the kitchen. "Nice place you have," she said, glancing around. The space had an open floor plan, and she noted the high ceilings and a few beams as they passed through the family room and stopped in the kitchen.

Brooke looked at her disapprovingly as she leaned against a counter. "Is that supposed to be a joke? Not one of your better ones."

Sam decided to just throw it out there. "I had some sort of accident and have amnesia."

Laughing at the statement, Brooke said, "Well, that's a little better." But when Sam just stood there, the expression on Brooke's face changed. She went to the refrigerator and pulled out a beer—the same brand as in Sam's apartment. She placed it in a koozie then handed it to Sam. After pouring herself a glass of wine, Brooke sat down on a barstool at the island to listen. "All right, go ahead."

Leaving out mission-essential details, Sam explained how she woke up in the hospital and then started her journey toward remembering who she was. She told her how she found Brooke's name in her phone and felt like she had to contact her. She was glad she did.

AT FIRST, Brooke didn't know what to say, but then she asked if Sam remembered anything about their relationship. Sam told her she knew she was teaching her how to shoot and some self-defense training, but other than that, nothing.

Brooke seemed disappointed but asked if she was okay. After Sam reassured her she was, Brooke wanted to know what she planned to do.

"Did you come back just to find out who I am and what you did?"

"I thought it might help. I was also hoping that maybe you'd take me back. I could continue to work for you." Sam told her she thought it might be the best way to regain her memory. "I still remember all my firearms and self-defense training." She looked away and mumbled, "Money's getting a little tight. I need a job."

"You were also hired to protect me, as a bodyguard. Do you remember that?"

"I did get the feeling there was more to it," Sam said taking a slow draw of her beer. "Hey, I understand if you'd rather just part ways. If you can just answer a few questions for me, I'll go, and you never have to see me again."

Brooke thought for a moment and took another sip of her wine. "Come on. I'll show you where you stayed. Maybe that will help with your memory."

Brooke took Sam upstairs to her room. It hadn't been touched since the day she'd disappeared. "Anything look familiar?"

"I'm not sure." Sam went in and had a look around. Brooke watched from the doorway as she picked up and studied objects she had held nearly five weeks ago. "These things are mine?"

"Yes. The postcards, magnets, and knickknacks. I had to take a trip to California, and you accompanied me. You said you'd never been and needed some souvenirs."

Sam picked up the postcards and magnet from San Francisco. Then the ones from the Sequoia National Park.

"You talked me into taking a few side trips."

Sam glanced at Brooke but then continued looking through the stack of postcards. Yosemite and then Reno was the last one.

"Side trips? Doesn't sound very professional to me."

Brooke shifted her weight, and a slight curve to her mouth appeared. "Okay, maybe the side trips were my idea. I had asked if you'd ever been to California, and you said you hadn't. I didn't have to rush back and so we did some sightseeing."

"I hope those memories return." Sam looked up at Brooke and smiled.

"Well, I'll leave you to it. Don't hesitate to ask if you need anything or have any questions. I'll be downstairs."

"Does that mean you're taking me back?" Sam asked setting the shot glass from Reno down.

"Why should I take you back when you can't remember anything?" Brooke asked.

The way Brooke asked was not in an angry manner. In fact, just the opposite. She was soft-spoken, and the question sounded almost like a test.

"You're right. You have no obligation to hire me back. Unless you haven't left your home while I was gone, you seem to be doing fine without me. So maybe I should just collect my personal things and leave."

Brooke stood in the doorway with her arms crossed, looking at her as Sam waited for some indication of what to do.

Sam was about to make up a story about how she needed the money or something when Brooke walked over and gave her an unexpected hug. "Welcome back."

"Uh, thank you."

SAM WASN'T sure what to make of the hug and sat down on the bed after the door was closed. It was getting late, and Sam was tired. It had been a while since she'd had a headache, but she felt one coming on. Sam wondered why Brooke hadn't packed up her stuff if she'd assumed she had left. Was she expecting her to return for her things? Maybe.

She opened the closet and found clothes similar to those in her closet at home. She saw a long black evening gown and suddenly remembered wearing it for the meeting with William. Flashes of that night came back into her mind. Feeling a little dizzy, she walked back over and sat down on the bed. That night suddenly became very clear.

Wow! That's the first full memory that has come back. More than just a snippet of a memory.

Brooke poked her head in and asked if she needed anything. Sam told her how she remembered meeting William that night in Venice.

"You were very impressive that evening," Brooke said. "I mean my father was impressed with how you handled your-self. Tell me, how did you know about all the security he had at the restaurant?"

"You had been threatened, right? It made sense that he'd increase security around you."

"But how did you know about the men out back and near the kitchen?"

"A good security team would cover all of that. It was an educated guess. But I was right, wasn't I?"

"Yes, you were." She couldn't help but smile. "As I said, you were impressive. The men were impressed as well."

"Your father's men?"

"All of them. I saw how the patrons watched you."

Sam blushed ever so slightly. "Your father chose a beau-tiful dress. That's it in the closet, isn't it?"

"Yes. Why did you leave the restaurant after accepting the job? You could have stayed."

"I'm not sure. Maybe I felt it was appropriate at the time."

"You certainly made your exit as memorable as your entrance." Brooke clarified when Sam tilted her head slightly. "The men. All eyes followed you out."

After a bit more reminiscing about that evening, Brooke decided to leave again. "Well, I have some things to finish up before I turn in, so I'll take my leave." She went to the door and stopped. "I'm glad you came back, Sam." Then she was gone.

Sam got ready for bed and set the alarm for six in the morning. She took a couple of aspirin she found in the bathroom and fell asleep quickly.

9

———————

Sam woke at five forty-five. After a minute of taking in her surroundings, she got up and took a shower. She dressed in workout gear she found in her closet, then went downstairs and found Brooke drinking a cup of coffee. While saying their good mornings, Sam went to the cabinet, grabbed a cup, and poured herself some coffee.

Brooke stopped her cup midway to her first sip and gave Sam a funny look.

"I'm sorry. Did I do something wrong?" Sam asked.

Not realizing it, Sam had gotten the same cup she'd always used. She hadn't hesitated to ask where the cups were. When Brooke pointed that out to her, Sam felt a sense of calm. She suddenly felt very comfortable being there.

"I guess coming back here was a good choice. I wish I had done it sooner, but it took a while to find my phone and unlock it."

"Why didn't you go to the police?"

"I don't know," Sam said, hoping Brooke wouldn't press the issue. She didn't.

Since it was Saturday, Brooke told Sam she could do

whatever she wanted. Sam wanted to know what their usual schedule was for a Saturday.

"You told me to vary my schedule, so I think a workout would be good," Brooke said.

Sam agreed, and they decided to go for a run. "I have to warn you that I'm probably not in the same shape I was before the accident."

"Good, maybe I'll have a chance." She smiled and took off.

After about thirty minutes, Sam's ankle began to bother her. She told Brooke about her ankle as they walked the rest of the way back home. Sam said she understood if Brooke didn't think she was up for the job anymore and wanted to let her go.

Finally, Brooke turned to her and said, "Ms. Barrett, do you think you're up for this job?"

"Yes."

Brooke was adamant about keeping her on. "Good, then stop trying to get me to fire you."

"Okay. What did your father say when I disappeared?" Sam asked as they walked along the street.

"He didn't say anything, because I didn't tell him."

Sam stopped walking. "Why didn't you tell him? Didn't he notice I wasn't around?" Sam asked.

Brooke turned to her and said, "I told him you were giving me a little more freedom at work. You've only been gone four and a half weeks, and luckily, we haven't had any parties or events yet, so I haven't really seen much of him."

"Well done. But you don't have to lie to your dad about me. I don't want to be the cause of any problems between you and your dad." That was important to Sam, and she remembered why. Her relationship with her father was strained, to say the least. She hadn't spoken to him or seen him since she left Italy at sixteen years old. The last thing she wanted was to disrupt Brooke and William's relationship.

Brooke smiled at her, and they started walking again. "We're fine. Don't worry about it."

"Maybe you don't really need me. It seems like you've taken care of yourself just fine."

"Oh my god. You're fired," Brooke suddenly said.

"Wait, what?" Sam asked confused.

Brooke stopped walking and gently touched Sam on the arm. "Yes, I do need you." She pulled her hand away. "I mean, you were hired to do a job. I'm not done learning from you." Then she continued walking.

The way Brooke had pulled her hand away and said that she still needed her was a bit concerning. *Maybe I'm imagining things. We're friends. Move on.*

Sam caught up to her and asked Brooke about the day she disappeared. It had started out like any other day. They got up, worked out in the garage-slash-gym, and since it was a weekday, went to the office. Sam had indeed started to give Brooke a little more freedom there. At about ten thirty that morning, Sam had left to run some errands but never came back.

Sam wondered if she'd retrieved the information and was leaving to meet Tom. He hadn't said they were supposed meet. Just that the last time they spoke she said she was close. "Was it normal for me to leave and run errands?"

"You were running to get a few groceries, and I was at the office. I'm relatively safe at my office. That's what you said, anyway. You need a key card to get into the building and past reception. We've always had that. I did hire an extra guard for the building, though. He patrols all the floors."

That made sense to Sam, and she was happy Brooke wasn't involved or hurt when she disappeared.

Brooke glanced at her. "I do have a question, though."

"Go ahead."

"There were times you would leave me alone. I thought bodyguards always stayed with their subjects."

"Many factors go into personal protection. Threat level, location, environment, and situational awareness are just a few. If I ever left you alone it was because it was low risk and felt you were safe. Did I ever leave you alone outside?"

"No."

"Good." Sam thought that if they retraced their steps that day, it might help jog some memories.

"Would you mind taking me to the office and walking me through it all? I think it might help me remember."

"Of course."

When they got back to the house, they showered, changed, ate breakfast, and drove to the office. Being a Saturday, no one would be there, so they could walk through everything. She doubted she'd have the chance to do any snooping while she was there. The mission came first, but finding out what had happened to her might help with that.

I need to find out what happened to me. How close was I to getting the information needed?

Sam had taught Brooke to vary her driving routes when she could. Sometimes, Sam would drive them in her car, and sometimes, they'd take Brooke's car. Today, they were in Sam's car, the same as they had been so many weeks before.

Suddenly, she had a thought. *If I drove my car that day, how did it get back to the storage unit?* It was a great question, but one that would have to wait for now. When they arrived at the office, Sam parked in the same place as that day, according to Brooke.

"Does it look familiar?" Brooke asked, getting out of the classic car.

"A little," Sam said, closing the door to her car.

They walked to the door of the building. Brooke entered the security code, unlocked the door, and they headed to the elevator. She placed her ID card over the security feature, which turned green, and pressed the button of the floor to her office. Once inside, they booted up Brooke's computer and pulled up her schedule for the day Sam disappeared. Sam noticed a sort of shorthand that she couldn't read. Brooke explained how Sam taught her not to be so open with her calendar, for safety. In other words, make it difficult for anyone but her to understand.

"Well, you must be a great student."

"It's not hard when you have a great teacher," Brooke told her.

Suddenly, Sam felt a bit uncomfortable. The feeling wasn't a bad one—just enough to keep her on edge. Sam was picking up on some signals from Brooke that she wasn't quite sure of. *Is she flirting with me?*

"So, did you leave the office at all that morning?"

Brooke said she did not. She'd had a meeting at nine in the morning in the conference room then was back in her office until Sam left.

"Where did I say I was going?"

"As I told you before, after I came back from the meeting, you said there were a few things we needed from the grocery store."

"So I wasn't at your meeting?"

"No, you waited here, in my office."

Hmm. She left me alone in her office. That would have been a great time to snoop and get any evidence. If there was any to get. Sam glanced around. The office was relatively sparse. No filing cabinets. Just a glass desk with computer on it and one chair. "Your office is sparse and lacks comfort."

Brooke smiled. "You commented on that the first time you came here. It's not meant for comfort. All I need is the computer, and I don't like people loitering in here. Present company excepted." Then Brooke added, "You're my body-guard, after all. I brought the chair in for you."

"All business. I respect that. Did your father teach you that?"

"He taught me to be professional. I've developed my own way of leading."

"So meetings are held in the conference room? Is every-thing digital? Do you have paper files?"

Brooke looked at her curiously.

Whoops? Did I go a step too far? Thinking quickly, Sam said, "I mean a possible reason to kidnap you would be corporate spying. I'm just wondering what vulnerabilities another company might try to take advantage of. Knowing the enemy helps me protect you."

"As with most companies, some things are still on paper, but we do have a lot digitized. Our cybersecurity is top-of-the-line. The file room is down the hall and has a numerical keypad for entry."

"Does it bother you that I asked those questions?" Sam could tell something concerned her.

"Security of the company isn't exactly in your area of responsibility, Ms. Barrett."

Ms. Barrett. Wow. I really stepped in it.

"I'm sorry. I'm just trying to cover all the bases and regain my memory."

Sam saw Brooke's shoulders loosen as she relaxed a

little. "No, I'm sorry. I should know that all your questions are based on my security. Where I work and live is part of that. You brought up corporate espionage before you disappeared. While you were 'away' I hired a consultant from the University of Texas to make recommendations to beef up our cybersecurity. Based on the recommendations she made, we've made some changes."

Cybersecurity. She? The University of Texas? No. It couldn't be, could it?

"What was that?" Sam quickly turned her head toward the door. "Stay here," she said as she walked out of the office and down the hall, drawing her weapon. She pretended to search for someone, but as soon as she found an open conference room, she went in.

Fuck! Sam didn't particularly like to cuss, but this warranted it. *Fuck, fuck, fuck!* It warranted the f-bomb. Sam leaned against the wall to think. *Could Leia be the one targeting her? The chance meeting in a nightclub. Was it planned? All this time, was Leia working for someone trying to get into Brooke's company? Someone was after Sam. Someone shot at her, twice. Was it to keep her from protecting Brooke? What the fuck was going on? Fuck!* She wanted to hit something but knew she couldn't.

Sam took a deep breath. In and out. When she calmed down, she went back to Brooke's office.

"Brooke?" She looked around but didn't see her. "Damn it. I told her to stay put."

"I'm right here," Brooke said suddenly appearing from a hidden door in the wall. Brooke pressed a button under her desk, and the door closed.

"What the... How long have you had that, and *why* do you have that?"

"I thought it'd be cool," she said with a straight face.

Sam was far from amused and her face showed it.

"I had it installed after my father received the ransom note. We moved the wall out, which makes the office next door smaller. The head of his security recommended it. It's a small panic room."

Sam was stunned. "Okay, whatever. Did you tell me about that?"

"Uh, no. I was told to not to tell anyone, even you. Unless necessary." Brooke stared at her. "Come on, Sam. You have to admit it's cool, right?"

It took her a few seconds, but then her face softened slightly. "Yeah. Okay, it's cool. You need a different desk. That glass one will not protect you."

Brooke smiled back at her. "I mentioned that, as well."

Sam moved on. "Tell me about this cybersecurity person. Why did you hire her?"

"It was the day you left. You said I may want to hire an independent contractor to check the computer systems."

Why would I do that?

As if reading her mind, Brooke said, "I'd mentioned to you that we'd had a couple of strange cyberattacks lately. They'd been dealt with, but you suggested it anyway. I agreed. I did some research and found that one of the top cybersecurity specialists in the country was right here in Austin. So I hired her."

"Keep going."

"She graduated from and teaches at UT. So a fellow Longhorn was a bonus."

Sam rolled her eyes. *Go Gators.* Even though she graduated from Sam Houston, her heart was with the Florida Gators.

"What's her name? Did your father check her out?" Sam

prepared herself for what she knew was coming. *Don't make any kind of reaction.*

"Leia Coventry, and yes, I asked my father's man to check her out. She's one of the best, and she's an Army reservist."

Sam's face never changed although her stomach was another story. She decided to move on for the moment.

"Was part of my job to run errands for you?"

"What? No, that wasn't your job. You said we needed some things. You volunteered!" Brook began raising her voice. "I never asked you to do things like that for me. You weren't my servant. You were my—" She suddenly seemed very upset and stopped speaking. She stood and walked to the other side of the room, facing away from Sam, and looked out a window.

"Take a step back from the window. I was your what?" Sam asked, wanting to know what Brooke was going to say.

Softly, she said, "My friend. You were my friend." Brooke backed away from the window, turned, and looked at Sam. Calmly, she said, "You were my protector for three months. You moved from the pool house into the guest room and almost never left my side. Then one day you went to the store and never came back."

Sam was as confused now as when she'd woken in the hospital. "Hey, I'm sorry. I didn't mean to upset you."

Brooke's tone changed. She said, "No, I'm sorry. It's just... that day was tough. Recalling it brings back those feelings. I didn't know what had happened to you and was worried. I spent a week trying to find you. I filed a missing person's report with the Austin Police and even thought of hiring a private detective to look for you. I thought I'd found you once. One of the hospitals said they treated someone matching your description, but the patient left before they could get any information."

I didn't find anything online from Austin PD about a missing person matching my description.

"You searched for me for a week?" Sam said to her. She was surprised and wondered why she would go through all that.

Brooke crossed her arms and sarcastically said, "Well, I was getting used to having my ass kicked in our workouts."

They laughed, and Brooke added, "Anyway, I stopped looking when I got the email from you. I even went back to the police and showed them the email and withdrew the report."

"What email?" Sam asked and Brooke pulled it up on her computer. It had been sent to her work account.

"Miss McKenzie,

I'm sorry, but I don't feel the job is working out. I resign. Thank you.

Samantha Barrett"

"I stopped looking for you after I received that. I had no indications that you weren't happy about the job. In fact, I thought things were going great. We were supposed to go to dinner that night and discuss my progress."

"I didn't send that email." Sam couldn't be sure of a lot right now, but she knew she would never resign like that. Not after working for Brooke for three months. *Unless I got what I needed. Did I finish the mission? But if I did, how did I lose my memory? No, it doesn't feel right.* "By the way, how do I normally dress for work?"

"I was surprised when I read it. I thought it was a joke at first. You sounded so formal in the email. But when you never came back... Anyway, you wear suits for work. But once every other week, I schedule a casual day here at work. That's why you were wearing a polo and your tac pants when you disappeared."

"Tac pants? Getting the lingo down, are we?" They smiled at each other.

Sam wanted to know if there was a particular store she went to for grocery shopping. There was one near the office.

"What time did I leave?"

"Ten thirty or so."

It made sense that she wouldn't have gone far since she'd had to get back to escort Brooke to her lunch date. Sam had noticed it on the calendar but had no idea who the lunch was with or where, since she didn't know Brooke's code.

Not important right now. I need to know what happened to me.

THEY DROVE to the HEB grocery store close by. Brooke asked if it seemed familiar, and Sam said she recognized it. After sitting in the car for a minute, Sam suddenly had a memory flash. She'd hit someone with her fist. Then she'd seen the inside of a van. She remembered running.

"Sam, are you okay? Do you remember something?"

Sam reached for a bottle of water that was near her. She took a couple of sips and then set the bottle down. With her left hand, Brooke touched Sam's leg and again asked if she was okay.

"Yes," Sam said and then started the car.

"Did you remember something? Don't you want to go inside and see if anyone recognizes you?" Brooke asked.

Sam told her it wasn't necessary.

The drive back home was quiet. As she got out of the car, Brooke looked at Sam and said, "I understand if you don't feel like talking, but just know that I'm here when—or if—you do."

Sam nodded and thanked her.

They went inside the house. Sam was going to go to her room and process the memory she'd had. Before going upstairs, she asked Brooke if there had been any more attempts to kidnap or hurt her.

"No."

"I'm glad to hear that," Sam said then went to her room. She needed to contact Tom. The night they'd spoken, she hadn't told him about the incident in the park. She had a burner phone she used to contact Tom in an emergency. This wasn't exactly an emergency, but it was important. Besides the van and running, she remembered a black SUV and a license plate. Before calling Tom, she wanted to check her apartment. Maybe she missed something that could help her with those memory flashes.

She went to find Brooke.

"Do you mind if I leave for a few hours? I promise I'll be back."

"Is there anything I can do to help?" Brooke asked.

"No. Don't worry, I'll be okay, and I will return," Sam said trying to reassure her. "There's something I need to take care of. I'll be back by five this evening. Do me a favor and stay in the house—and make sure the house is secure. I'll do a walk around before I leave."

Brooke looked puzzled but agreed.

Sam drove to the motel. She packed up what she had

there and put it in her car. No point in keeping a place she didn't need. She thought about keeping it because it would make a good safe house—if she needed it—but decided against it. After settling with the manager, she drove to her apartment.

Sam went straight to her bedroom. She picked up the picture of her and the man in their uniforms. She needed to find out about this guy. She took the picture out of the frame and looked at the back. Printed in pen was "Rick and Sam, Germany." Rick. She said his name aloud. She went to the closet and went through everything again. Everything was hers. As far as she could tell, she lived alone.

I need to check the storage unit again. So she drove over there.

She had looked through the few things in the unit, but it was just souvenirs—nothing that told her who she was. The footlocker showed promise, but it was locked. Sam wondered where she would have kept the key. Then she remembered her go bag in the trunk of the car. She grabbed the lockpick set from it and went to work.

Success.

After removing the lock, she took a deep breath and opened the lid. Inside, she found several types of male Air Force uniforms and footwear. The uniforms were in vacuum-sealed bags to keep them safe. Some certificates and awards were stacked in frames and folders. *Maybe he's on temporary duty overseas or somewhere.* On the awards was the name "Richard B. Adams." *Rick Adams.*

Then she saw a photo album. She started to get a bad feeling, and her hands began to shake. The album was white and large. On the front was a photo of her and Rick. He was in a dress uniform, but she was in a wedding gown.

It all came flooding back. She suddenly remembered it

all. Opening the book was just a formality to look at the pictures. Her wedding day to Rick. The photos were typical wedding photos except for one thing. No family on her side. Rick's family and friends, but she didn't have anyone there. Her bridesmaids were cousins of Rick's and friends of his family. She didn't even know them. His best man was the only one she knew. He had gone to OTS with them. As she turned each page, she remembered more and more. No mother of the bride. Sam sniffed as she thought of her mother missing out on one of the biggest days of her life. She wiped the tears as kept looking at the photos. No dance with her father. Was that her fault or his? Maybe a bit of both. She could have called him. But at that point, she felt it was too late to reconcile.

She closed the album then glanced back at the foot-locker and moved one of the uniform bags. An American flag folded in a triangular case. Sam closed her eyes before she could read the small bronze plaque on the case. *No.*

RICK HAD BEEN a year older than her and graduated from his university the year before she did. He was working on his master's degree after he graduated. Sam met him while at officer training school. They had an immediate connection. After graduating OTS, luck was on their side. Their first assignments were in Germany. While not at the same base, they were close enough to travel and see each other. They were married in June and were hoping their next assignments would be at the same base. But Rick was deployed to Afghanistan, and while on an escort mission, they ran over an improvised explosive device, and he was killed. He had been there eight months. Sam held the wedding album tightly as her hands continued to shake.

Sitting on the floor, Sam gently placed the album back into the footlocker. She was overwhelmed with feelings—surprise, sadness, a sense of loss, grief, among others. After a minute, she took a deep breath, wiped away the tears that were running down her face, and stood. It was a lot to take in. She remembered everything. Rick had been the love of her life. Her first love and she might have been blinded by that. They had been so happy together. Yes, there had been some issues, but what military marriage didn't have issues? They'd known the risks of deployment during a time of conflict, but she'd thought he would come home safe. Sam tried to push it all to the back of her mind. She had already been through this once. She felt like she was reliving it all over again, and she couldn't do that.

She reached in her pocket and pulled the photo out of her ID case. *I was married, Mom, but I guess you knew that. I hope you kicked his ass up there. Or maybe he went the other way. He was a jerk at times.* She chuckled. *Am I doing the right thing on this mission? This was my chance, but I must have made a mistake. Someone tried to take me, but I got away. I forged the path I wanted, Mom. I thought I did it on my own, but now I'm not sure. Did dad send someone to get me this assignment? I really hope it wasn't him. I need to do this on my own. Okay, enough bellyaching.*

Sam replaced the photo in its hidden compartment. She'd learned so much today, and it was weighing on her. Her thoughts were scattered, and she needed to get them in order. "Get it together, Sam. Suck it up, and get back on mission."

Rick is gone and has been. Leia. Was it a coincidence, or was she somehow involved? A betrayal from her would be very hurtful because I think I'm falling for her.

A sudden noise startled her, and she reached for her weapon. Slowly, she stood up and went to the opening of her unit. It was someone down the row of units moving things from their truck into their unit. Sam looked around but didn't see anyone else. She had been extremely careful and watched for anyone who might be following her. Stepping back inside the unit, she did some slow breathing.

Her mind clear, Sam also recalled the night before she'd disappeared. She'd thought someone was following her and Brooke.

AFTER WORK, the day before Sam disappeared, Brooke had plans to meet some coworkers at a local bar and grill. As they were driving, Sam spotted a black SUV that seemed to be following them. Brooke was driving her car, so Sam used this opportunity as a training scenario. She asked Brooke to use what she had taught her to verify a tail. Brooke used the driving techniques—like taking multiple right turns—and verified what Sam thought—they were being followed.

She didn't want to alarm Brooke, so she told her to go ahead to the bar. It would be relatively safe since it was a public place, and there would be the after-work crowd. Brooke pulled up in front of the door and got out. Sam told her she'd park the car and meet her inside. She kept an eye on Brooke and made sure she was inside before she found a parking spot. Sam parked the car and watched the SUV. Whoever was driving it parked as far away as they could while keeping a visual on Brooke's car. If they could see

Sam, she could see them. *Let's hope you stay there.* Sam exited Brooke's car and went inside the bar.

Ninety seconds later, after leaving through a different door and covertly making her way around to the back of the SUV, Sam snuck up and knocked on the driver's window of the SUV with the barrel of her gun. She startled the two men inside. The vehicle was still running with the air on since it was hot outside.

The driver put the vehicle in drive and sped off.

Sam let them go. She had written down the license plate number before she approached the driver. The next time she made contact with Tom, she'd pass the number off to him.

Tom had told Sam that one of the agencies was thinking of doing something small, but obvious, to make William McKenzie think his daughter was still in danger. Maybe another abduction attempt. It would be a good reason to keep Sam on the job. But this didn't feel like that, and Tom would've given her a heads-up if it had been approved.

The next day, she disappeared.

Since Tom hadn't mentioned the plate number at their last meeting or a vehicle that might have been following them, Sam assumed she'd never gotten the chance to report it.

A CAR DRIVING by snapped Sam back to the present day. She closed the storage unit and went back to Brooke's. On the way, she stopped at a store and bought a burner phone and made a call.

"Hello?" Leia said.

Sam was quiet. She shouldn't be calling even if it was a burner phone. So many questions. *Are you trying to kill me? Are you involved in this?*

Leia did the talking for both of them. "Is it you? You don't have to say anything. I understand if you can't talk. I'm just glad you called. I miss you, and I hope things are going the way you want." She paused. "You know I'm usually the one who takes the lead in a relationship. You surprised me on that last visit. You were so quiet and shy at first. But now, you're so different. That's not a bad thing. I want to get to know the real you. Anyway, stay safe."

Sam disconnected the call. It was enough to get her through for now. She wiped her misty eyes. She really hoped Leia wasn't involved, but she needed to find out.

It was four thirty in the afternoon by the time she returned to Brooke's. She headed straight for the refrigerator and grabbed a beer.

Brooke came around the corner and said, "Would you like some company?"

Sam hesitated, lost in her thoughts, and Brooke began to walk away.

"No, wait, it's fine. Stay. Care to join me?"

"Sure. I'll have one of those." Brooke gestured toward her beer.

"I thought you preferred your wine."

"I decided to expand my knowledge of the beer world."

"When did this happen?"

Taking a sip of beer, Brooke replied, "A little over a month ago."

The timing was not lost on Sam. About the same time she'd disappeared.

"So, did you get any answers?" Brooke asked.

"Yes. Yes, I did." Sam took a big gulp.

"Are you all right?"

"I will be," Sam said decisively.

10

S am had learned a lot about Brooke over the time she'd spent with her and was remembering more as the hours passed. Sunday was a day when Brooke took it easy. Learning her father's business wasn't as simple as some might think. Especially for the boss's daughter. During their conversations, Sam learned that Brooke wanted to make sure she earned her way in the company and that William also believed that. So after she'd gotten her business degree from the University of Texas, she started just like any other new hire—in the trenches. Once she moved up in the company and had her own department, she never asked her employees to do anything she wouldn't do herself.

Brooke had also revealed some personal things to Sam. She had always kept busy with school, sports, and going out with friends. She never had a problem getting dates, either, but the more responsibility she had at work, the less time she had for dating. When Sunday came around, she liked to veg out—watch TV or maybe read a book. This Sunday was no different.

After a morning run with Sam, she showered and went to the den to catch up on her shows. She always let Sam know her plans either the night before or in the morning. That way, Sam could plan accordingly. Sam had to work in training for Brooke as much as she could, but sometimes, it was difficult with Brooke's schedule. The next day, Sam would accompany her to the office, just like before.

OTHER THAN THE run with Brooke, Sam spent much of the day in her room. As much as she wanted to follow up on things, she felt the need to decompress. After a few hours, she decided to go to the range and let off some steam. She grabbed her gear and range bag and headed downstairs. She was going to go by herself, but since she hadn't seen Brooke shoot in over a month, she decided to ask her to go. But when she did, Brooke declined.

Sam was a little surprised and asked if she was sure.

Brooke told her she had been keeping up her training and had been going to the range once a week or so.

"Uh, okay." Sam was surprised. "Did something from work come up?"

"No," Brooke replied.

"Keep the doors locked and stay inside, please."

Sam waited a second to see if Brooke would say more, but when she didn't, Sam turned and left. On the way to range she got that funny feeling and checked her rearview mirror. She made a right turn and another. Coming up on a light, Sam sped up as it turned red and saw a black SUV do the same thing. She pulled into a fast-food parking lot and parked.

The vehicle continued by without stopping.

Paranoid? Maybe? Maybe not.

She went to Tom's range and passed him a note for a meet. After she spent an hour on the range, she cleaned her weapons and headed to the crowded sports bar where she was supposed to meet Tom. Sam went inside, ordered a beer and a water, and stood at the bar.

About ten minutes later, Tom walked in. Acting like they didn't know each other, Tom went to the other end of the bar. After the bartender brought Tom his drink, Tom said something to him. When she was almost finished with her beer, the bartender brought her another and pointed toward Tom. Sam acknowledged him with a nod, then Tom made his way toward her.

"Hi. I'm Tom."

"Sam. Nice to meet you, and thanks for the drink."

Down to business.

Speaking quietly, Tom said, "How are things going?"

"They're going well. My memory has returned. Well, I still have some gaps. But I know what happened the day of and the day before I went missing." She handed him a piece of paper with the license plate number of the vehicle that had followed her the day before she disappeared. "This vehicle was following us."

"You remember that number after all this time and your memory loss?"

"Yeah. I had written it down, but I don't know what happened to the paper. I use those word tricks to remember things like plate numbers. Like in school. Mnemonics, you know?"

"Yeah, I know."

She told him about being shot at in the park.

"Shit, Sam. Your cover is probably blown. You should come in," Tom said.

Sam didn't want to give up. "I can still do this. I'm back in with Brooke and can get what we need. Knowing what I know now, I'm being more aware. They might not expect me to come back."

She eventually convinced Tom to let her continue with the mission. He wanted to know what she remembered about her disappearance.

"I was placing groceries in my car, and two men tried to grab me. I was holding my own until I felt a sting in my shoulder. A third person must have shot me with a tranquilizer dart. Before I passed out, I remember being pushed into a white cargo van. I woke for a few seconds and found myself on the floor of the van. My hands and feet were bound with zip ties. I think I passed out again, but then woke up later, still in the van. The men hadn't searched me because I still had a boot knife strapped to my left leg under my pants. I was able to get it and free myself from the zip ties." Sam continued with the story. A partition separated her from the men, so they couldn't see her. She could barely hear them talking, but she heard one man ask what the boss wanted with her.

"What did they say?" Tom asked.

"They said they needed to find out how much I knew without hurting me too much." Sam smiled.

"Why are you smiling?"

"I broke one of the guys' noses." Sam remembered what else he said but kept it to herself. *"Yeah, the boss wasn't kidding when he said she was tough. She's also pretty hot."* Then they both started to laugh. "They stole my license and cards."

"Don't worry about it. We can take care of that. They didn't search you?"

"No, they were idiots. They checked my wallet but didn't search for anything else. Left me ten dollars as a joke."

"What about the third person?"

"I don't know. I didn't see the third person. I think it was just the two men in the front of the vehicle."

"Okay, go on," Tom said.

"I went to work on the back door of the van. Using my knife, I managed to pry the door open. Then I waited until they slowed down enough that I felt safe jumping out. When the opportunity came, I jumped and rolled down an embankment. The hill country can hurt." She smiled slightly.

Sam continued. "It was dark, and I had no idea where I was. I heard the van stop and the men get out. They started down the embankment after me. The area was very thick with trees and brush. I heard a shot, ducked, and ran some more. It was then that I stepped into a hole, broke my ankle, and fell. I must have hit my head because the next thing I remember was waking up in the hospital."

"How did you get to the hospital?"

"No idea." She also didn't know who put her car back into the storage unit.

"ONE MORE THING," Sam said to Tom. "Someone sent Brooke an email from me telling her I quit the job."

"I'll try and run that as well as the plate. I'll need the IP address to run the email. I'm glad you're okay, but keep your head on a swivel. Do you remember finding anything on KenzieCorp that might explain why someone's after you? We always suspected that any digital evidence would be at the company headquarters. In that office building."

"No. Not that I remember. I might still have some memory gaps." Sam couldn't think of anything specific. She had sat in on many meetings Brooke had with other companies. Maybe she had heard something she wasn't supposed to. From what she saw of Brooke's work, Sam didn't think she was aware of anything illegal.

"Okay. There's an exhibition in Paris coming up. McKenzie goes to it, and so does Brooke. Keep your eyes open while you're there."

"What am I looking for?"

"Illegal activities. Anything suspicious. There'll be vendors from all over the world, including China. See who they talk to. We don't know what KenzieCorp might be into but have reason to believe something is going on."

Sam hesitated over what to do next.

"Something wrong?" Tom asked her.

"I'm not sure."

"What is it?"

"I have a name I need you to run. She teaches cybersecurity at UT and may do consulting on the side. She consulted with Brooke during my missing time."

"What am I looking for? Anything specific?"

"Her consulting business. How long has she been doing it? Just anything else that stands out. Leia Coventry is her name. Let me know as soon as you can."

"Okay."

"Tom?" Sam paused. "Do you believe in coincidences?"

"In our line of work, I find they are rare."

Yeah. That's what I was afraid of.

Satisfied with their exchange of information, they finished their drinks and left. Sam left first. Tom stayed a while and finished watching a game on one of the TV monitors.

11

When Sam finally arrived back at the house, it was dinnertime. She ran upstairs and dropped her range bag into her closet. She then went to find Brooke to see if she had eaten yet. Sam checked all the rooms upstairs, but she wasn't there. She called out, but there was no answer. The house was a decent size, so Brooke might not have heard her. Upstairs were four bedrooms, one of which was Sam's. She headed downstairs and called out again.

Nothing.

She searched the kitchen, living room, dining room, and the den. She started to get worried. *I told her to stay here, didn't I?*

Brooke's bedroom was on the main floor at the back of the house. She knocked on the door, but there was no answer. Slowly, she turned the doorknob and opened the door. She called out again and went to check the master bath. Still nothing. She went out the French doors to the backyard to see if Brooke had gone for a swim, but she wasn't in the pool either. The only other place to look was the pool house. She knocked on the door and called Brooke's name. Sam had her hand on her sidearm, just in case.

Brooke opened the door and said, "Hello."

"Is everything all right?"

"Yes," Brooke said.

The pool house was fixed up like a guest house. It had a bathroom and small kitchenette and a pullout sofa bed.

"Are you getting ready for a swim?"

"I already went for one. I'm just watching a movie. I like to hang out in here sometimes, and it's a way to make sure there aren't any maintenance issues. You stayed here before you moved into the house."

Sam remembered staying there for the first month of her assignment. Then Brooke said she could move into the house if she wanted.

"I was thinking of ordering a pizza. Have you eaten yet?" Sam asked.

"No, pizza sounds great. Whatever kind you want."

Sam noticed that Brooke seemed different. She didn't sound like her normal happy self. "Are you feeling okay?"

"Yeah, I'm fine. I'll be up to the house in a minute."

Taking that cue, Sam turned and went back to the house. She ordered a large thin-crust meat lover's pizza. After grabbing a glass and filling it with water, she sat on a barstool in the kitchen and pulled over the crossword-puzzle book sitting on the counter. A pencil was inside the book.

Brooke walked in and apologized.

"I'm sorry, Sam. Nothing is wrong. I'm probably just a little drained from everything. It was a busy week," Brooke said.

Sam let it go at that. "Okay."

"Sam?"

"Yeah?" Sam said, looking up from the crossword puzzle.

Sam could tell that something was on her mind. "Uh, nothing." She paused then said, "By the way, we have another busy week coming up. We have some meetings at the office, and Friday evening is a party. Saturday night, we'll be leaving for Paris to attend Eurosatory. I think your passport is in your room."

"Great. What's Eurosatory?" Sam already knew because she recalled being briefed on it by an ATF agent. But she didn't want Brooke to know how much she knew.

"It's a global defense and security exhibition. One of the biggest in the world. There'll be vendors from all over the world there."

"Cool. I'm looking forward to it. Does your dad go to those?" Sam asked.

"Yes. We'll see him at the party and then meet him at the airport on Saturday."

"You'll have to help me pack. What's the dress code?"

"You can wear your suits, polos, tactical pants. Also pack some evening wear for any events we attend. We can always pick something up if you need it," Brooke said.

"Shopping in Paris. How will we survive?" Sam said sarcastically.

Brooke laughed and suddenly perked up. "I really missed your sense of humor. There's something I meant to ask you but never got around to it. When you met my father, you told him you were carrying. Was that true?"

Sam smiled and said yes, it was true. Brooke wanted to know how she had transported a weapon to Venice since they had very strict gun laws. Her father had a difficult time getting the proper permits for his security team. She also wanted to know where she was carrying it that night.

"I can't reveal all my secrets. If I do, I won't have anything left to teach you."

Just then, the doorbell rang.

"Saved by the bell," Sam said.

Brooke started to get up, but Sam said she'd get it. She checked the app on her phone. It was a girl with their pizza. Sam opened the door and tipped the girl, but as she thanked her, a flash caught her eye from the other side of the cul-de-sac. In the middle of the cul-de-sac was a circular landscaped green area with a couple of trees, flower beds and a cluster box unit for mail. The driveway was long and curved slightly, but Sam could still see the trees in the middle of the circle.

She took a few steps out and looked past the trees to see a vehicle parked on the street. Again, she saw a flicker of light and knew it came from the vehicle or something inside.

A memory back to when she was fourteen and Jimmy was eleven came to mind. They were searching for each other in the woods. It was a game to teach them the art of camouflage and evasion. Sam was quietly making her way down a thin trail. She knelt to look at the ground for some sign of her little brother. A rustle to her left made her turn and point the paintball rifle towards the noise. A rabbit hopped out and then scurried away quickly. Out of the corner of her eye she saw a flash to her right. Slowly, she stood and backed away from the direction she'd come. Ten minutes later, she stood over Jimmy and fired the paintball handgun she'd removed from backpack. "You're dead, little brother."

"Aww man. How'd you find me?"

"You were watching me with that range finder. The sun glinted off the lens, and I saw it."

"Well done, Samantha!" Her father stepped out from behind a tree. "Jimmy, you hid yourself well, but why did you use the range finder?"

"I wanted to see her face before I took a shot. I was waiting for her to get a little closer, but that rabbit came out and she backed away."

"You should have moved as soon as she backed away."

"Yes, sir." Jimmy said, standing up and hanging his head.

"Don't sulk, son. Samantha has more experience running around in these woods with me hunting her. You'll get there." He patted the boy on the back. "Go home and get cleaned up," he told both of them.

"You owe me a gelato," Sam told Jimmy.

Sam caught herself smiling and then quickly it faded as she turned to go back inside the house. She needed to confirm her suspicions without alerting them. In this gated neighborhood it was rare to see a black SUV sitting on the street for any length of time. Brooke lived at the end of a cul-de-sac and that was another reason Sam thought the vehicle was suspicious. There wasn't a lot of traffic there.

She closed the door, locked it, set the alarm, and took the pizza back to the kitchen. Brooke had already opened a bottle of wine and poured two glasses. She set the pizza box down and said, "I need to check something. Stay here." Then she thought of something. Turning to Brooke, she said, "Do you have a pair of binoculars or a telescope?"

"No." Sam began to leave and then Brooke said, "Would a golf range finder work?"

"Yeah."

"In my golf bag in the garage."

"Stay here."

Sam retrieved the range finder then went to Brooke's office and pulled up the video feed on the laptop. The system saved the recording for one hundred eighty days. Sam only needed a few hours. She found a camera the pointed out toward the street and saw nothing. She scrubbed ahead and stopped when she saw the vehicle park.

Shortly after I returned. Did they follow me?

Sam went upstairs to one of the bedrooms that faced the street. The window had wooden blinds, and she carefully stood to the side and looked down at the vehicle. Using the range finder, she peered into the vehicle. Two men were talking. Then one pulled a pair of binoculars up and looked toward Brooke's house.

Sam went back downstairs.

"Where's your weapon?" she asked Brooke.

"Bedroom safe."

"Go to your room and stay there. The alarm is on. Reset it after I leave."

"What?" Sam turned and grabbed her by the arm. "Okay. I'm going. Ow. Sam. I'm going."

Sam continued out the back and grabbed one of the chairs off the deck. She carried it over to a place she had scouted for a quick escape if needed and proceeded to place it near the fence then hopped over it. She followed the edge of the tree line down a few houses and then along the side of a house to the street. Carefully looking, she saw the black SUV still in the same spot. She took out her phone and tried to zoom in on the license plate number. Using the range finder, she looked at the plate and typed it in the notes app of her phone.

Sam wanted to get rid of them, so she decided on the most logical way to handle it. She called the police.

"Yes, I'd like to report a suspicious vehicle in my neighborhood. This is Brooke McKenzie." Sam gave them all the pertinent information. Using Brooke's name might get the police to respond a little faster. "It's just been there for hours. I think someone is sitting inside which seems strange. It's so hot out."

The dispatcher asked for her address, and Sam gave it to her. It only took a minute and a patrol car arrived.

Fast response when you live in a nice neighborhood.

"Yes, I see them, thank you." Sam hung up.

The patrol car was driving toward the SUV, and it started to move, but they turned on their lights and the vehicle stopped.

Sam crossed the street and walked up behind the vehicle and snapped a photo of the plate number, just to be sure she wrote it down correctly. Then she walked by the driver's window to get a look at the driver. She timed it just right. The patrolman had the driver unroll his window and was talking to him. The driver glanced at Sam as she walked by smiling.

12

———————

*S*hit. *This case sure is making me cuss a lot.*

Sam recognized the driver as the one that had tailed Sam and Brooke to the sports bar.

She continued up to Brooke's house and phoned her. "It's me. I'm coming in." She hung up before Brooke could say anything. She unlocked the door then went inside where she found Brooke walking to the kitchen.

Time for some unpleasantness.

She walked up to Brooke and stood inches from her. "You do not question me. You do what I say, when I say it. Is that understood?" Her voice was calm, but the order was more than clear.

"Yes." A bit of a timid response.

"The police may come and ask you about a black SUV that was parked out in the cul-de-sac. It was suspicious, sitting there for hours. You saw it earlier today and again when the pizza girl delivered the pizza. You thought someone was sitting inside. So you called the police. Got it?"

"Yes." This was not timid but leaning toward pissed.

Sam didn't care. These people were watching her, and she would not place Brooke in danger because of her.

Sure enough, fifteen minutes later, the police came and spoke to Brooke briefly. They assured her they would step up patrols in the area.

"May I ask what the person said they were doing?" Brooke asked the police officer.

"They said they were helping spread the word of God. But I think it was a lie, ma'am. We didn't have anything to take them in on. I gave them a warning for soliciting in this neighborhood. I don't think they'll be back. But call me if they do." He handed Brooke his card.

"Thank you, Officer. I really appreciate what you do. Please be safe." Brooke smiled and closed the door, locking it behind her.

She strode into the kitchen to find Sam eating the pizza and drinking her wine.

"Are you going to tell me what the hell that was about?"

"You already know. Suspicious vehicle. Could have been watching the house and you." *Actually they were watching me.*

Brooke stared at her.

"Sit down. Your pizza is getting cold," Sam told her as if it all had been a common occurrence.

Brooke strode over grabbed the box and her wine and went to her bedroom. The door slammed.

"Well, that's rude. I only got two pieces," she said, looking at her plate with the one remaining slice on it.

THE NEXT MORNING, Sam found Brooke in the garage working out. Part of the three-car garage had been set up as a small gym. Since this was Texas, Brooke had the air-conditioning and heating extended to the garage.

"Good morning," Sam said.

Brooke gave her a dirty look as she continued her dumbbell presses.

"Fine, ignore me, but I'm not going to apologize for doing my job." Sam placed some weights on the barbell and proceeded to bench press. After a while, she decided to test Brooke's self-defense. She grabbed Brooke from behind and placed her arm under Brooke's chin in a rear choke hold.

Brooke leaned over and moved her right leg behind Sam's. With her right arm, she grabbed Sam's right hip and pulled her to the ground, sending Sam to the floor. Brooke was now sitting over Sam, staring into her brown eyes. She had Sam's arms pinned to the mat and hesitated long enough for Sam to take advantage and flip Brooke off her. She landed with a thud, and Brooke groaned.

"Shit," Brooke said.

"What happened?" Sam stood up.

"What do mean? You kicked my ass as usual." Brooke sat up but looked down at the mat, avoiding Sam's eyes.

"You hesitated. That could get you hurt or worse."

"Well, it has been a while since I had someone to spar with."

Sam reached for Brooke's hand and helped her up. She had a feeling there was more to it but decided against saying anything else. Her gut also told her it wasn't relevant to the investigation.

Brooke grabbed a towel and walked out of the garage to the house. Sam was still a little behind in her workouts, so she was ready to end the workout early anyway. Brooke seemed distracted.

They ate breakfast, but Brooke didn't talk.

"Is anything wrong? You haven't said a word," Sam said.

Brooke was staring at her plate and then set her fork down when Sam spoke.

"What? Oh, sorry. No, I just... uh... it's nothing." Brooke stumbled to find the words.

This time, Sam wasn't letting it go, even if it wasn't relevant to the case. "Are you still mad at me about yesterday? You can tell me, Brooke. You can tell me anything."

Brooke drank some of her orange juice and forced a smile. "No. I'm sorry I got upset about that. I know you were just doing your job. That's what I'm paying you for. It's okay. I'm fine."

Brooke was obviously lying. She wasn't fine, but she didn't want to talk about it either.

"Okay, but like you once told me, I'm here if you want to talk." Sam reached over and touched Brooke's hand.

Brooke closed her eyes for a second then stood. "Thanks. I'd better go get ready. By the way, there's leftover pizza in the bottom crisper." She turned and left.

Sam had done what she could. She knew you couldn't force anyone to talk if they weren't ready, and Sam wasn't going to interrogate her like a suspect. She finished her breakfast, put the dishes into the dishwasher, then went to get ready for work.

Technically, Sam was always at work. Being a bodyguard was a full-time job. If this bodyguard assignment hadn't been a ruse, Sam would never have gotten this friendly with Brooke. A bodyguard should be aware at all times, and being too friendly with her charge might be a distraction. Although there did seem to be some sort of real threat, it was against Sam, not Brooke.

After showering, Sam picked out a navy-blue suit with a white dress shirt. She found a pair of black heeled dress boots in the closet. The last thing she did was put on her weapon. She went downstairs and found Brooke packing her briefcase in the den.

"Almost ready," Brooke said without looking up.

"No problem. I don't think the boss will fire you for being late."

Brooke laughed and closed her briefcase. When she looked up, she stopped and didn't say anything.

"What's wrong? Do I have deodorant on my jacket?"

Suddenly, Brooke seemed to realize she was staring. "No, sorry. You look great. I think that's my favorite suit of yours. I really like that color blue, but you should vary the shirt colors. You look like a government agent." Looking down, she paused and said softly, "I'm glad you're back." Again, she paused. "And on that note, let's go." She grabbed her brief-case and walked quickly past Sam toward the garage.

Once in the garage, Brooke asked who was driving today. Sam let her decide, and Brooke chose to drive her own car. In the car, Sam said, "Thank you, and I'm glad to be back too." The ride into the office was a quiet one.

ONCE AT THE OFFICE, Brooke went about her day. It didn't take long for Sam to get back into the swing of things. She remembered everyone she'd met and where everything was. No problems. She sat in on two meetings with Brooke. One meeting was to remind the heads of departments that she was going out of the country next week. She was briefed by each head on the status of all contracts, and they planned out the rest of the week. Brooke was a very attentive boss. She listened to her employees and let them voice any concerns.

"Brigette?" Brooke said.

"Just the usual wear and tear on factory parts. The increase in production for the DOD has us running at ninety-five percent currently. We may have to look at expanding the facility in the future."

"Good. Start checking into that. See if it's worth expanding the current facility or looking into a different location. Anything else?"

"No, ma'am."

Brooke looked at the man sitting next to Brigette. "Ted?"

"The dockworkers and union have threatened a strike and that might disrupt some supply chain issues. It's just talk for now, but I thought I'd give you a heads-up."

"Start looking into stateside alternatives. The Board would like for us to go totally made in the USA. It may increase prices, but it'll go a long way with our customers." Brooke looked around.

After continuing around the conference table, Brooke finished up by saying, "Anyone else?" Everyone was silent. "Okay, thank you, team. Keep up the great work."

At eleven thirty, Brooke was back in her office, making a phone call. When she finished, Sam asked if she had plans for lunch. She said she hadn't but that she was probably just going to grab a sandwich from the café downstairs. Sam offered to go pick up something from a restaurant and bring it back.

Almost before she finished her sentence, Brooke yelled, "No! You can't leave."

Sam got up from the chair she was sitting in and closed the door to the office.

"Hey, you don't have to worry about me. I'm not going anywhere."

"You don't know that. Sam, you're a great bodyguard. I've

learned so much from you. But you couldn't protect yourself that day. And you still don't know why you were abducted."

"To be fair, I held my own against two men. It was the third one who got me with a tranquilizer dart."

Brooke stared in disbelief. "Excuse me? Were you ever going to tell me that?"

"Only if I felt you needed to know. I think the people who tried to take you in Venice may have been trying to get me out of the way."

Sam used Brooke's "abduction" to stay close to Brooke and ensure job security.

"But once you were gone, why didn't they try anything?"

"You tell me. Put yourself in their shoes and think about what you might do. I escaped the same night they took me. So as far as they knew, I wasn't gone a month. They most likely didn't know about my amnesia. Now, what would you do?"

Brooke thought for a moment. "Since you escaped so quickly, they didn't have time to arrange another attempt on me. They'd have to wait and see when you'd show back up. And when you did come back, you'd be on high alert. Maybe you'd set a trap. No, it would have been too risky to try anything at that point. They'd have to abort the whole mission or wait a while."

Sam clapped her hands. "Excellent. I'm impressed. I guess you do have a good teacher."

"But wouldn't they have been watching me and wonder where you were?"

"Possibly. But if it were me, I'd still wait before making a move."

Without knowing it, Brooke had filled in some blanks for Sam. Everything she said made sense, so she went with it.

SAM COULD TELL that her praise had pleased Brooke and that she seemed to feel better.

"Thank you, Sam. You always seem to know just what to say."

"I do? In what way?"

Brooke sat down in her chair. "Well, when I'm stressed due to work, you were able to tell and would say something to help me. At home, you'd suggest a workout or a trip to the range. Sometimes, just talking would help." Brooke pushed a few strands of hair behind her ear and turned her eyes from Sam as if embarrassed to tell her these things. "You're a great listener, and I know that I tend to keep things bottled up, but talking to you feels natural, like a best friend. I don't know if you remember, but I once commented that I should pay you extra for being a therapist in addition to your other duties."

"You make it easy, Brooke. I've enjoyed working for you." That being said, Sam got the impression there was one thing Brooke just wasn't ready to talk to her about.

13

———

Because of the party Friday night, Brooke only went into work for half a day. The party was work-related, so Brooke let everyone go home at one.

It was one thirty by the time Brooke and Sam left the office. Something Brooke had said stuck in Sam's head. When she got home, she did a sweep of her car. Under the right wheel well, she found a tracking device.

"Son of a biscuit." She replaced the tracker since she wouldn't be using the car for at least a week. That would give her the time to figure out what to do. Then she swept Brooke's car, but it was clean.

Heading inside the house, Sam took the time she had to start packing for the trip. She set one dress aside for that night. After finishing most of her packing, it was time to start getting ready for the party. The dress she wore was dark blue. Sometimes, when the light hit it exactly right, it looked black. Simple, yet elegant. It had a slit up the side. Sam placed her left foot on the bed and strapped her .380 to her thigh—the same place she had carried it when she met William. The garter holster was what she'd needed to buy before meeting him. After giving herself one more look in the mirror, she grabbed her purse and left the room.

Sam went downstairs just as the doorbell rang. Checking her app, she made her way to the door. She opened it and acknowledged the driver.

"Brooke, the car is here," she called. William sent a car whenever he had parties. Brooke came down the hallway in a red evening gown. Her blond hair was tied up in a perfect bun. Sam had seen Brooke dressed up before, but this was different. She had an air of confidence about her.

"Ready to go?" Brooke asked.

Sam hesitated and then said, "Yes."

As they walked out the door, Sam told her how stunning she looked. Thanking her, Brooke then turned to the driver. "Jesse? Home from college already?"

"Hi, Brooke. Yes, done until the fall. How have you been?"

"Good." Brooke smiled and quietly asked, "How's Kevin doing?"

Sam noticed the way Brooke's behavior changed when she mentioned Kevin. Obviously, they had some kind of history.

"He's back at Texas A and M, working on his master's degree. You should call him, just to say hi." He shifted uncomfortably as he spoke and ran a hand behind his neck. Sam noticed. Something was bothering him.

Jesse helped Brooke into the back of the car, but Sam hesitated before getting in.

"Is there a problem?" she asked Jesse.

"Uh, no."

Sam didn't believe him. "I've been hired to watch out for her. You need to tell me if there's a problem." Sam stepped close, and Jesse relented.

"Don't say anything, but Kevin wanted to surprise her. That's it. I swear."

Sam took a second and then got in the back seat with Brooke. Jesse closed the door then drove off.

Sam asked about Jesse. Their fathers had been in the Army together. After Jesse's dad retired, William hired him as his head of security. Jesse drove for them every summer.

"And what about Kevin?" Sam knew there was a story there.

Kevin was Jesse's older brother. Brooke and Kevin met while both were home after their freshman year. Kevin was in the corps of cadets and was planning on the Army as a career. They had a wonderful summer and made the long-distance dating work. Their respective schools were only two hours apart. But after a while, things stopped working out and they grew apart. They graduated and went their separate ways—Kevin to the Army and Brooke to work at her dad's company. She had only seen him a couple times since graduating.

As they pulled up to William's house, Sam was in awe. The sprawling mansion sat on a few acres of land.

Jesse helped the ladies out of the car. Just as she was about to go inside, he said, "Brooke? Don't be mad."

"What do you mean?"

"You'll see," Jesse said.

Brooke and Sam went inside. They made their way to the room where everyone was gathered. Looking around, Sam recognized a few of the employees. Brooke was looking for her father when a young man in an Army dress uniform rolled his wheelchair out of the crowd and made his way toward them.

"Hello, Brooke," he said.

Brooke stood there, not saying anything. Sam extended her hand and introduced herself.

"Hi. I'm Sam."

Snapping out of her daze, Brooke apologized, "I'm sorry. Samantha Barrett, this is Kevin Malone."

"Nice to meet you. Thank you for your service," Sam said.

"It's a pleasure to meet you, Miss Barrett."

"Sam is fine," she told him.

After an awkward silence, Sam excused herself and went to the bar. She ordered a club soda and scanned the room, keeping Brooke in her sights. She received her drink and saw William speaking to a man and looking her way.

He motioned for Sam to join them.

William introduced the man as retired Colonel Patrick Malone. He was Kevin and Jesse's father and head of security for William and KenzieCorp.

"I've been looking forward to meeting you again. To see the woman Brooke said could run circles around some of my men. You'll have to come out with us on a training exercise," Colonel Malone said.

"Sounds like fun." Sam smiled.

Again? What did he mean 'again'?

Kevin and Brooke joined them, and more pleasantries were exchanged. Patrick kept looking at Sam, and finally she needed to say something. "Sir, is there something on your mind?"

"You don't remember me?"

"I'm sorry, have we met before?"

"Yes, briefly." His voice changed to become solemn as he continued. "I suppose I shouldn't be surprised you don't remember. It was a difficult day for you, and I'm sure you had a lot on your mind."

"Sir?"

"You were Lieutenant Barrett when I gave my condolences. You were married to Lieutenant Rick Adams. I attended his funeral. I'm deeply sorry for your loss," Patrick said.

Sam was totally caught off guard by what the colonel said. She really didn't have any choice but to confirm what he said.

"Thank you, sir. I'm sorry for not recognizing you. How did you know Rick?"

Patrick paused before he spoke. "Let's step over here." Patrick gently took Sam's elbow and guided her a few feet away so he could talk to her without anyone else hearing. "Normally, I wouldn't volunteer this information, but it was recently declassified, and you were his wife. I was in the convoy he was escorting. There was more to it than just hitting an IED. He saved my life. I can't go into detail. At least not here, not now. But when or if you want to know, call me, and I'll set it up." He handed Sam his business card.

Suddenly, Sam was very uncomfortable. Her stomach felt like she had just been punched, and memories of the funeral swirled around in her head. She glanced over at Brooke and then said, "Sir, would you excuse me, please?"

Sam turned and went to find a bathroom. She reached for the door handle with a sweaty palm. Closing the door behind her and locking it, Sam tried to slow her now increased breathing. She had to regain her composure. Even though Rick's death had been a few years ago, regaining her memory after opening the footlocker had stirred up all those feelings. Sam hadn't thought she'd run into anyone who knew about her and Rick. OSI should have known. One of the agencies should have known and told her. That part made her angry. *Didn't this come up in their research?*

Surely they knew Colonel Malone was with Rick. Maybe they did tell me and I forgot. She kept her maiden name, and they weren't married that long before he was killed. The link between Sam and Rick wasn't obvious. Hopefully, this wouldn't hamper her operation. The background that was written for her was remarkably close to the truth. The only thing that was changed was what happened after Rick died. The story they came up with was that staying in the service was too much of a reminder of Rick, so she resigned her commission and went into business for herself as a firearms instructor.

What did Patrick know? Only that she was married to Rick. He might know that she had been a security forces officer. She'd worn her uniform to the funeral, and the distinctive blue beret and her badge gave away her job. No, Patrick would have no reason to doubt her cover and look into her further.

I'm being paranoid. Everything is fine, so get it together. Having doubts keeps you alive. Just don't overthink it. Sam took a few more slow deep breaths.

Brooke knocked on the door and called her name. After two more deep breaths, Sam opened the door.

Sam smiled and said, "I'm fine." She walked out past Brooke. Turning her head, she asked Brooke if she was coming and then began walking again.

"Sam, wait."

Reluctantly, Sam stopped and turned around.

Brooke stepped closed, speaking softly. "I know you have a past. I mean a life before we met. Did you remember that part? About your husband?"

"Not until recently."

Brooke's face softened. "I'm so sorry for your loss."

"Thank you. I'm fine."

"You can go back home if you're not up to this. I should be safe here with my father, Patrick, and everyone."

"No. My personal life doesn't matter. I have a job to do, and it's here with you."

"Sam, you can't turn off your feelings like a switch."

I have to. Sam forced a smile. "I'm fine. I went through all this when the memory returned. The colonel just surprised me. I didn't expect my past to come up here."

Brooke stepped even closer to her. "You are human and are allowed to have feelings."

"I said I'm fine. Please forget it." It was a lie. Sam was not fine. But it wasn't running into Patrick and the memory of Rick and his death that bothered her. She dealt with that already. Those feelings had been placed in a box and shoved deep down. She was more upset with her reaction and having to step away to compose herself.

I should have been able to stay there and deal with it. I can't run when things get uncomfortable on a mission.

Sam smiled even brighter in an attempt to convince Brooke.

"Come on. You have a client to shmooze."

Brooke gave it a few seconds and said, "My father will win him over without my help."

They made their way back to William, Patrick, and Kevin. Patrick apologized for upsetting Sam. She told him it had just been a while since she had run into anyone who knew Rick.

After a few moments, Brooke excused herself to make her obligatory rounds, and Sam followed her. Dinner followed and a little more mingling. At that point, Brooke was ready to go. The party was a success, and the potential client seemed happy. Brooke and Sam said their goodbyes to William and Patrick. Kevin followed them to the door.

"It was great to see you again, Brooke. Are you leaving?"

"You, too, Kevin. Yes, we have to pack for our trip."

"Do you think I could have a moment?"

Brooke hesitated but agreed. She looked at Sam and said, "I won't be long."

"Take your time." Sam watched as they went to what was probably her father's study, just off the foyer. Kevin waited and let Brooke go into the room first. As he closed the door behind him, he caught Sam's eyes. The look he gave her was one of contempt.

Sam didn't know what was being discussed, but slowly, the muffled voices got louder. She was standing about twenty feet away but took a few steps closer as she grew worried about Brooke. Suddenly the door opened and Brooke bolted out, obviously upset.

"Nice meeting you, Sam," Kevin said rolling past her.

"You too." Sam turned and went after Brooke. She was waiting for Jesse to get the car. "Are you all right?"

"Not now," Brooke said, tightening her jaw.

Jesse pulled up in the car and ran around to open the car door for them. Brooke looked at Jesse as he said, "Sorry. He didn't want me to say anything." Looking at her face, he said, "What happened? Did he do or say something?"

Sam saw her soften her features. "It's okay. It's just been a while." Brooke smiled and gave his arm a light squeeze before getting into the car.

Sam followed Brooke into the back seat.

"Damn it. I forgot to tell you that you need to speak to my father, Sam."

"About what?"

"Just go back inside and ask him about the letters."

"What letters?" Sam said it slow and raised her voice slightly.

"We'll wait for you."

Sam sighed and exited the vehicle. She found William and asked to speak to him alone.

"Brooke mentioned some letters I needed to speak to you about."

"Yes. I've received a few that threatened Brooke's safety. The latest one threatened you."

"Why didn't you tell me?" Sam was furious but maintained her composure as best she could in front of William.

"I told Brooke. I thought she'd have mentioned it already. The first two came about two months ago. The third about three weeks ago and the last one came last week. I gave them to Patrick, and he put some men on it." He didn't take his eyes off Sam. "I can see you're upset about not being informed, and I apologize for not following up."

Teeth clenched, it was all Sam could do not to lose her temper at that moment. Slowly, she said, "Please send me copies if you don't have the originals."

"I'll do it now." He took out his phone and emailed them to Sam. "There. Sent."

"Thank you, sir." Sam left him and stopped in the foyer to make sure the email arrived. She pulled up the letters one at a time and skimmed over them. They were from an environmental group protesting the sustainability of Kevlar. They threatened to step up their protests by attacking William's family. The last letter told William that Sam couldn't protect Brooke. "You made a poor choice in security for your daughter. A failed military officer who doesn't know what she's doing. She's an easy target as well."

Well, that's a bit harsh. They should have told me about these.

The more she thought about it, the angrier she got. Angry that Brooke hadn't said anything. She read the third and fourth letters again. Something seemed different about them. The way they were written and the fact that she was mentioned specifically.

Ten minutes later, Sam returned to the car, and she was pissed. Jesse closed the door, but Sam needed to release some anger. She opened it and slammed it closed. Then she did it again. One more time for good measure. Brooke jumped at the first slam, but not the second or the third.

Jesse turned around from the driver's seat and looked at Sam. "Uh, ma'am?"

"I'm done! We can go!"

Halfway home Sam finally spoke. "You lied to me. I asked if there had been any attempts while I was gone and you said no."

"There weren't any physical attacks. Just the letters threatening me. Then last week Dad told me about the one threatening you."

"I can't protect you if you aren't honest with me."

"I know!" Brooke yelled at her.

Brooke kept her head turned away from Sam and looked out the window. She stayed that way most of the trip home. Sam was pissed at her but also knew seeing Kevin had upset her, so she gave her the space she needed and didn't say anything else.

Jesse let them out and stopped Sam before she went in after Brooke.

"I didn't mean to upset her. He made me promise not to tell her." He was visibly bothered. "She hasn't seen him since the hospital, after his injury. Please tell her I'm sorry."

Sam could see that he had more to say and waited a few seconds for him to continue.

"They meant a lot to each other at one time. She's like a big sister to me. We all care about her, Miss Barrett. Uh, if it's not out of line, may I ask if she's in danger or something? I didn't mean to eavesdrop, but as I said, she's like a big sister."

Sam hesitated and said, "I'm here to protect her. Don't worry. I'll tell her what you said." She continued inside. After closing and locking the door, she called out for Brooke, but there was no reply. She wasn't surprised.

Sam went through the kitchen, grabbing a glass of water on the way. She knocked on Brooke's bedroom door. Slowly, she pushed it open and saw Brooke lying on her bed. She went over and sat beside her.

"I brought you some water," Sam said. "I need you to understand that I have to have all the information in order to protect you. No matter how insignificant you think it is. As soon as I came back you should have told me about the letters."

Brooke didn't move. Sam set the water on the nightstand next to the bed. "I know seeing Kevin tonight upset you. I'm not great at relationships, but I am a good sounding board if you need me."

After a few minutes, Sam started to get up, but Brooke turned and grabbed her around the waist. She hugged her tight, and Sam could tell she was fighting back tears. Sam stayed there, brushing Brooke's hair out of her eyes as she sobbed.

It seemed Sam was better at compartmentalizing her feelings than Brooke was. But Sam still needed to do better, especially while on a job. When Patrick had mentioned her husband, she didn't handle it as well as she should have. She couldn't let personal feelings affect her on the job.

"I'm right here," was all Sam said.

Eventually, Brooke cried herself to sleep, and Sam covered her with a nearby afghan and left.

14

The next morning, Sam was scrambling some eggs when Brooke came into the kitchen. She poured a cup of coffee and sat down at the kitchen bar.

Sam spoke first. "Good morning."

"Good morning. Look, I want to explain about last night."

"You don't have to. We've all had our hearts broken at one time or another," Sam told her. She didn't need to get into the situation about the letters again because she knew Brooke got the message.

"It would seem so. Well, thanks for being there. It means a lot. And if you ever need anything, don't hesitate to ask." Brooke paused and then said, "So, you were married."

"Don't go there, Brooke," Sam told her as she set the spatula down and grabbed the bacon.

"All right. I'm sorry."

Sam didn't want to get into her history with Rick. She was irritated enough that Tom hadn't reminded her about Patrick. She needed to focus on the mission and getting the information they needed. Perhaps this trip would yield some results. She hoped it would, because she felt like she was living on borrowed time concerning this mission. If she couldn't produce some results, how long would it be before they pulled her? Then what? Back to security forces in Germany. Her dream of being an OSI special agent would be gone. Sam knew she could be a good investigator. She just needed a little more time.

Well, I guess there's always CID or NCIS. She laughed to herself. *No way! Fly, fight, win!*

"What's so funny?" Brooke asked when Sam laughed.

"Oh, nothing. One of the men tried to pick me up last night with the worst line ever," Sam said.

"What did he say?"

"Are you a magician? Because whenever I look at you, everyone else disappears."

Brooke almost choked on her orange juice. Then they both started laughing. "That is terrible."

"Yeah." Sam was glad to see Brooke laughing.

"So, if not for the corny pickup line, would you have considered dating him?"

"No."

"Why not?"

"I have a job to do, Brooke."

"You can take a few hours to go out on a date. Or was he on the wrong team?"

Sam knew she was fishing. She served up two plates and sat down. "I was married to a man."

"I know. I date men. That doesn't mean I don't find women attractive."

Sam didn't say anything and began eating quickly.

"I'm sorry if I hit a nerve."

"I just don't want to talk about my personal life, Brooke."

"Okay."

"May I ask a question about Kevin?"

"Your personal life is off-limits but mine isn't?" Brooke said disapprovingly.

"It's not about you. It's about him. I was curious about his injury. I assume it happened in combat."

"He was shot. His Kevlar failed, and he was paralyzed. He's still bitter about it."

"How does that happen? Don't you make Kevlar plates?"

"I don't know the details of why Kevin's plate failed. I can tell you that we have the highest standards and rigorous testing for our equipment."

"Glad to hear that," Sam said. "The testing, not Kevin's injury." Assuming Brooke didn't want to talk about it anymore she ended the conversation.

After a big breakfast of eggs, bacon, and sausage, Brooke went back to her room to finish packing for the trip.

SAM ALSO WENT to her room to pack. Last night had been overwhelming—for her and, apparently, for Brooke as well. Sam hadn't felt that vulnerable in a long time. She needed to focus and stay on target. Adapt and overcome. Her job was to gather intel for the DOD and the others. Last night was a great start because it gave her a chance to meet some of the players in this game. She had been watching the interactions of William, Brooke, and others, but nothing stood out as being suspicious. She also needed to talk to Tom again.

Sam checked the hallway to make sure Brooke was downstairs. She closed her bedroom door, locked it, and grabbed the phone she'd hidden inside her concealment shelf that she'd brought. It looked like a shelf but had a hidden compartment that dropped down under it. She had a pistol, an extra magazine, and the burner phone in it. Quickly, she called Tom. She let Tom know they were leaving for Paris and Eurosatory that evening—another opportunity to meet some of the people KenzieCorp worked with. She could also check for any black-market dealings or whatever she could find. Sam gave Tom as many names and companies as she could remember from last night.

Finally, she told him what Patrick Malone had said about Rick. "Did you guys know about Patrick?" Then she realized that they had to know. "Of course you did. He must have come up in the research about KenzieCorp."

"Yes, and you were briefed about him in the original mission planning. You must have blocked it out, or you still have bits of memory missing." He paused, waiting for confirmation. Her silence confirmed it. "We left that part in your background. We knew you'd probably run into Patrick and that he'd recognize you."

"Are there any other surprises I should be aware of?" Sam asked.

"No, I don't think so, but if you continue with this, you need to prepare for anything that might come up."

"Did you run that name for me?" Sam wasn't going to ask but she really needed to know about Leia.

"Yes. Soon-to-be Captain Leia Coventry is one of the top cybersecurity experts in the country. You didn't tell me she was Army Reserve."

"Had to let you find something out on your own."

"She's been consulting since she was in high school. She's one of those tech geniuses. Picked up computer programming and wrote code for her high school after some football players got caught hacking into the system to change their grades so they could stay eligible to play."

"I'll bet that made her popular. Go on."

"Got a soccer scholarship to college, got hurt and came back to Texas where she enlisted. Obtained her degree on the GI Bill and teaches at Texas."

"Hmm. Anything pop?"

"Not really. Not a parking ticket. Clean as a whistle. Army record is outstanding. Why she's not at the Pentagon or Langley I don't know. They had to have offered that."

"Maybe she doesn't like the weather in DC."

"She's got some coin in the bank, if that matters. Sold some of her programs to school districts when she was a senior. I don't know why she didn't use that money to pay for college after losing the scholarship."

"Any other relatives in the military? Maybe it was a sense of duty."

"I didn't check. Did you say she consulted for KenzieCorp?"

"Yeah." Sam said it with a sigh and rolled her eyes. *At my recommendation. But I didn't mean her. But then again, I didn't even know her when I made that recommendation to Brooke.*

"Shit. She's one of the best. You'll have a hell of a time getting into their system if she beefed it up."

"Let's see if anything happens on this trip. Maybe we won't need to take that route."

"We need some evidence, Sam, and soon."

"I'll contact you when I can. Oh, Tom, they may be rare, but I think there are coincidences," she said and disconnected the call. She was irritated about Patrick but knew it wasn't Tom's fault. She looked at her gear bag and took out the other burner phone.

She'll hate me if she ever finds out I ran her name. I think it was a chance meeting and Brooke hired the best. Leia is the best.

"Hi," Leia said. "I hope you're well. I really miss you."

"Hey, Sam!" Brooke yelled.

Damn.

Leia laughed. "Well, I didn't get to say much. You need to go. I hope you'll finish soon and come home. Stay safe."

Sam hung up, answered Brooke, and went downstairs after hiding the burner phone. Brooke told her she could pack one handgun and one fifty-round box of ammo. They had all the necessary paperwork for TSA since they were flying commercial. Anything else she needed they could probably get her. Sam wasn't worried since she had a contact in Paris that could get her whatever she needed. It had been the same in Venice. The contacts were actually Tom's, but she knew she'd have whatever she needed.

WILLIAM HAD A PRIVATE JET, but sometimes, he flew commercially—first class, of course. Jesse picked them up and took them to the airport.

"Brooke?"

"We're fine, Jesse. I'm not upset with you."

Sam could see the young man's shoulders visibly relax.

They met William in the club lounge. When it was time to go, they went to the gate and boarded the plane. The only time Sam had flown first class was when she escorted Rick's casket back to the States. The airline had upgraded her. She was glad to be flying under better circumstances.

They had to fly from Austin to Chicago and then on to Paris. Sam sat next to Brooke for the first leg of the trip. The second leg, they sat in what was called Polaris Business, which had individual seats that reclined almost completely for sleeping. For the first time, she felt rested after an overseas flight, and it was definitely better than a webbed seat on a C-130.

They arrived Sunday morning at Charles de Gaulle Airport. A car took Sam and Brooke to Le Royal Monceau, which was right down the road from the Arc de Triomphe. Brooke had a two-bedroom suite with separate living and dining rooms, a bathroom, and a fully equipped kitchen—everything they'd need for a week or so in Paris.

"You know, I could really get used to this," Sam told Brooke as she looked around.

"I highly recommend it," Brooke replied.

The bedrooms were at opposite ends of the suite. Sam took the one on the left and started to unpack her things. After she unpacked, she went to the kitchen area and grabbed a bottle of water. She then asked Brooke what the plan was for the day. The Exhibition started the next day and ran through Friday. So today was a "free" day.

Brooke asked if Sam had ever been to Paris before.

Sam's face suddenly changed to sadness. "Yes, it was about four years ago or so." Sam didn't say anything else for a moment.

"You don't have to talk about it if you don't want to."

Sam suddenly spoke. "No, it's okay. Maybe it's time I did. Rick and I came here just before he deployed." Sam told her how they met and were both stationed in Germany, but at different bases. They took leave together and got married back in Texas. About three weeks before he was due to leave, they took a long weekend in Paris. The trip was wonderful. They did all the tourist things, but it was also very romantic, like a honeymoon. He deployed, and eight months later, he was killed by an IED. He died two weeks before their first anniversary.

Brooke moved closer and touched her on the arm. "Sam,

I'm so sorry you had to go through that." A slight squeeze of compassion then the hand was moved.

"Thanks. I feel a little better saying it out loud. Like a weight has been lifted." Sam hadn't really spoken about Rick's death to anyone. She put it in a box and buried it, along with a lot of other feelings. But with everything that had happened recently, she felt it would help both her and Brooke. It would reinforce her friendship with Brooke by revealing some personal details. And she really did feel better after sharing it with her.

"If you'd rather not go anywhere, that's fine. I can find something to do. In fact, if this is all too much for you, I'd understand. As much as I'd hate to lose you, I can hire someone else," Brooke said.

Sam reassured her that she was fine and could do her job, protecting Brooke. She asked her if she'd show her the sights, and Brooke jumped up and told her to get ready.

They went down near the Seine River and had a late lunch. Then they walked along the Seine to the Louvre Museum. Brooke seemed to be having so much fun showing Sam around that she asked her about it.

"You're really enjoying this, aren't you?"

"Yes. I've been coming to Paris for a few years, and it had started to feel mind-numbing. Eurosatory is only every other year, even years. So, sometimes I come just for pleasure. It's nice to have someone I can share the beauty of the city with."

As they kept walking along the Seine, Sam started to get a funny feeling. She noticed a man who had recently walked by them now seemed to be up ahead of them under one of the bridges. He was reading a newspaper, leaning against the wall.

She stopped to fix the lace in her boot. Discreetly

glancing behind her, she saw another man who suddenly stopped and took out his phone. Something just didn't feel right. A small motorboat was also slowly making its way toward them. Sam stood up and pulled Brooke close as if she was about to kiss her.

Brooke inhaled.

"We don't have a lot of time. Be ready and remember your training," Sam whispered in her ear.

Just then, the two men closed on them, and the boat pulled up to the wall. The men pulled out handguns, and one tried to grab Brooke and push her near the boat. Sam kicked the gun out of the other man's hand and punched him in the face. They fought, while the other man kept trying to get Brooke into the boat. Just as Sam knocked her guy down, she turned and pulled her gun on the man holding Brooke. She could see the muzzle of the man's handgun pressed into Brooke's side. He moved behind her and put his left arm across Brooke's neck and held her right shoulder. Sam really didn't want to shoot him.

Moving closer to the boat, Brooke suddenly stepped to the left and punched him in the groin with her right hand. Her elbow came up and made contact with his chin, and she was able to step away from him.

That gave Sam the second she needed to move in and kick the man into the water. Brooke ran as Sam followed her. They ducked into the nearest public place, which happened to be a bar.

"You okay?" Sam asked.

Shakily, she said, "I will be." She motioned to the bartender. She ordered two shots of whiskey, looked at Sam, and said, "Did you want anything?"

Sam laughed.

When the bartender came back with the shots, Sam

ordered a bottle of wine. Eventually, a table opened, and Sam and Brooke grabbed it. Sam kept her eyes on the front door and the entrance to the patio.

"Brooke, I need you to keep your eyes on the front door while I monitor the patio." Sam used the unexpected opportunity as a teaching moment. "Whenever you enter a room or building, always look around for the exits."

"Place yourself against a solid wall, if possible. Monitor exits and stay away from the cash register but keep it in view, if possible. In case of robbery," Brooke told her.

Sam raised a brow.

"It was one of the first things you taught me," Brooke said, smiling. "I thought Paris was becoming a bit mundane, but after that..." Brooke took a deep breath and let out a sigh of relief.

"You did great out there. I'm proud of you."

"Must be that great teacher I was telling you about. A toast," Brooke said, raising her glass of wine and waiting for Sam to raise hers as well. "To a great teacher and friend."

Sam smiled. "To a great student and friend."

After they toasted each other, Brooke started to tell Sam something.

"Sam, there's something..." But then Brooke stopped talking.

"Are you sure you're okay? That's not the first time you've tried to tell me something and stopped."

Brooke nodded and took a sip of her wine.

"We'll stay here for a while. We should be safe in a crowded, public place." Sam continued to be on alert and keep an eye out for anything unusual. She told Brooke to turn off her phone and remove the sim card as she did the same. They ordered some food and talked about what had just happened. Sam told Brooke it was important to talk about it while it was still fresh in their minds. They "debriefed" each other and discussed what they could have done differently, if anything.

"What gave them away? How did you know something was coming?" Brooke asked.

"I noticed one of the men had passed us and then he was under the bridge ahead of us. When I tied my lace, I saw the man behind us stop walking and use his phone. It just seemed off. The boat was coming in too slow, as well. Plus the hair on my neck was standing up."

"You have good instincts. I knew I made the right choice."

Instincts and a father who taught me things other kids didn't have a clue about. "Who knows that you come here?"

"The team at work, the post office to hold my mail, Jesse, my father and his people. It isn't exactly a secret. My father has been coming for years. When I was younger, we all came and..." She stopped speaking. Sam could see it was a memory that brought her discomfort.

"Brooke?"

"Sorry. I haven't thought about it in a while."

"I didn't mean to bring up something uncomfortable. I never asked, and I hope you won't be offended, but... where's your mother?"

Brooke looked up at her. "I guess it was just a matter of time before you asked. She was killed in a car accident after leaving me at my dorm my sophomore year of college."

"I'm so sorry, Brooke."

"Thank you. You know what it's like, don't you?"

Sam straightened up and took a sip of her wine. *Yes, I know what it's like to lose a mother. You're lucky to have as much time with her as you did.* Sam remembered her cover identity said both parents were dead. "Did your father tell you my parents are dead when he did his background check on me?"

"No. He didn't tell me anything. I ran my own. I can't let him do everything for me. Patrick gave me the name of an investigator. But he couldn't access your military record. I had to get that from Patrick. I'm sorry."

"For running a background check, don't be. You're the daughter of a wealthy man who has a company that has a defense contract. You should be careful who you choose to place in your orbit." Then Sam remembered something. "You told me your father didn't tell you I was married. But you ran your own check. Didn't it come up?"

Brooke couldn't look at her as she confessed. "I did know you were married, but I stopped reading at that point. I felt guilty about it. Like I was spying on you. I'm sorry I lied."

"You shouldn't feel guilty for checking out a potential employee. People do it all the time. If I ever have kids, I'll probably run backgrounds on their dates."

"Okay, first off, that is really wrong." Brooke cracked a smile.

"And second?"

"It may have been after you'd already been working for me." She said it quietly and almost mumbled it.

"You ran your own check after I'd been working for you?"

"Yes. I'm sorry."

Sam wondered why she would do that. It didn't really bother her, but she wanted to know why. "Didn't you trust me? Did I do some—"

"No! Sam, I trust you with my life, and you didn't do anything. I just..."

Sam decided to give Brooke the easy way out. She had been curious about her and ran the check herself. "Had you ever run a BI on someone before?" When Brooke gave her a funny look she knew the acronym threw her. "Background Investigation."

"No."

"So, you wanted to try. It's fine, and I understand." When Brooke began to say something, Sam said, "It's fine, Brooke. Let it go." Sam changed the subject. "So, you've been here many times, and it's not a secret."

"Correct."

"Your father has security. Why haven't you?"

"Actually, I did have security up until I fired him. It was one man, and my father insisted."

"Is there a story there?" Sam smiled, hoping for details.

"No, not really. Kevin was jealous. He convinced me I didn't need security in college. After we drifted apart, I never hired anyone else, and by the time my father found out, I convinced him I didn't need it." She looked toward the door. "Guess I was wrong."

"Well, maybe so. But we'd have never met otherwise," Sam told her.

Brooke smiled and gave a little laugh.

They continued talking, but Sam kept thinking about what had happened. She had so many questions. *Are we safe going back to the hotel? How did those men find us?* If they followed them from the airport, then the hotel probably wouldn't be safe. They had three choices, as Sam saw it. They could stay at their current hotel, move to a different hotel, or go back to the States. Leaving the country would be a last resort. From the outside, this attack appeared to be on Brooke, and Sam didn't think it was a ruse from her people, but she needed to verify that by contacting Tom. Most likely, it was an attack on her. Someone was trying to get her out of the way, and this time, Brooke was there.

They left the bar and, on the way, stopped at a convenience store. Sam picked up three prepaid burner phones and a couple of bottles of water using the little bit of cash she had. She handed Brooke one of the burners.

"Brooke, can you get your hands on some cash so we don't have to use cards?"

"Is it okay if we go to a bank? I have a safe-deposit box with emergency cash in it."

"Really? You have one here in Paris?"

"We come here every year, and my dad taught me to be prepared."

"I thought Eurosatory was every other year."

"It is, but I like to shop."

Sam laughed and said going to the bank would be fine. It would have to wait until tomorrow, though. It was getting late, and Sam wanted to find a place for the night. They took to the streets and began walking.

"Why can't we go back to our hotel? I'm sure Dad can get some more men for security."

Sam stopped walking and so did Brooke. "We don't know who is behind this. It's safer if we hide for the night."

"You don't trust my father's men?"

"I don't trust anyone I don't know." She considered what Brooke said and began having second thoughts. "I don't know, maybe I'm being overly cautious."

"No, I trust you. I don't mean to make you doubt yourself. I'll do whatever you say. But once we go to the exhibition won't they be able to find us and follow us back to the new hotel?"

Smart girl.

They resumed walking. "Probably, but I'll be aware and prepared. Think of it as a strategic retreat or regrouping."

"Dunkirk."

"What?"

"Dunkirk. The British and allies evacuated France so they could defend Great Britain." When Sam gave her quizzical look, Brooke added, "I took a class in college. Military History. Something I could talk to Kevin about, but I enjoyed it."

"Yeah, kind of like Dunkirk." *I just hope we don't have to deal with a force like the Luftwaffe.*

"Sam, I don't like this area, and I'm getting tired of walking," Brooke finally said.

A man crept up to them and in French said, "Come with me, ladies. I have men and drinks."

Sam saw him as he approached. "No," Sam replied in French, grabbing Brooke's hand. "We're fine, thank you."

"Ahh, I have women too," he said, smirking at her.

"Tell me where we can find a room for a few hours." Sam pulled Brooke closer and wrapped her arm around her waist.

"How much?"

Sam sighed. "Fifty euros."

"Show me."

Sam took the money out of her pocket and showed him.

"Two blocks down to the right. Tell him André sent you."

"Merci," Sam said, handing him the money. She watched him leave and then started walking holding Brooke's hand again.

"Sam. Is this necessary? The hotel—"

"The hotel may not be safe. Someone could be watching it and waiting for our return. Trust me." Sam gave Brooke's hand a slight squeeze.

"There's no one I trust more," Brooke said quietly, but Sam heard her.

"Don't worry. We'll be fine."

They found the pay-by-the-hour motel near the red-light district. Sam went in while Brooke stood just inside the door.

A man with a scruffy beard and wrinkled clothes came out from another room. He was quiet as he looked past Sam to Brooke and leered at her. His sunken cheeks and jaundiced pallor told Sam he was probably an alcoholic. It was confirmed when he spoke in French. It was difficult not to smell the aroma of cheap whiskey.

"*Oui?*"

Sam spoke back in French. "I need a room for the night. André sent us." The man grinned and gave Brooke another once-over. Then he looked at Sam.

"She is too expensive for you."

"The coke I have says otherwise. She's slumming and wants to walk on the wild side. How much?"

"One fifty."

"I can go somewhere else." Sam started to turn around.

"Discretion is our forte. One twenty-five."

"Seventy-five."

"One hundred."

"Seventy-five and a bottle of whatever," Sam said.

He scratched at the three-day scruff on his chin. "Deal." The man reached around and grabbed a key hanging from a hook and placed it on the counter. "Towels are fifteen. I guess you don't need condoms. Anything else?" he snickered again, giving Brooke another once-over.

"No." Sam reached for the key, but his hand slapped on it first.

"Whiskey."

"Where's the nearest off-license?"

"Four doors down on the left. No cheap stuff."

Sam sighed. She turned to Brooke and said, "Come on."

"Slumming? I don't appreciate that."

"Hey, he said you were too expensive for me. That's a compliment. How much cash do you have?"

"Two hundred euros."

"Okay."

They walked into the off-license and bought a bottle of whiskey and a bottle of wine and a few other things. Quickly, they retraced their steps to the motel.

"Wasn't sure you'd come back," the man said, wiping his nose. Sam placed the money and bottle on the counter.

"Key." Sam snatched it from his hand as he leered at Brooke again. She took the towels even though they probably wouldn't use them.

"Let me know if she's too much for you. I'd take a ride on that."

Sam grabbed him by the shirt and yanked him close. "She'd break your neck, and if she didn't, I would. Understand?"

"Yeah. Sure."

"And if I find anything out of order in that room, I will be back. Get me?"

He swallowed as he nervously took her threat seriously. "Uh, yeah. Wait." He reached around and offered a different key.

Sam growled and took it, tossing the first key at him.

As they walked to the room, Sam saw Brooke smiling.

"What?"

Brooke grabbed her arm and said, "My hero."

"Seriously? I save you from armed men and a kidnapping, but telling the skinny Frenchman off makes me your hero?"

Brooke laughed as Sam unlocked the room and said, "I know this probably isn't what you're used to, but it's just until morning." She flipped the light switch, and a dim light flickered on with a buzz. Before them was one bed with a nightstand next to it and a lamp on top. A small table and chair were in front of the window. The carpet, curtains, and bedding looked to be about fifteen years old, and the paint was peeling from the walls. In the small bathroom, the faucet was dripping water into the rust-stained sink.

Brooke walked in and carefully sat on the corner of the bed. Sam set the bag of water bottles, phones, and wine, on the table. Then she checked the room. Brooke watched as she ran her hand over the walls and moved the cheap pictures.

"What are you doing?"

"Looking for peepholes."

"Sorry I asked."

When Sam was satisfied, she pulled out the plastic cups she'd bought and poured Brooke and herself a cup of wine. Handing it to Brooke she said, "I'm sorry about this."

"It's not your fault."

Yeah, it kind of is. Pretty sure they were after me.

"If anything, I should be apologizing to you," Brooke said. "Thank you for being here today." Brooke gulped down the wine. "May I have some more?"

Sam handed her the bottle. "Try and get some sleep."

Brooke looked at her and sarcastically replied, "No problem. I'll sleep like a baby."

It was just before midnight, and since it was Sunday night, it was relatively quiet. Sam kept watch by the window. She saw a few working ladies out, and occasionally, a man would approach one. They would disappear into one of the rooms.

After a few hours, Brooke managed to fall asleep on top of the bed. Sam took the opportunity to step outside with one of the phones she'd bought. She called Tom to brief him on what happened and make sure this was a real threat. Tom confirmed that there had been no plans for another fake abduction.

"Have you been sending letters to her father?"

"Yes, we sent two."

"Her father received four. Two from you and two from someone else. The last one included me in the threat."

"How? Can you send me copies?"

"I'll forward photos of them when I can. Her father showed me. His man Patrick has them and is checking them out."

"So, someone is really after Brooke?"

"I wouldn't disregard that, but I think it's me. I think I got too close or got the evidence and that's why they took me."

"Maybe it's about KenzieCorp." Tom was just throwing out ideas.

"That's a possibility, as well."

"I don't believe it's a coincidence that we sent two letters and two others showed up. Sounds like someone on the inside knew about the letters we sent."

"They showed up while I had my memory loss, but I don't know the order of their arrival. I'll see if I can find that out. I do agree that it's highly unlikely it's a coincidence," Sam said. "I'll see if I can find out who knew about the letters you sent."

"Sounds good. I'm going to see if there's an agent in your area to assist you, if you need it. Don't be surprised if someone contacts you. Use the code. Do you remember it?"

"Yes."

"Sam, be careful."

Although he knew Sam could take care of herself, Tom let Sam know he was still concerned about this new development. He told her he would check with his intelligence sources and try to find out who might have wanted to abduct Brooke. There could have been several reasons for the attempt. Someone might have just wanted her for ransom because her dad was wealthy. Or someone might have received "bad gear" or gotten stiffed on black-market items from KenzieCorp and was trying to take revenge through Brooke. The latter would have tied into Sam's original mission. Or they were after Sam. Trying to keep her from investigating, which Sam was starting to believe. She was afraid she was putting Brooke in danger and wasn't happy about that. Tom would check things on his end, and Sam would do the same. She'd make contact in two days.

She pulled out another burner phone and thought about calling Leia. *Keep your friends close but your enemies closer. Leia isn't exactly my enemy. More like a person of interest. I should stay in contact.*

"Hello?"

"Hi." Sam decided it was safe to talk to her. "How are things?"

"Fine. I miss you."

"I miss you too. I'm sorry I wasn't able to speak to you those other times."

"It's okay. I understand. Can I see you?"

"No. I mean it's not possible right now. I'm not done and not exactly close."

"I see. Well, remember that promotion I was telling you about?"

"Yes."

"I was hoping you could come to my ceremony."

"I would love that, but I don't have a timeline."

"Again, I understand."

Sam gave a quiet chuckle. "You're very understanding."

"Next time I see you, I'll show you how understanding I can be," Leia said.

Sam cleared her throat and smiled. "That is a date I will be looking forward to." Sam looked around, keeping an eye out for anything suspicious. "I should go."

"Stay safe."

"You too."

Sam hung up and went back inside, quietly opening the door. Brooke stirred and asked if everything was all right. Sam said it was and told her to go back to sleep. But Brooke got up and reached for a bottle of water. She took a sip and asked what the plan was. Sam said they would leave in a few hours and go to Brooke's bank as soon as it opened. They'd get the cash and then go to a different hotel. Brooke asked about their luggage and how they'd move it.

"I'll take care of it. Don't worry." Sam would take care of it later, but she wasn't sure how. *One problem at a time.*

15

Sam and Brooke freshened up as best they could. Neither one wanted to take a shower in that place. After getting the cash from the bank, they found a different hotel that was more than accommodating. Brooke knew someone who had stayed there once. This hotel was known for its discretion since many wealthy and famous people stayed there.

"Sam, they want a card," Brooke said after trying to get a room.

"Put your sunglasses on and just stand there. Give me three thousand euros. Look important."

Brooke discreetly handed her the cash.

Sam walked over to the person at the desk. She began speaking French. Another man came out from a back room and spoke to her. Every now and again, Sam glanced over at Brooke as they spoke.

They only had a room with a king-sized bed for now. A suite would be available on Wednesday. Sam said that was fine, and they took it.

As they walked into the room, Brooke said, "What did you say to them? I couldn't hear what you were saying."

"I was trying to be discreet, Your Highness," Sam said, winking at her.

"You didn't."

"Don't worry about it. We have a room for now, and on Wednesday, a suite will be available. We're booked under the name Laurent, and you're a distant cousin of Grand Duke Henri of Luxembourg."

"You're crazy. No one will believe that."

"They know I was lying. At least about the name. It's part of the discretion they offer here."

In a voice made for royalty, Brooke said, "Be a dear and order me room service, Samantha."

Sam stared at her, and then they both burst out laughing.

Brooke ordered room service herself and gave Sam some more cash when she asked for it. "Don't spend it all in one place, sweetheart."

She was going to go take a shower and get cleaned up when Sam told her to stay there and not to leave or tell anyone where she was. She also told her not to open the door for anyone else after the room-service delivery. Sam thought twice about leaving her alone but decided it would be okay.

"Maybe I should wait until after room service comes," Sam said.

"I'll be fine, Mom."

"That's not funny. Do you have a weapon?"

Brooke hesitated. "In my suitcase."

Sam hung her head. She pulled up her pant leg and removed a knife and sheath and handed it to Brooke. "Always have a backup."

"I'll add it to the list."

"List?"

"Sam's Rules."

"I don't have rules."

"Yes, you do. Now go get my clothes, please. Unless you want me to wander around here naked?" Brooke said flirtatiously.

Sam wasn't sure if she was kidding around or serious until she began undressing. Sam quickly left the room.

SAM WENT DOWNSTAIRS and hailed a taxi. She talked the driver into taking cash and had him drop her off a couple of blocks from Le Royal Monceau. Sam thought it possible that someone was watching the hotel, so she carefully approached and watched the entrance from a safe distance. She stayed hidden as best she could in an alley across the street. She spotted a car with two men in it down the street from her. They looked like they could be watching the hotel as well.

Suddenly, Sam got a strange feeling in her gut, and the hair on the back of her neck stood up. She felt like someone was watching her. She turned and walked down the alley. Finding an open door leading to the back of a café, she walked in and went into the ladies' room.

As she opened a stall door, another woman came up behind her and pushed her against the wall. The woman said "Police" and then began frisking her. She started by putting Sam's arms out and slowly began squeezing from her hands in toward her torso. The woman was slow and methodical. When her hands arrived at Sam's waist, she paused at the pistol Sam had concealed there. Instead of removing it, she left it and placed both hands on Sam's waist.

"What are you doing?" Sam asked.

With a thick Russian accent, but in English the woman replied, "Patting you up."

"I think you mean down. Patting you down."

"*Da.*"

"Did I do something wrong? Are you Russian? What police agency are you with?"

Sam turned her head to see that the woman suddenly had a look of bewilderment. With less of an accent, she said, "I thought you liked this game."

"Game? May I see your badge?"

"Sam, what are you talking about?" the woman asked as she let Sam turn around and face her.

"You know me? Who are you? How do you know me?"

"Maybe this will help." The woman placed one hand gently on the side of Sam's head and leaned in for a kiss. It was a gentle, familiar kiss. As she stepped back, she asked, "Now, what's going on, Sam?"

Sam was stunned. During the kiss, she inhaled a familiar scent of lavender. A flash of a memory suddenly appeared in her mind. Through her own eyes, her lips touched someone's sleek, flawless neck and bare shoulder. The flash was gone as quickly as it came. Her eyes glanced to this woman's neck but quickly darted back to her eyes. She thought for a moment, not knowing if she could trust this woman.

"Tell me who you are first."

"Katrina. I'm an analyst with the agency, and we met at an FBI seminar a few years ago. I was in the area, and Tom contacted me and said you might need some help."

"You know Tom?"

"Yes. He also told me you had an accident and may or may not remember me. So—do you still have doubts about me?"

Something had changed, and Sam felt she could trust Katrina, but she wanted more information. That scent she'd smelled during the kiss took her back to a familiar time and place.

They left the ladies' room and found a table to sit and talk. Katrina told her about the weeklong intelligence seminar they'd attended. They became friends, and by the end of the seminar, they had become very close.

As Katrina spoke, Sam started to remember the events of that time. It had been a great week. She'd made friends and contacts she hoped she would keep, including Katrina.

A FEW YEARS AGO...

Sam had been called in by her commander and told she had orders to Quantico to attend a seminar. It would enhance her decision-making as an air force officer as she led her troops in protecting base assets and personnel. She was excited to attend and looked forward to the opportunity to advance her career. The attendees came from many different agencies, such as the DEA, NSA, CIA, and local and state police. Sam was the only military.

They were split into groups to work on projects. Katrina and Sam were in the same group. On Wednesday at a group lunch, Katrina asked Sam about her personal life. Sam had avoided telling them too much about herself. She wasn't comfortable talking about her past and either excused herself to go to the restroom or managed to chang the subject.

While others were talking, Katrina placed a hand lightly on Sam's knee and said, "I noticed you don't like talking about yourself, Samantha."

Sam looked at her knee, and Katrina moved her hand. "No. There's not much to tell. Please don't call me Samantha. It's Sam."

"I'm sorry, Sam." She smiled brightly, trying to make up for her blunder. "I'll bet you have a very interesting life. I already told the group that I grew up in Russia to American parents."

Sam thought she should give her something, so she said, "I was born in Italy to American parents."

"See, we have something in common. I love Venice. I was able to go a few times. Have you been? Or did you live in the south?"

"We didn't live far from Venice. It's a beautiful city," Sam said.

"I loved this little café near St. Marks. They served a wonderful plate with six different types of biscotti. They also had a wonderful ice *cioccolato*." She said the last sentence in Italian. "What was the name of that place? Café—"

Sam immediately was intrigued, and it showed on her face. "Café Florian?"

"Yes! That's it. You know it?"

"Yes. I loved their gelatos." Sam smiled back at her. "You speak Italian?"

"Yes. Russian, Italian, and French."

Sam relaxed and said in Russian, "I can speak those languages as well." She asked where else Katrina had traveled in Europe, and they spoke of the places they'd both visited.

Occasionally, Katrina or Sam would say something to

the other in one of their shared languages. Up until that point, Sam had been very professional and a little stiff. Now she was relaxed and was enjoying speaking with Katrina.

On the last day of the seminar, a group of them went to a local bar. Almost everyone was flying back to their respective homes the next day, so no one stayed out too late. Sam and Katrina were about the last of the group to leave. One of the guys, Joe, offered to walk with them back to the hotel. The dormitory on the grounds of the FBI Academy was undergoing renovations, so rooms were limited. For this weeklong seminar, they were all put up at the same hotel, so it wasn't a big deal. A bus had come and picked them up each morning and dropped them off at the end of each day. Just as the elevator stopped on Sam's floor, Joe asked if she'd like to join him for a drink. She politely declined by saying she was tired.

Sam and Katrina were on the same floor, about four rooms apart. They came to Katrina's room first.

"You know, I was going to ask you the same thing Joe did. I have a bit of wine I need to get rid of before flying out tomorrow. But since you said you were tired, I'll let you go. It was great getting to know you this week. Stay safe." They said good night, and Sam continued walking toward her room. Katrina went into her room, and Sam stopped at her own door. She glanced down the hall toward Katrina's.

Throughout the week, Sam had made friends with a few of her colleagues in the seminar. Katrina had taken a seat next to Sam on the very first day, and they got along. They'd had lunch together in a group setting. Since Wednesday Sam had thought she was getting signals from Katrina and was pretty sure she'd been flirting with her the past couple of days—the way Katrina would steal a glance or touch her arm or hand. Sam found herself liking it. She'd never thought about dating a woman before, but then she'd never felt this way about one. Not until now. *Why not? Take a chance.*

She couldn't explain how she felt. She had butterflies in her stomach. She wasn't sure why, but she turned and went back to Katrina's room. Hesitating, she took a deep breath and knocked on the door. When Katrina opened the door, Sam said she couldn't remember if they had exchanged contact information. They both knew they had done that earlier in the week. Katrina reached out and took Sam's hand, pulling her into the room and close to her.

"I've never done this before... with another woman, that is," Sam admitted.

Katrina said she didn't want to pressure Sam into anything she felt uncomfortable with. She reassured her and said they could stop anytime she wanted. Sam was the one who leaned in for a kiss. Their lips met, and Sam ran her hand through Katrina's long hair.

WHEN SAM OPENED HER EYES, she saw Katrina was already awake. She must have been watching her as she slept.

"Good morning," Sam said.

"Good morning. How did you sleep?"

"It was probably one of the best nights' sleep I've had in a long time," Sam admitted.

Katrina smiled.

It was early, and Sam's flight back to her base in Germany wasn't until one fifteen that afternoon, but she still had to finish packing since she hadn't gotten to it last night. Katrina had an evening flight, but she also needed to pack.

Sam wasn't in a hurry to get out of bed. They stayed in

bed and talked for a while. Sam told Katrina how she surprised herself by coming back to her room last night.

"I hope you don't have any regrets," Katrina said.

"No. Not at all."

For the first time in a long while, Sam was happy. They decided to make the most of what time they had left.

They shared a shower, then Sam went to her room and put on fresh clothes. She finished packing and met Katrina in the hotel restaurant for breakfast.

"Back to your base in Germany?"

"Yes. You said you have a late flight? West Coast?"

"No. I have an appointment at two at Langley."

"Heading on a secret spy mission?" Sam teased.

"Hardly. I'm just an analyst."

"Right." Sam didn't believe her. "Come on. You can trust me. I'm an Air Force officer. Why would 'just an analyst' need this intelligence course?"

"The same reason an Air Force cop would."

"I aspire for better things," Sam told her.

"Maybe I do too."

"Fair enough. This was fun. Can we email or text?"

"I'll do my best."

They walked back to Katrina's room after finishing their meals.

"Well, I guess I'd better get my stuff and head to the airport," Sam said with reluctance in her voice.

Katrina stepped closer to her, and they hugged. "Live long and prosper, Samantha."

Sam smiled at the reference to their shared interest—science fiction TV and movies. With one last kiss, Sam turned and left. They again said they'd try to keep in touch, but their jobs would make that difficult.

16

———

P*resent day...*

In what only took a moment, Sam remembered that week with Katrina, and a wave of emotions flooded over her. The memory of that night put a smile on her face. She put her arms around Katrina and hugged her tightly. Anyone could have seen what had attracted Sam to Katrina. At five foot eight with sandy-blond hair and a slender, flawless body, Katrina was a beautiful woman.

"It's nice to see a friendly face," Sam said. "Oh, wait. You wouldn't happen to have a pack of Pall Malls, would you?"

Katrina rolled her eyes at the code phrase. A way to ensure she was who she said she was. "No, I prefer Lucky Strikes."

"Had to do it."

"It's okay. I understand. I've missed you," Katrina said, almost tearing up. "So, how can I help?"

"Before I tell you, why didn't we stay in touch? We said we would, didn't we?"

"As soon as I left the seminar, I was given an assignment overseas." Katrina set her hands in her lap and looked down at them. "I'm sorry, but reaching out could have compromised my cover." She smiled and brushed some of her locks behind her ear. "I thought about you, though." Katrina reached to Sam's hand and grasped it gently. "So many times I wanted to try and contact you. I really missed you."

Sam didn't know how to respond. "I still have memory gaps. I guess I went back to work as well. But I remember that night. Your hair is different, though. The color. Weren't you a blonde?"

"Yes. I've been trying something different."

Her smile lit up the room and Sam's heart. It caught her off guard.

"You could say that fate has brought us back together. Maybe that means something."

As happy as Sam was to see Katrina, she needed to stay focused, and there was Leia. She needed to file all those feelings away but found it difficult. Her memories of that night with Katrina invaded her mind.

How could one night have such an impact on me?

She slid her hand away and placed it in her lap. *Get down to business.* "I'm on an assignment."

"I know. Now tell me how I can help you. Please." Sam took a moment and then Katrina said, "Sam?"

"Yes, sorry."

Sam trusted her completely now and brought her up to speed. They went back to the alley, and Sam pointed out the car she thought might be watching for her and Brooke, which was still there.

"Katrina, would it be too much to ask for you to go to our rooms and get our stuff?"

"Of course not. Anything I can do to help."

Sam gave her the key card and told her which suite to go into. About twenty minutes later, Katrina came back downstairs and flagged down a taxi. The luggage was loaded up with the help of a valet, and she had the taxi driver pull around the block.

Sam met her at the other end of the alley and got into the taxi. They drove to the new hotel, and the valet helped Sam and Katrina take the luggage back upstairs. Sam knocked on the door and then entered.

"Brooke? It's me," Sam said quietly.

Brooke came out from around a corner, holding the knife Sam had given her.

"We got the luggage from the hotel," Sam told her as they moved aside to let the young man pushing the luggage cart inside. He quickly unloaded the bags, and Katrina tipped him as she waited by the door.

Brooke saw Katrina come in behind Sam.

"Brooke, this is Katrina. She's a friend."

"Nice to meet you, Katrina," Brooke said with surprise in her voice. "I didn't expect Sam to return with anyone."

"Nice to meet you, too, Brooke." Katrina's Russian accent became thick again. "You are Brooke McKenzie, yes? Your father owns KenzieCorp, no?"

"Yes, he does. How did you know?"

"I have come to Eurosatory before. I work for company that wishes to do business with KenzieCorp," she said in a bit of broken English.

Sam noticed that Brooke seemed to relax a bit.

"Oh, great. We're always looking for new clients and business partners. How do you know Sam?"

"Ah, yes. Samantha and I met during, ah, how you say, officer exchange program. I was at same base as Samantha in Germany. Samantha was assigned to keep an eye on me. Make sure I didn't steal any secrets."

She laughed. Then they all joined in.

Sam was a bit startled that Katrina played it out the way she did, but she was sure Katrina had her reasons. She figured Tom must have given her Sam's cover story.

"So, how did you run into each other today?" Brooke asked.

At this point, Sam took over. "Remember when I said I have contacts? Well, I remembered that Katrina did business here in Paris, and I took a chance and called her. I didn't remember until you told me about Eurosatory. I never thought I'd need to call her. She was here, so we met near the hotel, and I sent her up to our rooms to get our stuff," Sam finished and thanked Katrina again for her help.

"This was no problem. Well, I'd better be getting back to my boss at the exhibition. Hopefully, I will see you both again this week. Maybe we all have lunch or dinner," Katrina said.

"I'll walk you out," Sam said.

Brooke thanked Katrina as they shook hands. Sam and Katrina didn't speak again until they were in the elevator.

"That was quite a performance you put on," Sam said.

Going back to her normal voice, Katrina said, "It ties in with why I'm here. I think we're on similar missions. Tom briefed me on that and your cover story. My 'boss' has been trying to find equipment and gear through less-than-reputable channels. And he doesn't always check to see if it's bottom-of-the-barrel stuff. Although I have noticed he doesn't buy from those companies or individuals. Anyway, I was sent in to gather intel. Sam, if you need anything else, please, let me know." Katrina handed her a card with a phone number on it.

After glancing at the card, she placed it in her pocket. "Katrina, your boss wouldn't have any reason to abduct Brooke, would he?"

"I don't think they've done any business yet. He only recently mentioned KenzieCorp. But I'll discreetly check into it for you. If I hear anything, I'll let you know."

Sam and Katrina went just out the front of the hotel entrance where Katrina quietly told her how much she wanted to kiss her.

Sam felt the same but was also conflicted. It was even more important to try and keep Brooke safe and continue with their respective missions.

Why did I have to start a relationship when I had memory loss? Idiot.

She remembered how Katrina made her feel, and she still felt something for her, but she was seeing Leia now.

"Sam? Did you hear me?"

"Yeah."

"Oh, you don't feel the same anymore. I guess that shouldn't surprise me. It has been a few years. I'll check into those things for you."

An overwhelming feeling pulled at Sam's heart. Sam grabbed her hand, and they went around the corner to a doorway that was set back a few feet, most likely a delivery entrance. Sam led her down the two steps and pulled her close. They kissed just as they had that night back at the hotel. For Sam, it was almost as if no time had passed. She reached under Katrina's shirt and trailed her fingers up the smooth skin of her back, slowly moving her hand over a breast while brushing her hair back with the other. Katrina had one hand on Sam's waist and was moving toward the small of her back.

Katrina pulled away and said, "I have to go, and you have to get back to your bodyguard duties."

Sam knew she was right. She gave her one last quick kiss and let her go. As Katrina walked up the two steps, she looked back at Sam and said, "By the way, I think your girl might have a crush on you."

Sam looked up, but Katrina was around the corner and gone by the time Sam straightened herself up. Katrina had stunned Sam with what she'd said about Brooke. For Katrina to make that assumption so quickly only verified what Sam had thought but hoped wasn't true. Thinking back, it made sense. It would explain some of the things Brooke had said—what she hadn't said—and the way she'd been acting.

Sam decided she'd wait to deal with that when it was necessary.

Great. This is great. She thought sarcastically. *I'm such an idiot. Not to mention a cheater. Maybe a little horny too.* Sam was torn between the two women. *Focus, Barrett!*

She made her way back up to the room to clean up. She was suddenly aware that she was in the same clothes she'd worn yesterday. Brooke had already changed into clean clothes by the time she returned to the room, so Sam took her turn to shower and change.

17

By the time Sam had cleaned up, it was already late afternoon—too late to go to Eurosatory. Brooke asked if they were going to be able to go to the exhibition tomorrow as planned. Sam said they needed to be cautious, but yes.

"Do you need to touch base with your father?"

"Not really. Do you think I should tell him what happened? Maybe he can help us figure out who is doing this. He'll probably wonder why we're not at the hotel."

Sam considered it for a moment. "I'll tell him."

"Okay. If we go to the exhibition center tomorrow, I can catch up with him. He'll let me know if he needs me for anything. Otherwise, I have my own agenda. What about this phone you gave me? Am I still supposed to use it and not any other phone?"

"I think it's safer that way for now. Your regular phone can be tracked. I know it's an inconvenience, but for your safety, I think it's best. They may know you're at Eurosatory, but with so many people in attendance, I don't think anyone would try anything. You're not an exhibitor, right?"

"Not yet. Maybe in the future."

"Good. We'll stay mobile. Besides, I'll be right by your side the entire time." Sam smiled at Brooke. "Okay?"

Brooke agreed and smiled back. The hotel had a three-Michelin-starred restaurant, so they decided to stay there to eat dinner. Tables were difficult to get, and one was supposed to have reservations. Sam said it was okay if they couldn't get in. They could always walk somewhere else.

But Brooke told her to get dressed up. So they put on some evening wear and went downstairs to the restaurant. As the maître d' approached, Brooke took the lead and spoke to him for a minute. He glanced at Sam then turned and started walking toward a table. Brooke motioned to Sam, and they were seated at a corner booth.

"I'm impressed. What did you say to him?"

"You have your superpowers. I have mine," Brooke told her.

They ordered drinks and entrées, although Sam didn't say much throughout dinner. Brooke asked if anything was wrong. Sam said no and apologized for being so quiet.

Brooke asked quietly, "You're trying to figure out the abduction plot, right?"

"Uh, that and other things." In reality, Sam was concerned about Brooke becoming too attached and having feelings for her.

Then there was Leia and Katrina. *This is nuts. I didn't even date until after OTS. Now I've got two women and a third who hasn't made her move yet.* This was a distraction Sam didn't need right now. She wished Katrina hadn't said anything about it. Sam decided she had to put it out of her mind—for now.

They finished their meal and went back to the room. The suite still wasn't available until Wednesday, so they had to share this room and the one bed for two nights. Sam hoped it wouldn't become too awkward. Before turning in, Sam excused herself to make a call.

"William McKenzie speaking."

"Sam Barrett, sir."

"Yes, what can I do for you, Ms. Barrett?"

"I thought I should inform you of an incident that took place yesterday. Brooke is fine, but two men tried to abduct her." Sam smiled and added, "You'd be proud of her, sir. She reacted with strength and courage. Again, she's fine."

His voice was calm. "I see. I assume you are fine as well?"

"Yes."

"Well, it seems Brooke made a good choice in you, Sam. Give me the information on the men, and I'll have Patrick look into it."

"Sir, I've already contacted some old friends to look into it for me."

"Patrick has other resources."

"Sir, I need you to trust me for now. If I feel we need help, I'll give you what we have."

William thought about it. "This is my daughter's safety we're talking about."

"I know, and I won't let anything happen to her."

"Ms. Barrett, I hired you to protect and teach my daughter. Let me help find these men. I can't stand by and do nothing. Is there a reason you don't want Patrick to help with the investigation?"

Sam was just trying to keep things in-house for the time being. Her house, her people. She didn't think Patrick's investigation would lead back to her true purpose for being involved in Brooke's life or KenzieCorp, but she'd contact Tom and give him a heads-up. She heard that voice in her head say *be a team player.*

"All right, sir. I'll give you what I have."

"Thank you. We're a team, Sam. You don't have to do everything by yourself. Use the resources at your disposal. I'll have Patrick contact you directly."

"Yes, sir." Before disconnecting, Sam quickly said, "Sir?"

"Yes?"

"Would you mind telling me who knew about the letters besides you, Brooke, and Patrick?"

"I turned the letters over to Patrick as soon as each one arrived, and I didn't tell anyone else. Speak to Patrick about it."

"Yes, sir. Thank you."

Sam disconnected the call, and Patrick phoned her within a minute. She gave him a description of the men and told him what happened. He said he would get right on it.

"Colonel, would you humor me and tell me who else knew about the letters?"

"The letters? William gave me the first one, and I sent it to an old friend to check out. He was CID and works as a private investigator. I sent them all to him. No prints on the letters or envelopes except post office employees. They were typed on a computer and printed out. Nothing special about the paper."

He hadn't answered her question. "Sir, did you personally send the letters to your friend?"

"No. I put them in large envelopes and had Jordan overnight them to him. He lives up in the Dallas area."

"Jordan?"

"He's one of my men. Former army. Helps with security for William. Why? Is there a problem, Ms. Barrett?"

"No, sir. I didn't know about the letters until just before we left Texas. One threatened me in particular. You can see why I'd want as much information as possible about them."

"Yes, of course. I apologize for not informing you myself. I'll keep you advised."

"I'd appreciate that, Colonel."

Sam called Tom and let him know that Patrick would also be investigating the attempted kidnapping.

"Tom, I need information on one of Patrick's men. A former Army guy named Jordan. He mailed the letters to Patrick's friend to check out."

"Jordan. Last name?"

"He's a member of the team. I'm sure you have it."

"Anything else?"

"Not right now. Thanks."

He let her know he appreciated the notification and hung up.

She paused before going back into the room. Something she hadn't considered but should have. Could William McKenzie be defrauding the government? Was he behind it? Then when Sam got too close he had someone attempt to take her and find out what she knew. Steal back any evidence she had. But she couldn't remember if she had the evidence back then or not. That might not matter right now. She needed to get evidence. Find out if KenzieCorp was defrauding the government and how. That was her mission — and to stay alive while doing it.

18

S am woke up on Tuesday morning glad that Brooke hadn't made a move during the night. She'd become too close to Sam. She originally thought that would help her to access the information she needed. Now she had her doubts. She kept going over it in her mind. *No, I never led her on or did anything more than be her friend. Friendship sometimes turns into more than that. It happens.* Realizing she was overthinking it, she put it out of her mind again and rose to take a shower.

~

"SAM? PENNY FOR YOUR THOUGHTS," Brooke said during breakfast.

"Just mulling over everything." She took a sip of her coffee. "May I ask a question about the company? I'm curious, and it might help me figure out who might be after you."

"Of course. You can ask me anything."

"How is the company doing? Financially. Any issues or problems?"

Brooke didn't hesitate. "No, none at all. We're very sound and have been." She paused and moved close. "You signed an NDA, right?"

"Yes. I remember signing one." Sam wondered what she was going to say.

"I'm trusting you, and you can't let this out."

"Who would I tell?"

Brooke's voice lowered, and she leaned in to whisper. "Dad's been considering taking the company public in order to expand. You were in the meeting the other day when I mentioned keeping everything made in the USA and expanding." She looked around and then said, "Our R and D has also been working on something that would be a breakthrough in the industry." She leaned back. "The company is doing well."

Crap. R and D. That brought corporate espionage back on the table. Cybersecurity. Leia. Crap. If someone was trying to hack into and spy on KenzieCorp, did they think I'm trying to do the same? Maybe they think I'm just another hired corporate spy. Not after evidence of illegal activities, just trying to get intel on this new product or word of taking the company public. Damn. Fudge-nuggets! Better than the f-bomb.

Sam's eyes met Brooke's, and she saw the grin on her face. "What?"

"I love watching you when the wheel is spinning. Concentrating, thinking about something."

Sam ignored the comment. "You said you'd been having hacking attempts. Have you had any since you hired that cybersecurity expert?"

"Ms. Coventry? Yes, but whatever she's done has worked extremely well. Our IT guys were beyond impressed. I thought we had the best until she worked her magic. She's well worth the price."

I'll bet she is.

"How do you know she can be trusted? I mean that would be a great way to spy on the company. Hire a cyberse-curity expert, she does her 'magic,' puts in a patch or what-ever they do, steals your secrets without you knowing."

Brooke glared at her. The silence took Sam by surprise.

Finally, Brooke spoke to Sam in a way as if she was explaining herself to a colleague. There was no malice in her voice. She was calm. "I did my due diligence, Sam. Checked her out. She signed the necessary nondisclosure agreement like you did and additional paperwork. If I felt it necessary, I could take that building she owns, her parents' house, and her company. Not to mention her Army career if she screws up or does anything like that. I will protect KenzieCorp with my last breath." Her mouth turned to a slight smile. "But I don't believe it would come to that. I trust her."

Building she owns? Her parents' house? Tom, you bastard! You didn't tell me any of that. Side-gig my ass.

Sam took in a breath and smiled. "I'm sorry if I upset you. I'm sure you took all necessary precautions."

Brooke relaxed a little more. "When it comes to the company and my actions concerning it, I tend to get a little protective. Sam, I'm sure you realize what it's like being a woman in a male-dominated industry. Not to mention rumors of nepotism."

Nepotism? What did she mean by that? As far as she knows, my father is dead. How would nepotism play into it? She thinks my father was a businessman.

"Nepotism?"

"Not you, me. I know people think I got this job because

my father gave it to me. I told you this. I've worked hard and earned my place in the company. I spent time in the trenches. My only advantage was I was able to start from a young age. Weekends and summers."

Maybe you should change your last name. It helps.

"Brooke, I'm not questioning your abilities. I've seen that you're more than capable, and I predict you will be running this company one day. You're a smart and talented individual. I just need to explore all possibilities and ask the questions."

"You're right. Thank you."

BROOKE AND SAM took a taxi to the Paris Nord Villepinte Exhibition Centre, where Eurosatory was being held. They wore business suits since Brooke would be speaking to potential buyers and sellers. They first had a walk around to check out the layout of the area. It was a large convention hall, but Brooke took the lead. At times, Sam walked beside Brooke, but whenever she stopped to speak with someone, Sam would back off. This gave her the advantage of better protecting Brooke. She stayed close enough that if someone tried to grab Brooke, Sam could react.

What are you doing? She's not the one in danger. I am. I'm the one they're after. But keeping up appearances is important. Watching out for her will keep me on my toes.

Brooke had a few exhibitors she was particularly interested in. After casually speaking with some of them, they went to watch one of the live demonstrations taking place in an outdoor area, off-site. The area was mostly mud and dirt. The spectators sat in bleachers under a large metal covering. This demonstration showcased the French Army. There was a large video screen to watch the movements of the vehicles and personnel. The military vehicles drove up and down the hills and set up their weapons. Tactical units searched and cleared a wooden structure built for that purpose. Small drones with cameras relayed the video to the big screen. Sam enjoyed it but wondered how KenzieCorp fit in to that part.

"Hey, you don't sell your body armor to foreign military, do you?"

"There's a list of sanctioned countries through the Office of Foreign Assets Control. Right now, we just supply law enforcement in the States and our military."

"That military contract must have been big for you."

"It is. We're not the only ones that supply the military. Oh, look. They're bringing out the puppies."

Sam laughed. "Puppies? Is that why we're here? You wanted to see the K-9s."

Brooke nudged her with her shoulder. "Who doesn't love a dog?"

"The guy who gets his ass bit by one."

SAM WAS IMPRESSED with how big Eurosatory was. Brooke's list of all the exhibitors included well over eighteen hundred. She had done her research ahead of time, so she knew who she wanted to talk to. After the live demonstration, they returned to the main area of the hall. Brooke also wanted to listen to some of the speakers presenting in one of the conference halls. Her schedule showed that one was taking place that afternoon.

Brooke was to meet her father for lunch to see if there had been any changes to who he wanted her to speak with.

The first time Brooke came to Eurosatory, she stayed with her father and watched how he conducted business. Slowly, over time, Brooke was left on her own. She had learned a lot from her father about how to deal with people in this profession. Her only disadvantage was being a woman. This was a predominately male profession. Although, at times, being a woman had helped her. Sam saw how professional Brooke was when speaking to others. She seemed to have been born for it.

They met William at a restaurant nearby.

"Are you all right, honey?" he asked as he greeted Brooke.

"I'm fine, Dad. I take it Sam told you about our incident."

"Yes. I'm glad the both of you are okay."

"We didn't get a chance to go to the exhibition yesterday," Brooke told him. Though Brooke had missed the Eurosatory events the day prior, it wasn't a big deal. Her schedule was very flexible, and she could catch up during the week.

"Do you need me to adjust my schedule? Talk to any vendors?"

"No, I can handle it, Dad."

William smiled at her and said, "Yes, I know you can."

William had his own security man, and Sam noticed him at a nearby table. She excused herself and went to sit with him. Based on the threat level, bodyguards didn't always sit with the people they were protecting. You stayed close enough to react to danger but didn't interfere with their business. The professional relationship needed to be maintained. Sam knew she had gotten too close to Brooke, and the professional line had blurred. But her mission was two-fold. Protect Brooke and get the information about alleged fraud and defective equipment. The latter was her main mission, and she had to remember that.

She felt it might be good to get to know this other security guard and maybe gather some intel. *Could this guy be Jordan?*

Bodyguards must eat, too, so she ordered a light meal and water. William's bodyguard was an American as well, and it just happened to be Jordan. He was a former Army Special Forces noncommissioned officer and had worked for William for about eight years. He was older than Sam, about forty years old or so, but was still in peak physical condition. Sam didn't want to raise any suspicions, so she only asked a few basic questions. It wasn't unusual for someone like William to hire former military personnel, especially in his line of work. Sam found out that Jordan had been recommended by Colonel Malone. Not exactly a red flag, but it was interesting.

Sam saw William get up from the table and nod toward Jordan.

"Looks like we're on the move. It was nice meeting you. I'm sure we'll cross paths again."

Sam said goodbye and looked toward Brooke, who motioned for her to come and sit with her. Sam had finished her lunch but grabbed her water and took it with her to the table.

"You could have sat and ate with us, Sam."

"I didn't want to give your father the wrong idea," Sam said.

"What do you mean? Wrong idea about what?" Brooke asked.

Sam needed to be careful. She didn't want to hurt Brooke if Katrina was right about her having feelings for her.

"I just want him to see that I'm a professional and take my job seriously."

"He knows that. Are you sure there's not more to it? Please, talk to me."

Sam didn't think she'd be having this conversation already, but Brooke was pushing her.

"Most bodyguards aren't as close as we are. They don't insert themselves into their employer's lives as much as I have. There needs to be a line, an employer–employee line. I think I may have crossed it. You didn't do anything wrong. It's my fault." As she was talking, she could see Brooke's face change. The light in her eyes seemed to dim a bit.

Brooke looked down. Suddenly, Sam noticed she looked very uncomfortable. Brooke took a sip of her wine before speaking.

"It wasn't you who crossed the line. It was me." She finished her glass. "You're so easy to talk to and get along with. I thought you could be both a protector and a friend." Brooke hesitated as if she was considering something. "The day you disappeared, we were supposed to have lunch together. I was going to tell you how I felt... about you."

Sam sighed and sat back in her chair. So it was true. Brooke did have feelings for Sam. She wasn't quite sure what to say.

"Brooke, I'm sorry if I led you on. The last thing I'd want to do is hurt you." Brooke had her hand on the table, and Sam reached for it. But Brooke pulled it away before Sam could touch her.

"See, doing things like that is what made me fall in love with you." Brooke stood up, and Sam quickly asked if they were leaving. Brooke told her she just wanted to freshen up before they left. Sam stood and stopped her.

"I still have a job to do." Sam escorted her and checked

the ladies' room to make sure it was safe. "I'll wait out here unless someone comes in." Sam left the room and stood nearby.

This was way more than she expected. *Fall in love with me? Crap.* She looked up at the ceiling. *What are you doing to me? Every time I turn around, you throw a new wrench in the works.* She wasn't exactly speaking to the deity she prayed to as a child. She'd given up on that after she left home.

"Praying for divine intervention?" Suddenly Brooke had returned and was watching her.

Sam turned her head and said, "No. We're not on speaking terms." They hadn't been for years. No matter how many times someone tried to explain it to her, she never forgave Him for taking away the best person in her world, her mother. Her father still took her to church occasionally, but it was the nanny-slash-housekeeper that took her every Sunday as time wore on. Then when her brother died and her father turned against her, she gave up on Him or any other deity the world made up. "I don't see you going to church or Mass on Sundays," Sam muttered under her breath.

Brooke stopped walking and turned to her. She stepped so close Sam could feel her breath. Calmly, she said, "That doesn't mean I'm not a Christian. It doesn't mean I don't pull out the Bible my mother gave me when I was a little girl and talk to her." Staring into Sam's eyes, she said, "Two things I won't discuss with you. Politics and religion. But I will leave you with this, Samantha Ellen Watson Barrett. You can never hide from Him. Anger can revert to joy, wrath can revert to delight, but a nation destroyed cannot be restored to existence, and the dead cannot be restored to life."

Then she turned to walk away.

Sam didn't appreciate the last thing that Brooke said and

grabbed her arm. That last quote was familiar, but Sam couldn't quite place it.

"What was that? Some Bible quote? I don't need that."

Brooke looked down at Sam's hand clenching her arm. She smirked. "I'd have thought a warrior such as yourself would know Sun Tzu's *The Art of War* when she heard it. And I have no idea what you need. Now, if you don't mind..."

Sam released her arm. "Sorry. I read Sun Tzu when I was a kid." Another of her father's teachings. *Might be time to brush up.* "Yes, I do mind. I'm not your enemy, Brooke. Look, I don't want to fight with you."

"I didn't realize this was a fight. More of a discussion. Boy, you are quick to anger."

"What? No, I'm not angry.

"Intense?"

Sam tried to relax by taking a deep breath. "Why that quote?"

"It just seems appropriate."

"Why? Tell me, please."

"I'm not sure you want to know what I think."

"Yes, I do."

"Ever since you came back you haven't really seemed happy. Before your memory loss, you were driven, but you were fun to be around."

"I have a job to do, and I lost my memory. I'm trying to put the pieces of my life back together."

"It's not just your memory loss. The last part of the quote was the important part. The dead cannot be restored to life. You've lost your family, and you still haven't gotten over it. You lost your mother, Marie, when you were four and then your father, James Watson, a few years later. He was a businessman in Italy who died in a private plane crash. It seems to be bothering you more since you came back. You can't bring them back, Sam. The dead cannot be resurrected. Let them go and stop being mad at Him."

My father's death was part of the cover story. Sam had forgotten it until now. Brooke's insight surprised Sam, but this topic was not one she wished to continue. She was probably right about Sam not being able to forgive. Even though her father was alive, her relationship with him was dead.

Time to move on from this subject.

"Let's stay away from the topics of politics and religion and get back to the original one," Sam said.

Sam asked her to sit down so they could finish the conversation.

"I don't think there's much more to say. I told you how I felt, but you... but you don't feel the same. So I think it's best we just go back to that professional relationship. Unless you'd rather quit."

"Brooke, sit down, please." She waited for Brooke to sit down then continued. "I'm not quitting. I'm sorry if I'm different or more intense, but I won't apologize for doing my job. Look, I care about you, and if you got hurt on my watch, I don't know if I could live with that."

"It's fine. After meeting your friend, I realized the two of you had unfinished business."

Crap.

"Am I that easy to read?" Sam asked.

"No, you are definitely not an easy person to read."

"Then how did you know?" Sam asked.

"I didn't. You just confirmed it," Brooke said.

Sam smiled and said, "Touché. I think the student has become the master. Are we okay?"

Brooke said, "Yes. I feel better now that everything is out

in the open. It'll be a little easier to live with knowing you are unavailable."

"Brooke, I don't know where my relationship with Katrina stands. It's been a few years since we've seen each other."

I also started something with Leia, and I don't know where that relationship is going either. I really like her too. But she might be a suspect.

"You care about her more than you think. Your eyes light up when you see her."

Sam was uncomfortable. She wasn't used to all this talk about her feelings and deep conversations. "You said I wasn't that easy to read."

"You're not, but when you were together, there was something there. It was subtle, but it was there. Now that I know, I realize you still have feelings for her."

Sam shifted in her seat. *It was one night years ago.*

"May I ask you a personal question?"

"I would think by now you would know you can ask me anything."

"Why are you attracted to me? I mean have you always liked women? You dated Kevin."

Brooke took a moment. "Yes, I've always found women attractive. Men as well. You're not the only fish in the sea, Samantha Barrett. I'll get over it. In fact, I already have."

Sam knew it was the first time Brooke had lied to her. She had spent enough time with Brooke to read her body language, and she knew it would take more than a few seconds for Brooke to get over her. Brooke wore her heart on her sleeve when it came to personal relationships. She remembered comforting her after seeing Kevin. But Brooke knew where she stood, and Sam needed to get back to her mission, so she let it be and decide not to call her out on the lie.

There was one thing she needed to know.

"You called me by my full name. A name I don't use."

"You don't use it anymore. Watson. You want to know how I got that information?"

"Yes."

"Sam, it was in your background information. Why did you change your name?"

Changing my name wasn't part of the cover story. I did that on my own because I don't want to ride his coattails.

"Personal reasons. I'd appreciate you forgetting that name."

"Very well. Let's go. I have more people to talk to," Brooke said, standing.

WEDNESDAY MORNING, before they left for the exhibition, the desk clerk let them know a suite would be available that afternoon. They were both a little relieved at the prospect of more space. Things weren't exactly awkward, but their relationship was different now. Tense. They weren't having as many conversations as before. Nevertheless, Sam was determined to protect Brooke and complete her mission, no matter what.

Sam followed Brooke around as she met with different exhibitors. While keeping an eye out, Sam saw William's security guy, Jordan. He must have been off duty because he was dressed in business casual instead of a suit. He was speaking with one of the exhibitors. From the way they acted, it looked like they knew each other. As Sam watched them, she noticed that Jordan seemed a bit uncomfortable and kept looking around. His left hand was tapping the side of his leg, another indicator of anxiety. Considering the way he acted when they met, she believed something was going on with him. She was also concerned that he was involved with the additional two letters.

As they finished their conversation, he wiped his right hand on his slacks. The two men then shook hands, and Jordan walked away.

Sam positioned herself so Jordan wouldn't see her as he walked through the crowd. She was curious about their conversation and thought she should find out who Jordan had been talking to. It wouldn't be difficult. Although they weren't near an exhibitor booth, Sam watched as the man walked toward one that was nearby. He was in a suit and had exhibitor credentials.

Sam was just barely able to see the name of the company on the exhibitor's table cover. She looked it up on the paper list that came in their registration bags. Brooke had circled all the exhibitors she wanted to speak to ahead of time. This company was circled. From what Sam had learned, this company was a potential client, or they already did business together and Brooke just needed to touch base.

Sam had decided that while they were in the building, they could go back to using their smartphones. She opened the app for the exhibition and looked at the map of the convention floor. She verified the name of the company. Now she just needed to find out that guy's name.

Brooke had just finished speaking with someone and was moving on. Sam needed to steer her toward that guy. They only had until Friday, and Sam didn't want to wait until the last minute in case she needed to follow up on anything.

She had an idea. She texted Katrina to see if she was in

the building. She was, and Sam asked if she could get the name of the guy for her. She sent the name of the company and a brief description of the guy. Katrina replied that she would.

Fifteen minutes later, Sam had his name—Nicolas Boucher.

Since Sam had sent Katrina to get the name, she moved on with Brooke. They listened to a few presentations and saw more live demonstrations outside. That evening, a cocktail party was scheduled at a nearby hotel, hosted by one of the French companies at the exhibition. By invitation only, the party was another way of networking with some of the more established companies. KenzieCorp was invited, and William usually attended. This time, he had a conflict and asked Brooke to attend for him. So Brooke and Sam went back to the hotel, moved into their suite, and got ready for the black-tie event.

19

———

When they arrived at the hotel, they followed the signs to the party room. A gentleman in a tuxedo checked their names against a list. Brooke's father had called ahead and made sure they would have no trouble getting in.

Waiters walked around with trays of champagne, and Brooke took two glasses and handed one to Sam.

"I'm on duty," she said.

"I'm sure you can stay sharp while having one glass," Brooke told her. "Besides, you're always on duty."

Brooke started mingling and talking to people. She introduced Sam as her associate because she didn't want to draw any unnecessary attention to having security. But Brooke and Sam had already drawn attention from the men in the room just by entering.

Brooke was just finishing a conversation when Katrina suddenly came up to her.

In her thick Russian accent, she said, "Miss McKenzie? It is a pleasure to see you again." She shook her hand and asked, "May I introduce you to my employer, please?"

"Yes, of course. Please, call me Brooke. It's a pleasure to see you again as well."

"Sergei Rogov, this is Miss Brooke McKenzie. Brooke, this is Sergei."

Sergei was a tall, handsome, broad-shouldered man with dark hair and a close-cropped beard. He took Brooke's hand and kissed the back of it. His accent was also Russian. "A pleasure to meet you, Miss McKenzie. May I ask who your lovely companion is?"

Brooke introduced Sam. Sergei took her hand and kissed it as well. He then said something to Katrina in Russian.

Katrina smiled. "He said he could, ah, die happy tonight after meeting two such beautiful women."

They smiled and thanked him for the compliment.

Brooke asked Sergei if he'd like to tell her about his company and what he was looking for.

"Da. Straight to business. Yes, I'd like that."

Brooke whispered in Sam's ear, "Give me a moment with him."

Sam excused herself.

Katrina spoke to Sergei in Russian. "If you don't need me, I'll be nearby." He nodded his head and turned his attention back to Brooke.

Katrina followed Sam to a less-populated area of the room where Sam could still see Brooke. They stood next to each other, facing the crowd.

Sam spoke first in a low voice. "Thanks again for getting Nicolas's name for me."

"No problem. I have some information about him. He recently popped up on Interpol's radar for illegal activity, but they haven't been able to get anything on him yet. He's a French national. Also, after I got his name, I saw him speak with one of the exhibitors from China. It may be nothing, but I thought you should know. Sergei also spoke to him on Monday. So there could be something there."

"Is Sergei going to do business with him?"

"I'm not sure. Nicolas was cagey when he spoke about protective gear. Sergei sent me for coffee and spoke to him alone. I'm not sure what his plan is."

"Interesting. By the way, you look beautiful too. In case Sergei didn't say," Sam told her.

Katrina took a sip of champagne to hide her smile. "Are you flirting with me, Ms. Barrett?"

"No. Just stating the obvious. Don't read into it." Sam needed to tread carefully. "How'd you like to help me again? I think we need to clone Nicolas's phone. See what we can glean from it. What do you think?" Sam asked.

"I think that's a great idea, and I'd love to help. I have what we need, so we can do it tomorrow at the exhibition. By the way, what led you to Nicolas?"

"I saw one of William McKenzie's security men talking to him. He was acting nervous. Jordan might also have something to do with some threatening letters that were sent to McKenzie."

"That's thin."

"I know, but I have to start somewhere." *My gut is telling me to follow up.* "So let's figure out what we're going to do."

After coming up with a plan, the conversation turned personal.

"You were right," Sam told her. When Katrina looked at her, Sam continued, "About Brooke. And she knows about us. Not the details, but that we were more than friends."

"Were?"

Sam looked at her. "I guess we'll just have to take it day by day. Things are complicated for me right now." *That's an understatement. I may be dating a suspect.* "I need to complete this mission and then I can figure the rest out. I might be headed back to Germany after this, if not before."

"That doesn't sound like the Sam Barrett that came to my hotel room and—"

"And I need to focus and stay on target," Sam said, cutting her off.

"I found this little café that serves a decent gelato, if you're interested."

"You did not. The only decent gelato is in Italy."

"You're right, but they do have something called a chocolate coconut spindle."

Sam sighed and said, "I know what you're trying to do."

"What's that?"

"Trying to connect with me on an emotional level through our shared love of certain foods."

"We have some things in common, Sam. Not just food. You can't deny that."

Katrina was right. The physical attraction was undeniable, but there was an emotional attraction as well. Sam enjoyed the time they'd spent together at the seminar, and when they parted, she found herself still thinking about Katrina months later. She liked her sense of humor, and they had spoken about how they both enjoyed science fiction.

Katrina leaned close and whispered, "You're thinking about the time we spent together at the seminar, aren't you?"

Damn, how does she know? She's wearing that perfume again.

"No," Sam said unconvincingly.

"Remember teaching me to play darts? The way you placed your hand on mine as you leaned against me. Your left hand on my waist. It was so comfortable, even though you were using your nondominant hand."

Sam remembered, and again Katrina was right. It was very comfortable. It was more than flirting. Deep down, Sam knew they had a connection.

Katrina smiled. They were standing in front of a wall, and Katrina sidestepped closer to Sam. Behind their dresses, she reached for Sam's right hand. In a faint voice, she said, "Imagine me turning toward you, running my hand through your hair, and slowly moving in to kiss you."

Sam couldn't help herself and squeezed her hand. "You really know how to get a girl going."

"And, hopefully, leaving her wanting more." Katrina took another sip and then walked back to Sergei, who had just finished talking to Brooke and was looking for her.

Brooke walked over to Sam. "Did you two get a chance to catch up?"

"We did."

But I can't do this. I'm involved with Leia. Maybe. I have no idea what I'm doing on the relationship front. This is stupid. Stop thinking about your personal crap.

"How does business look with Sergei?"

"Promising, but this was just the first step. More meetings to come," Brooke told her.

"Seriously, you may do business with him? I heard he might be shady."

"Who I consider doing business with is not your concern." Brooke cocked her head and said, "Or does it bother you that I might do business with your ex and her boss?"

Crap. My mouth just keeps getting me in trouble.

"No, that's not what I meant. She's not my ex. I mean... we're not... we weren't..."

Brooke laughed. "Lighten up, Sam. I'm just messing with you."

SAM WATCHED Katrina and finally got up the nerve to approach her for what would be an unpleasant task.

"May I have a moment?" she asked.

"Of course," Katrina said.

They walked away from the man that Sergei was speaking to.

Sam was nervous because she still had feelings for Katrina, but the situation needed to be rectified. "I think we've been leading each other on. The flirting and touches. I'm seeing someone."

She may be a suspect, but then again, she may not. It doesn't matter. Maybe I should end things with her as well. Why is this so hard? I hate relationships. I'm never dating again. It's nothing but a distraction. No men, no women, ever.

"I see." Katrina looked down and then stepped close. "Are you sure I can't change your mind?" she said, whispering in her ear.

Her warm breath made Sam shudder and close her eyes. Quickly, Sam stepped back and said, "Yes, I'm sorry. Thank you for your help, and I understand if you want to end your assistance."

"Hmm. So formal. I'm not that petty. If you need my help, then that's what I will do. Do you still need my help, Ms. Barrett?"

Sam knew she did. Katrina had the equipment to clone the phone. *Maybe I can figure out another way. No, I'm on limited time. I need her help.*

"Yes."

"Fine. We'll get started tomorrow." Katrina gave a curt smile and walked back over to Sergei.

Sam sighed and joined Brooke.

Telling her there was no chance for us was the right thing to do.

Brooke and Sam stayed for another hour or so then left for their hotel. Sam noticed that there wasn't as much tension between them now. This made things easier, and Sam felt better.

20

Sam and Katrina's plan was to try to clone Nicolas's phone via Bluetooth. That was the safest way without physically having the phone. They just needed to be close enough. Katrina had a laptop with the software on it, so she was going to make the attempt. She set up close by his booth and tried to hack the phone, but it wouldn't work. Nicolas's phone had recently been updated, and cloning via Bluetooth was easier done when it didn't have the newest update.

Katrina texted Sam and told her it was a no-go. Katrina had already warned Sam of this possibility, so they came up with a backup plan.

Plan B. They'd have to physically access the phone to install the spyware. Someone would have to lift the phone from Nicolas, install the spyware, and return it. Sam knew that Brooke still needed to contact Nicolas since he was on her list, so Katrina waited until they approached him.

While Brooke was speaking to Nicolas, Katrina caused a distraction by bumping into him, pickpocketed the phone, and dropped a folder of papers. She discreetly handed the phone off to Sam, who quickly installed the spyware.

Katrina had used her connections at Interpol to get Nicolas's cell phone number and sent a text to it a few minutes before. Sam quickly scanned the text messages and clicked on the malicious link, thus opening the door for the hack. She then deleted it. Hopefully, he wouldn't check his deleted texts.

"Katrina, are you all right?" Brooke asked as she helped Nicolas pick up the papers.

"Da, yes. I'm just clumsy." She made eye contact with Nicolas and smiled. "But my clumsiness might be an opportunity. I am Katrina."

"Yes, we met on Monday. Nicolas."

"You remember me?"

"I remember beautiful women."

Katrina blushed and moved her hair behind her ear. "Thank you, Nicolas. I meet so many, I apologize for not recognizing you."

"You are quite welcome, and it's understandable," Nicolas said, smiling back.

As Katrina began to walk away after her papers had been returned, Sam slipped her the phone. Katrina then did an about-face and returned to Nicolas.

"Nicolas. If you don't mind." Katrina handed him her briefcase horizontally and opened it. She placed her folders into it and closed it. "I appreciate your assistance, Nicolas." While she spoke and he was occupied gazing into her blue eyes, she was able to discreetly slip his phone back into his suit jacket pocket. She took the briefcase back and handed him her card. "In case you care to do business."

"Your boss already gave me his card."

"Da. That one is mine." She winked at him and walked away.

Brooke looked at Sam who rolled her eyes. "Is she trying to make you jealous?"

"I don't know. It doesn't matter. I have a job to do with you. I don't have time for games." Sam tried to play it off, but in reality, the flirting did bother her a little. *It was a distraction. She was placing the phone back in his pocket. That's all it was, and I don't care.*

Katrina found an empty table and sat down. Via her laptop, Katrina went through the call logs and texts and was able to see the numbers Nicolas had called and texted and where he had been.

Brooke decided to grab a light lunch at the exhibition center. Sam texted Katrina to let her know where they'd be. Katrina found them and discreetly passed a note to Sam. Brooke asked her to join them.

"Thank you, but I have to get back."

Sam stood to gather her trash and was bumped into by a young man.

"Oh my gosh, I'm so sorry, ma'am," he said.

Before Sam could say anything she was standing face-to-face with Leia.

"Stroud, what happened?" Leia asked him.

"I was about to apologize for my clumsiness, Professor."

Leia looked at Sam.

Sam spoke in Russian to the young man. "It's all right. No harm done."

"I'm sorry. I don't understand."

Katrina translated. "She said it's all right and no harm done."

"Thank you. Are you sure you're all right? Maybe I can

make it up to you by buying you a drink later?" He smiled his best smile at her, and everyone knew he was flirting.

"Stroud," Leia said.

"Sorry, ma'am. Just trying to keep international relations friendly."

"Such a player," one of the young women in the group mumbled.

Sam looked at Katrina, waiting for the translation, even though she didn't need it.

Katrina grinned. "He's a little young for you, but he's cute," she told Sam in Russian.

"I'm not interested," Sam said.

"No, I think it's the professor that has your attention," Katrina said to Sam.

Sam was emotionless and not in the mood. "Just get rid of him."

"She says thank you, but a handsome man such as yourself must have plenty of women fawning over him, and she wouldn't want to get lost in the crowd."

Stroud blushed slightly and stood a little taller.

Leia spoke. "I'm really sorry. We have to go. Stroud," she said trying to move the young man along.

Before Leia could leave, Brooke spoke up. "Hello, Ms. Coventry."

"Ms. McKenzie, I didn't see you there. How are you?" Her eyes darted from Brooke to Sam whose face had not changed in the slightest.

"Fine, thank you. I see you've met my friends. This is Katrina Davis and Samantha Barrett."

"Yes, one of my charges was attempting to engage in a conversation," Leia said.

"Samantha Barrett? Doesn't sound very Russian to me," Stroud said.

Then in Italian, Sam said, "I'm not Russian. But you should never assume where someone is from just from their name."

He responded back in Italian. "You're right, ma'am. My mistake." Then he smiled. "Are you sure I can't buy you a drink?"

Sam stared at him with a straight face, and he shifted uncomfortably. In Arabic she said, "Go back to the fraternity, young man."

"What did she say?"

"It's Arabic," Leia said. "She said it's time for us to go, and she's right."

Sam finally blinked, and her eyes darted back to Leia. *You have some questions to answer. Not here and not now.*

"Would you like to join us? For lunch?" Brooke asked Leia.

"No, thank you. We have a schedule to keep." Leia began to walk away, but Brooke spoke again.

"Ms. Coventry, I've been meaning to follow up with you about that work you did for me."

"Is there a problem?"

"Not at all. I'm very impressed and pleased."

Leia looked at her watch. "I'm sorry. We really are on a tight schedule. Ms. McKenzie, you can call me if you have any issues with the program. It was a pleasure Ms. Davis, Ms. Barrett."

"It's Doctor Coventry. She's a PhD, ma'am," Stroud corrected in an almost protective manner.

"My mistake," Brooke said.

Sam watched as Leia led Stroud to a table to join their small group.

Brooke laughed. "Wow, she seems so young to be a PhD.

That was fun to watch. Why the subterfuge, Sam? Speaking all those languages."

"Because it's fun," Sam said. "I like to see how others react. It's also a good way to get rid of someone you don't want to talk to."

Once again speaking Russian, Katrina said a little more quietly, "I think you would have loved to talk to her." Switching back to English, she said. "I need to find the boss. Perhaps we see each other soon. Goodbye, Brooke."

"Bye, Katrina."

Katrina glanced briefly at Sam and said, "Samantha."

The way Katrina had used Sam's entire first name bothered her. There was a sudden lack of feeling. A coldness. *Jealousy? It doesn't matter. You're not dating anyone. Not anymore.*

"Katrina." She said it with the same coldness.

After lunch, Sam had a chance to read the note. Katrina had found some phone numbers based in the United States. The ones with Texas area codes stood out to Sam. She also noticed that Nicolas had been to a building in an industrial area of Paris many times. She thought it might be worth checking out but knew she shouldn't go alone. She still needed Katrina for backup and assistance.

SAM

Checking on a building tonight. Want to come along?

KATRINA

Love to.

SAM

0230 hrs, out front of mine.

KATRINA

See you then.

AT TWO THIRTY in the morning, Sam dressed in dark clothes, snuck out of the suite, and met Katrina in front of the hotel. Since Katrina had a car, she drove them to the building, which turned out to be a warehouse.

"Hey, I really appreciate your help. Are you ready for this?" Sam asked, trying to forget what happened during the day. Her flirting with Nicolas and Sam knew she suspected something was going on with Leia.

Stay mission focused.

"No worries. I'm glad to help." Katrina grabbed her backpack and put it on.

"Why do you have that software and stuff?" Sam asked.

"I have my own mission, Sam," Katrina said.

Sam started walking, but Katrina pulled her arm down. As they squatted, Katrina whispered, "I know this is our first time working together, but don't forget about the cameras."

Fudge-nuggets. Pull your head out, Barrett!

Katrina pulled out a gizmo that was about five inches long and turned it on. Sam recognized it as a camera and bug detector. Katrina extended the short antenna and popped open a red lens. Looking through it, she pointed to a camera to the right of the door. Then she pointed a laser at it, which knocked it out. "Do your girlfriends always show up on your missions?"

Girlfriends. Plural.

"Tom called you. I didn't even remember who you were."

"What about the professor? She's your new girl, right? The one you're seeing?"

Damn spy. Can't fool you, can I?

"Focus on the mission, please."

They walked to the door when Katrina said it was clear. Sam picked the lock with some tools Katrina had brought. "Do you always travel with spyware, lasers, camera finders, and lockpicks?" Sam whispered as she worked.

"I like to be prepared." Katrina smiled as she kept watch. "Need help?"

"No," Sam said as she stood. She smiled as she set her hand on the knob, but Katrina stopped her from opening it.

"Alarms?"

Mother fu—

"Don't you have a gizmo for that?"

What the hell is wrong with me? Stop making mistakes!

"Just wait." Katrina looked around for wiring but didn't see any. Checking the door frame for sensors or magnets, she found two. "Magnetic sensor." She dug into her backpack and pulled out what looked like a piece of flexible plexiglass with wires going to another gizmo that had a red light and green light on it. When the plexiglass was placed between the doorjamb, the green light went on. "Negative pole." She checked the other sensor and took out another magnet. "They're both negative." She took out two magnets and handed one to Sam. "Place this in this exact way down there." She retrieved a magnet and placed the negative side of the magnet near the sensor. Then she looked at Sam who did the same. "Slowly open the door."

Sam took a breath and slowly opened the door while holding the magnet in place.

"No alarm," Sam said, smiling. "Doesn't the agency have more high-tech ways of bypassing alarms?"

"What fun would that be?" Katrina said. "The magnets trick the sensor into thinking the connection is still there.

But you need to make sure the pole is correct. Negative or positive."

Once inside, they carefully looked around, hoping they wouldn't find any manned security. Again, Katrina searched for cameras. After she killed another two, they walked further into the building. Crates were stacked all around.

Sam whispered to Katrina, "We need to see what's in the crates."

Katrina agreed, and they picked one to open. They found military-style body armor inside. Sam picked up one of the vests and looked it over. Nothing seemed out of the ordinary.

Katrina dug deeper and pulled out another one. This one seemed a bit on the light side. It didn't have any plates inserted into it. A box within the same crate held the inserts.

Sam looked the plates over and recognized the company stamp on them. She remembered reading an article that said plates from RedLine Company had a high failure rate. If those plates were used as the body armor, they would never stop any kind of ammunition.

Sam told Katrina, and they looked through the rest of the crate. Some of the plates had KenzieCorp's stamp, and other plates had the RedLine Company stamp. The bill of lading attached to the crate was marked "US Army, Stuttgart, Germany." It had KenzieCorp's logo on it as well.

Katrina said, "We need some pictures."

Sam agreed.

Katrina snapped some pictures with her phone. Just as they were putting the lid down on the crate, Sam saw a red dot on Katrina's chest. She quickly pushed her down as a shot rang out.

Sam drew her gun and fired two rounds in the direction she thought the shot had come from. As they crouched behind the stack of crates, she looked at Katrina and asked if she was okay.

Then she saw the blood coming from her shoulder.

More shots rang out, and a crate broke open. Plates fell on the floor nearby. Sam quickly glanced at them and saw the ones marked RedLine were broken, cracked, or shattered. Ones marked KenzieCorp were intact. A testament to what Brooke had told her about their plates being sound. A piece of paper floated nearby and Sam grabbed it and shoved it in her pocket.

"We need to get out of here—now. Ready?"

Katrina nodded and pulled out her gun. She had been shot in her right shoulder, so she put her gun in her left hand. Sam told her to go, and Katrina ran for the door. Sam covered her then followed her out as more shots rang out. They made it to the car, and Sam drove back to the hotel.

"How bad is it?"

"Just another gunshot wound," Katrina said, breathing fast and pressing on the wound with her left hand to stem the bleeding.

Sam glanced over at her. She was in obvious pain.

"You've been shot before?"

Katrina tried to laugh. "No. First—" Katrina groaned as Sam turned a corner, causing her to slide against the passenger window. "—time. Ow!"

"Sorry. Keep pressure on that."

"Slow down. Don't get the police on us."

"I need to get you back and look at that." Sam felt terrible. "I'm so sorry. I should have gone alone."

"You wouldn't have made it past the cameras." Katrina laughed.

"How can you joke at a time like this?"

"It's that or cry."

Sam glanced over at her. Seeing her grimace in pain just made her feel worse. "I'm so sorry."

"Stop it. You saved my life. I'll have something to remember you by when we part ways."

"A photo would have been sufficient." This time Katrina was silent. "Katrina? Hey, stay with me. Stay awake, Katrina!" Sam saw Katrina's left hand fall from the wound and into her lap. "No, no, no. This is not happening. Katrina!" She reached over and lifted Katrina's hand to press it onto the wound.

"S-Sam. I need you to tell Sergei—"

"No. We're almost there. Just hang on. You'll be fine."

"My s-s...Ale..."

Sam really didn't want to pull up out front, but she had no choice. Stopping short of the drive leading to the entrance of the hotel, Sam quickly looked in the back seat and grabbed the lightweight jacket that was back there. Luckily, the blood was contained on Katrina's clothes and not the car. She draped the jacket over Katrina's shoulder. Then Sam pulled the car up to the covered entrance. She quickly exited the vehicle and ran to the passenger side just as the valet came out.

The young man spoke in French to her. "Do you need help, madame?"

Sam reached in her pocket and gave him a hundred euros. "No, my friend just overdid it with your wonderful wines. A good night's sleep will take care of it. Everything's fine, understand?"

"Yes, madame."

Sam was able to get Katrina out of the car. The motion caused Katrina to wake and she groaned.

"Hold on, honey. I got you," Sam told her.

"I knew you still cared."

It was three forty-five in the morning, and the hotel lobby was empty. The man at the desk gave them the evil eye.

"She loves her French wine," Sam told him in French.

She helped Katrina into the elevator and then to the suite. They tried not to make a lot of noise, but Brooke came out of her room when the main door slammed shut before Sam could stop it.

"What's going on? Where were—" Brooke saw blood dripping from Katrina's right hand. Sam had managed to stop a blood trail until now.

Sam told her to get some towels as she took Katrina into her room and onto the bed. She gently laid her back while keeping pressure on the wound. Brooke brought the towels and placed one underneath Katrina's shoulder. Sam took another and applied pressure with it to the front of her shoulder.

Brooke had been standing there, watching. "What can I do to help?"

Sam told her she needed the first aid kit—it was actually more of a small trauma kit—in her suitcase. Brooke went to the closet, opened the suitcase, and found the kit. She gave it to Sam. It had just about everything she needed.

Sam put the latex gloves on and grabbed the shears. She cut Katrina's shirt up the middle and moved it to the side to get a good look at the bullet wound in her right shoulder. She already knew she wouldn't find an exit hole.

"Well, you finally got me to take my shirt off," Katrina said through a groan.

"And now it looks like we may have to play doctor."

Katrina forced a smile. "Are you flirting with me?"

"No. It was a joke." Sam checked the wound. The

bleeding had slowed a little. "I need to get the bullet out." She asked Brooke if they had any alcohol.

"Sam, she needs a doctor," Brooke said.

Then the police would get involved.

"No, I can do it. I learned a thing or two in the Air Force. Combat training and basic emergency field medicine."

"Were you a medic?"

"No, I was a cop. Security forces. Besides, a good body-guard needs to know these things in case of an emergency." She took her eyes off Katrina's wound and looked up at her. "Brooke, I need to do this."

Brooke went out to the kitchen and returned with a bottle of vodka.

Sam reached for the vodka and took a swig. Then she asked Katrina if she wanted any.

Katrina nodded.

She helped her take a big gulp and asked if she wanted to bite down on a towel. She took the towel but also reached for Brooke's hand. Brooke held her hand while Sam poured some of the vodka on the wound. Katrina bit down and made a muffled yell through the towel.

"Vodka!" Katrina cried after Sam finished.

Brooke helped her take another large gulp of the alcohol.

"This might hurt." Sam then took the tweezers and went to work removing the bullet.

Katrina groaned through the towel as Sam dug into her shoulder for the bullet. "Almost got it. Come on. Gotcha," she said, slowly removing the tweezers with the bullet. She set it aside and began stitching up Katrina's shoulder. She covered the wound in gauze then wrapped Katrina's arm tightly to her chest to limit movement.

When Sam had finished, she asked Katrina if she needed anything.

"Unless you have some pain medicine, another shot of vodka will have to do."

Sam smiled and gave her another sip. She told her to try and rest. Sam and Brooke left her and went to the kitchen area.

"I'll bet you have some questions," Sam said.

Brooke sat at the table and poured herself some of the vodka. "If you want to tell me, I'll gladly listen—as long as it's the truth."

"Do you think I've lied to you?"

"Honestly, I don't know what to think."

Sam thought for a moment. *How much should I tell her?*

When Brooke started to get up, Sam stopped her. "All I can tell you is that I was helping Katrina with something. We were gathering some information and ran into trouble."

Brooke took a drink, and all she said was "Okay." She got up and headed toward her room.

"Brooke, thank you for your help and for understanding. I hope I'll be able to tell you more very soon," Sam said before Brooke went into her room.

"You're welcome, and I hope so too."

Sam was too wired to go back to sleep. She went to her room and grabbed an extra blanket from the closet and covered Katrina with it. She then lay on the bed next to her. Katrina was asleep, but Sam reached for her left hand and held it.

21

———————

Sam woke and looked over at the empty space next to her. Katrina must have been up already.

I hope she didn't leave.

Remembering the events that took place a few hours ago, Sam reached in her pocket and fished out the paper she'd taken from the warehouse. It was a partial bill of lading that had Walker Logistics on it along with a French company called Expédition Rouge and a signature. Nicolas Boucher's signature. *Boucher. I knew it.*

Sam left the bedroom and padded over to the kitchen-slash-dining area and made herself a cup of coffee. Brooke and Katrina had been talking but became silent when Sam entered the room. Taking her cup, she sat at the table with them.

"Good morning. Hope I didn't interrupt anything."

"Not at all. Katrina and I were just discussing business opportunities," Brooke said.

"Da. Sergei wants to conduct business with Kenzie-Corp," Katrina said in Russian to Sam. "Brooke thinks this might be a problem for you. Working with your ex." Then in

English with a thick Russian accent, she repeated the sentence.

Brooke smiled.

Katrina must have come clean about the ruse. They're messing with me.

"I don't care who she does business with, and you are not my ex." In Russian, Sam said, "We had one night together. That hardly makes it a relationship."

Sam took a sip of her coffee as they exchanged glances. "Do you care to share what's so funny?"

"No," Katrina said.

"Okay, fine. How's your shoulder, Katrina?"

Dropping her accent, Katrina answered. "Hurts like hell, but I'll live. You did a good job, from what I can tell. Can I have the bullet as a souvenir? Something to remind me of you." Katrina placed her left hand on top of Sam's, but Sam withdrew it.

"It's in a glass in the bathroom."

"Oh, that reminds me. I may have something for you." Brooke got up and went to her room. She came back with a bottle of pain pills and set it on the table near Katrina. "I happen to still have some of these pills left from an injury. Twisted my ankle during a volleyball game at a company picnic. Use whatever you need."

"Thanks," Katrina said, taking a couple of pills and swallowing them.

Sam commented, "So, no accent anymore?"

"No. Brooke and I talked. We're good."

"Really? Okay. So, you guys are buddies now?"

"Jealous?" Katrina smirked.

"Hardly. I've decided relationships aren't for me."

Brooke almost dropped her coffee cup. A little spilled over on the table. "I'm sorry, you what?"

"You heard me."

"Does the professor know that?" Katrina asked in Russian.

"It's none of your business."

Katrina switched back to English. "Sam, may I borrow a shirt? Mine seems to have a hole in it and a rip up the center."

Brooke and Katrina laughed.

Sam told her yes and that she could stay with them until her people could get her out.

"Your people? Are you a spy?" Brooke asked.

"No, by people I meant Sergei and his men," Sam said quickly.

"Thank you, but I need to get back to work."

Sam stared at her.

"Brooke, would you excuse us?" Sam asked her.

"I need to get dressed anyway." Brooke took her coffee and headed to her room.

Sam looked at Katrina and began the conversation in Russian to make sure Brooke didn't understand. "What are you talking about? Your cover's probably blown, and you have a hole in your shoulder that needs medical attention. I got the bullet out, but you need someone to look at it."

"I can't leave."

"You need to contact your handler and let him know what happened. We both got a big lead here. They can get you to Germany and take care of your shoulder." Sam was getting upset.

"I can't. There's more to it than you know."

"Why the hell not? What do you mean more?" Sam was angry now.

"I'm... in too deep."

"Too deep? How long have you been undercover?"

"What does it matter? You want me to quit? You lost your memory and didn't quit. What's the matter, Sam? Afraid I can't keep up with a little hole in my shoulder?"

"What? It's not a competition."

Katrina couldn't contain her laugh. "That's rich coming from you. You thrive on competition. They gave us four assignments during that seminar and you had to do better than the other teams in every single one. All so you could have bragging rights."

"I didn't brag."

"No, you didn't. But it's true, isn't it?"

"What's wrong with trying to be the best to get the job done?"

"Nothing." Katrina sighed.

"Answer the question. How long?" Sam needed to know how long Katrina had been on this mission of hers.

Katrina told her she'd started right after the seminar where they had met. That was three years ago. Sam couldn't believe it. Three years was too long. Yes, deep-cover assignments sometimes took years, but she hadn't expected Katrina to be involved in one.

Katrina explained that it wasn't supposed to be that long, but she was making steady progress, so they let her continue. The longer she was undercover, the "bigger the fish" she helped them catch. The people Sergei met and spoke to had paid off for the CIA, especially the ones Sergei contacted but didn't do business with.

"I don't care. You were shot. This changes things. Make the call!" Sam was adamant, her voice rising.

"Sam, if I could leave, I would."

"Give me one good reason, just one—"

"Sergei is my husband!" Katrina nearly shouted.

At some point during the conversation, Sam had gotten up. When she heard Katrina's words, she stopped pacing.

Katrina told her how she'd started working for him at the company. He wasn't a bad guy. He just made some deals that fell into a gray area—legally. That's how she was able to report illegal and shady activities and people to the CIA. Sergei turned down business with shady people, and Katrina was able to pass that info on. She married Sergei about a year and a half ago.

Sam couldn't believe her ears. "Why doesn't he introduce you as his wife?"

"To keep up appearances for work. It gives him more freedom when making his deals. He can flirt with the women and keep a 'playboy' image with the men."

Sam needed to know something, so she asked, "Do you love him?"

"I did at first—or at least I thought I did. I don't know anymore. Things haven't been good the past few months. We've grown apart," Katrina said.

"I don't get it. You're on a mission. How could you take it that far? Did your people tell you to marry him?"

"No, they didn't. I thought I was in love with him. And it helped my mission. I was able to get closer than ever and feed more information to my superiors. Pillow talk, you know."

"No, I don't know! You need to get out. Screw the mission." Sam walked back to the table and pulled her chair closer to Katrina's before sitting. She looked her in the eyes. "Katrina, I am so sorry I asked for your help. You got shot because of me. But it's over now. You can't go back—you might be in danger. We don't know how deeply Sergei is involved. You said he wasn't a bad guy. Will he hurt you if you leave?"

"No. He's not that kind of person, and I don't think he's involved with this."

"Then what is it? Why won't you leave?" Sam asked.

Katrina's eyes welled up, and she began to cry.

Sam reached for Katrina's left hand and held it. With her other hand, she gently brushed away a tear from her cheek. "Just tell me. I'll help you, whatever it is."

What came next made Sam wish it wasn't so early in the morning—she needed a drink.

"We have a son. He's six months old," Katrina told her.

Sam was floored, but now she understood. Katrina didn't want to take the baby away from his father. It would have been easier if Sergei was abusive or a jackass, but she claimed he wasn't. After the initial shock had settled, Sam was able to speak.

"Right. I get it. What do you want to do?" Sam asked her.

"I need to get back," Katrina said.

Sam capitulated and said, "What will you tell Sergei? Surely, he'll question where you were and what you were doing. Not to mention your shoulder."

Katrina thought for a while. "I slipped in the shower, dislocated my shoulder, and broke my clavicle."

"Hmm. Not a bad story. Except shouldn't it have happened at your hotel? And won't he see the hole in your shoulder?"

"Sergei and I haven't been together in over six months. We have separate rooms. We have an understanding," she said, implying that they had an open marriage. "I haven't been with anyone. I don't know about Sergei. Our marriage is over, but we love our son."

Sam sighed. "So you slipped in someone else's shower?"

"Care to be that someone else?" Katrina asked her.

Sam told her she would do anything for her.

"Except date me?"

"I need one more answer from you."

"Shoot." After the look Sam gave her, Katrina said, "Poor choice of words."

"Have you been playing me? Leading me on? Was it all part of some other game?" Sam looked serious and stoic when asking. She hated to think Katrina could have lied to her about her feelings.

Without hesitation, Katrina looked into Sam's eyes and told her, "Absolutely not." She took Sam's hand. "Seeing you on Monday morning brought back all those feelings I had for you. I would give anything to be able to be with you, if that's what you want, Sam. But right now, I can't. I have to go back." She cupped her cheek. "Besides, I thought you made your choice. The professor is very pretty."

Sam moved Katrina's hand. "I told you I'm done. That doesn't mean I don't care about what happens to you. But all this flirting. I don't know if it's real. How do I know you're not just using me to advance your own mission?"

Katrina stared at her with daggers in her eyes, and Sam didn't need a verbal answer. Her face told her all she needed to know. But Katrina did speak. "Fuck you."

Brooke came out of her room, dressed and ready for the day. "I'm sorry to interrupt, but I was wondering if our plans for the day have changed?" It was Friday, and the exhibition was ending. "I understand if we can't go."

Katrina obviously felt she must go back to Sergei, so Sam replied, in English, that the plans hadn't changed. "I just need some time to shower and get ready to go to the exhibition."

"You don't have to go with me. I'll be all right," Brooke said.

But Sam disagreed. "No. It's the last day, which might

make it even more dangerous." *For me, anyway. After last night, I really need to watch my back.*

"Take your time," Brooke said.

"Before we go, I'd like to redress your shoulder," Sam told Katrina.

"No. I'll go now."

"I said I'll redress your shoulder!"

"Fine."

They went into Sam's bathroom, and she helped Katrina take her robe off. Leaning against the sink, facing Sam, Katrina watched as she carefully unwrapped her arm. Sam took the bandages off carefully and grabbed a washcloth. She ran some warm water into the sink to wet the cloth. She then slowly and carefully cleaned around Katrina's wound. She didn't look Katrina in the eyes at all. Sam poured some hydrogen peroxide from her trauma kit onto a clean swab and dabbed over the wound. Katrina flinched as the antiseptic went to work, but Sam still avoided eye contact.

"Why didn't you use the hydrogen peroxide last night?" Katrina asked.

The corner of Sam's lips lifted slightly, but she didn't say anything. She remembered all the movies she'd seen where someone cleaned a wound with alcohol before removing a bullet.

Because it was cool. I can't tell her that. It was kind of exciting, though. Just like the movies.

"Sam!" Katrina raised her voice to get Sam's attention and took a breath. "Sam. We may never see each other again," she said quietly.

"I thought you were pissed at me."

She quoted Sam's words back to her. "It doesn't mean I don't care about you. I can be pissed at you and still care."

"You run hot and cold. I don't know how Sergei puts up with you."

Sam didn't see it coming, but she definitely felt it. Katrina's hand left a sting on Sam's right cheek.

"I'm sorry, but it's kind of like the pot calling the kettle black."

"I guess I deserved that," Sam said, rubbing her cheek.

"Sam, we had something."

"Had being the operative word."

"We still do. Look, I understand that you're probably under pressure with this assignment, but you seem really wound tight. That's not good for an undercover operative. You get angry quickly. I'm not the only one running hot and cold. Although I disagree with that assessment of me."

"I had a concussion and lost my memory. Maybe my short temper is a side effect. Maybe you just don't know me well enough."

"You're right. Maybe a week wasn't very long, but I still think we have a connection and could be good together."

Sam picked up the cloth again and wiped Katrina's shoulder without looking at her or saying anything.

"Samantha," she said again, reaching for her hand and stopping her.

Sam lifted her head and gazed into Katrina's eyes. She couldn't disagree with her. There was something there. Something between them, but it wouldn't work. They moved toward each other but Sam stopped short. "This isn't going to happen."

"I don't give up so easily. Remember the shower that morning?" Katrina ran her fingers slowly up Sam's arm. "You know, there's a bathtub right there," Katrina reminded her.

Sam smiled at her and started running a bath.

"Let me know if you need help," Sam said, walking out of the bathroom adjacent to her room. She grabbed a robe from her closet and stuffed her burner phone in the pocket.

"Brooke, I need your shower. Would you keep an ear out for Katrina?"

"Uh, yeah. No problem."

Sam turned the shower and fan on before undressing. Then she pulled out the burner phone and made a call.

"I'm so sorry," Leia said.

Sam spoke in Arabic, just in case. "What the hell are you doing here?"

"Every summer, I find a conference to take a few of my students to. Cybersecurity goes in hand with cybercrime. I also arrange tours of the local law enforcement agencies. I swear this trip has been on the books for months."

Sam took a few heartbeats to consider what she said. "You did work for KenzieCorp. Is that a coincidence?"

"Yes. She called me. She told me someone recommended we upgrade our systems. She did some research, and my name popped up."

"You failed to mention that you are a tech genius, your side job, and company. Not to mention the fact you speak Arabic. Or that you're a PhD." Sam was livid.

"I wasn't hiding those things. I would have eventually told you. Sam, please. I understand why you're upset. You're working, and I suddenly show up, and your... friend happens to be a person who recently hired me for some work. I suppose I'd be questioning that, too, if I were in your shoes."

There was silence as Sam considered it all.

"Sam, I'm telling you the truth. I don't know how to prove that to you."

I do. Answer some questions.

"Where did you learn Arabic?"

"The Army. At the Defense Language Institute."

"Where is that?"

"Monterey, California."

"What was the first program you sold and to whom?"

"It was to my high school. I called the program 'A-Gap.' It's a football term I used because some players were hacking their grades. The entire school district bought the program. I still update it for them."

Silence.

"You did a background check on me, didn't you?" Leia asked.

"I had to."

"I understand. Am I a person of interest in whatever you're doing?"

"I can't answer that."

"I have resources, as well, Ms. Barrett."

Without getting upset Sam said, "Is that a threat?"

"No. I shouldn't have said that. I'm sorry. Sam, if you need anything, any help at all, I will assist you. Whatever it is, all you have to do is ask."

"I have to go. I'll contact you when I can."

"Hey, it was good to see you. I didn't know you spoke Russian or Italian or Arabic."

"It seems we don't know a lot about each other."

Just like Katrina.

"We've had two dates and a few minutes on the phone. Some were one-sided conversations. We need time to get to know each other. I'd like the opportunity to do that."

"Thanks for not blowing my cover." Sam disconnected the call before she could respond.

22

———————

Sam had returned to her room to finish getting ready, and she exited it while pulling on her suit jacket. Her phone rang, and she saw it was Patrick. Closing the door behind her, she glanced at Brooke, who was finishing her coffee on the couch.

"Hello?"

"Ms. Barrett, I have some information I'd thought you'd find interesting."

"Go ahead, sir."

"My CID friend says the third and fourth letters are different than the first two. The writing styles between them are different."

"The writing styles? That is interesting. How does your friend know that?"

"Obviously, handwriting analysis wasn't an option since the documents were computer generated. So they used something called stylometry. I don't know the details, but a computer program looks at sentence structure and length, word choice, punctuation, and other things. It's not infallible, but it helps."

"So we're dealing with two different people within a group or two different groups." Sam knew it was the latter and figured the ex-CID person would figure that as well. That wasn't what was important to her. She wanted to know if Jordan had opened the envelope and had written the third and fourth letters. Another possibility was he was working with someone who wrote them.

"It would appear so," Patrick said.

"Anything else come up?"

"Not yet. I'll let you know."

"Thank you, sir. I appreciate you keeping me in the loop," Sam told him. She disconnected the call and thought for a moment. *Jordan is my most likely suspect. Who else would know about the letters and try and intercept them? No one. According to Patrick, only Brooke, William, and himself knew about them. I need proof Jordan wrote the letters or he contacted someone about them. Crap.*

Looking over at Brooke, who was still on the couch, she told her she was ready to go. Katrina came out, wearing one of Sam's polos, with her shoulder wrapped again in clean bandages and her right arm in a sling made from a T-shirt.

"Brooke, I want to thank you for everything. I'm sorry we met under these circumstances, but I'm glad I got to meet you." She walked over to her and hugged her with her left arm.

"I'm really happy to have met you too. Can we give you a ride somewhere? Please, I insist."

"Yes, we'll all go together," Sam said.

Katrina's car was downstairs, and Sam said she would drive it to her hotel. Then Sam and Brooke would take a cab and go to the exhibition. No one spoke as Sam gave the valet the keys to Katrina's car. The ride was just as quiet. Sam and

Katrina didn't have much left to say to each other, and Brooke was uncomfortable with the tension.

Sam was going to contact Tom and tell him what they had discovered in the warehouse. She pulled up in front of the hotel where the valet was and exited the vehicle while handing the keys to a young man. Another young man helped Katrina out. Brooke exited the car from the back seat and stepped away to give them some privacy, but Sam noticed she couldn't help but glance over at them.

"Goodbye, Katrina."

"Take care of yourself, Sam. I really hope to see you again someday. Maybe work together."

"I wouldn't hold my breath."

"Can't you be civil?"

No, I can't. Because if I let my guard down, I will melt.

"Safe travels."

"Live long..." Katrina didn't bother finishing because Sam turned and walked away.

Katrina walked inside the hotel as she wiped her cheek.

Seeing Brooke, Sam told the valet to hail a cab, then she waved Brooke over. Brooke looked at her and came over, but she didn't say anything. The cab arrived, and they went to Eurosatory. Brooke had already completed her most pressing business, so today was a light day. They could take in the last of the live demos and presentations. Some of the exhibitors had already packed up and left. Due to the time difference, Sam waited until after lunch to contact Tom.

While Brooke was listening to one last presentation, Sam took the opportunity to make a discreet call. She sent him the photos taken in the warehouse and let him know what they thought Nicolas was doing.

Tom let her know that the license plate of the vehicle

that had followed her and Brooke belonged to a shell corporation, Walker Logistics. Not a shocker.

Sam told him about what Patrick found out and that Jordan might have been the one to write them.

"Don't follow up on Jordan until you get back. I'll work it from my end," Tom told her.

"How?"

"I'll look for traffic cameras to follow Jordan's route to the post office. You never know what might turn up."

Sam said she would talk to him again when she returned to the States.

There was one last party Brooke wanted to attend that evening. "Sam, given what you've been through today, you don't have to go to the party."

"No, it'll be a good distraction for me, and if you want to go, we will. It's my job to accompany you. Don't worry about me," Sam told her.

ONCE AGAIN, Brooke and Sam turned heads as they entered the room. Brooke mingled, making small talk and introducing Sam to others. This party was less about networking and business and more about just having fun. Some of the men had brought their spouses or dates.

Sam was alert and very aware of her surroundings. She was keeping an eye on Brooke and got that funny feeling when someone came up behind her. He touched her on the arm and whispered in her ear.

"Samantha, I must speak with you, please." Sam spun on her heel ready to attack as soon as she felt his touch. "Damn it, Sergei."

"I am sorry if I startled you. Please."

She then moved toward Brooke and whispered, "I'll be close."

They moved away from the crowd, but as always, Sam kept Brooke in her sights.

"Sergei, it's good to see you again. What can I do for you?" Sam sounded almost matter-of-fact about it.

Sergei looked like he was on edge, and Sam could tell he was upset. "Da, tell me who hurt Katrina."

Sam took a sip of her champagne and asked what he meant.

"To quote from one of your TV shows, 'A lie is a very poor way to say hello,' Samantha." He told her that he knew about their relationship, and that it was fine. He just wanted Katrina to be happy. But he also knew she didn't slip in the shower like she'd told him.

Sam wasn't quite sure what to say. His quote was from *Star Trek*. One of her favorite sci-fi TV shows. Only Katrina could have told him that. *It must be her way of telling me to trust him.*

"It is okay. I will continue to show you can trust me." Sergei said he knew that Katrina was really an American sent to spy on him. He found out a year after she worked for him, but he was falling in love with her. He never told her he knew. He also told Sam he was a confidential informant for Interpol. "Now, tell me who hurt my wife."

Sam looked him in the eyes and saw his pain. He appeared to still care for her. This bear of a man who flirted with her and other women and kept up the playboy persona for his colleagues cared about his wife.

Sam wasn't sure she believed his story about Interpol. He told her it was true and gave her the name of his contact. He wanted to know what Katrina was doing last night and where.

Sam asked him if she could make a call.

He said he would wait.

Sam stepped away from him and made a call. About five minutes later, she returned. She looked at him and asked, "Do you love Katrina?"

Without hesitation, he answered. "I do. But I always knew her heart was not mine. It belonged to someone else, and now I know who. She gave me a son, and I will always love her for that. But she needs to be with the one she truly loves. Now, tell me what you know."

She won't leave her son, and I'm not sure you'll give him up.

"There's nothing between us. Not anymore. Not from me. Besides, we barely know each other."

Sergei huffed, and in his native Russian said, "Destiny does not ask permission—it simply unfolds."

Sam stared at him.

"Lyudmila Ulitskaya. A Russian novelist."

"You believe in destiny?"

"Too a degree, yes. Your time might have been brief, but was it not memorable?"

It was. It was very memorable. Sam thought about that week and that night for months afterward. Now was not the time for this.

"She was at a warehouse that Nicolas Boucher frequented when she was shot. Sergei, I'm sorry I couldn't have protected her from that. I can't tell you why we were there, but I am sorry she was hurt. I got her to safety and got the bullet out as soon as I could."

As soon as Sergei heard the name, he cursed in Russian in a low, angry voice. Sam understood him and asked if he knew Nicolas.

"Nico. Da, yes, I know him. A bad man. Also sneaky like

fox." His broken English made Sam crack a smile. "I will take care of Nico."

"No. Let the authorities handle it. I promise you they'll get him. And if they don't, I'll help you. I didn't see who shot her, so it could have been someone else. I do believe he is involved in something, though. When are you going home?" Sam asked.

"I send Katrina home already. She needs hospital for shoulder. I leave in a day or two."

"Good." Sam was glad that Katrina was going to get help for her shoulder. "Go ahead and conduct your business as usual. No revenge. May I contact you if I need anything?"

"Yes, yes. Okay. I only trust you because of Katrina. How was my old friend at Interpol?"

"He said you owe him a case of vodka. To be honest, I believed you before I called. You said all the right things. I knew I could trust you when you quoted from one my favorite shows. Katrina told you that, didn't she? That quote from 'City on the Edge of Forever'? *Star Trek*."

"Da. Yes. Captain Kirk." He waved his hand as if to dismiss the conversation. "Mr. Chekov is my favorite."

"Of course he is." Sam chuckled.

Brooke was walking toward them.

"Ah, Miss McKenzie... Brooke. A pleasure to see you again. I regret I have... how you say... monopolized Sam. And now I must go. I hope to do business with you in future." He held out his hand and kissed Brooke's hand once again.

Sam rolled her eyes.

Sam and Brooke stayed for a while longer then left.

23

———

Their flight back to the States wasn't until Sunday, so they could do whatever they wanted before then. They enjoyed Saturday by taking in a few sights. The day was pleasant but uneventful, and Sam was fine with that. She'd been on alert all day, waiting for something to happen. Exhausted, she slept the entire flight back home.

BACK HOME IN AUSTIN, Sam kept thinking about the operation. She needed to find out who, besides Jordan, was involved. He was just a middleman between Nicolas, in Europe, and whoever was running the op stateside.

What do I have so far? Nicolas is on Interpol's radar and makes a lot of calls to a Texas number. Nicolas and Jordan talking at the exhibition. A warehouse in Paris full of body armor. Some of the plates are okay, but some are from a company that does substandard work. A bill of lading with Nicolas Boucher's signature accepting goods on behalf of Expédition Rouge from Walker

Logistics, a shell corporation. Follow the evidence. I just need to give Tom what I have so far.

Finding another paper trail—digital or otherwise—would be the best way to move forward.

SAM SET up a meeting with Tom. She briefed him on everything she knew about the operation, and he told her everything he'd found out about the shell corporation. The bill of lading was the link between KenzieCorp, Walker Logistics, and Expédition Rouge.

"Is that enough? This is the connection, and we have Boucher's name and what we found in the warehouse."

"We'd like more. They want more. We need to get the files from KenzieCorp. There's a mole in the company but we don't know who or where they work. We also don't know who is in charge."

Tom gave Sam a flash drive with special software on it so she could hack into the computers at KenzieCorp. Everything was up to her now.

"How do you know this will work? I told you that Dr. Coventry made upgrades to their system."

"Yes. I had to get permission to contact her. That will work. She assured me."

"You contacted her? What did she say?"

"Nothing. She seemed eager to help. All she knows is that we needed to get into KenzieCorp's files as a matter of national security. Why? Is there something I should know?"

"No. I mean I ran into her at Eurosatory. She was chaperoning some of her students. But she played it off. Didn't give me away."

"Why would she give you away? Do you know her?"

Shit.

"Yes. I met her during my memory loss."

"Is that the coincidence you were trying not to tell me about?" Tom eyed her intently.

"Yes. I've ruled her out as a suspect."

"Good. She needs to come work for the agency."

"Ha, I knew it was Langley," Sam said as if she had solved a great mystery.

"I didn't say which agency."

"Come on, you sent Katrina to help me. I know who she works for."

He sighed. "All right. Yes, I do work for them, and I know she was hurt helping you get those photos. She's doing fine, by the way. Now, go finish your job."

Before she left, she said one more thing. "Tom, can you make sure Dr. Coventry receives an 'attaboy' or some kind of recognition for maintaining her composure when we ran into each other and for her help with this program? It was a public place and Brooke was there as well as her students."

"Sure. I'll see what I can do."

They parted ways, and Sam began to come up with a plan.

SHE HAD to decide the best time to try and get the information. Daytime would mean trying to avoid any employees. Breaking in at night would be more difficult because of security.

Sam waited a few days, and an opportunity presented itself. Brooke left her office for a meeting. Alone in her office, Sam sprang into action. She inserted the drive into the computer. She was able to bypass passwords and the firewall to look at shipping documents. She also searched for anything related to the shell corporation, named Walker Logistics.

Suddenly, a screen came up stating "Hidden folder found—continue? Y or N"

Sam pressed Y, but nothing happened. "Shit."

The screen looked like it was frozen. *What do I do?* She didn't have time to mess around and didn't want to yank out the drive because she didn't know what that would do. She pulled out her phone and called Leia.

"I need your help, and you can't say anything," Sam said quickly.

"What's wrong?"

"I'm in front of a computer and a message came up." Sam explained what the message on the screen said and that nothing happened when she pressed the Y button.

"Hidden folders? That shouldn't matter."

"Now it's glitching."

"What do you mean?"

"Glitching, like an old video."

The line was silent.

"Are you there? I don't have time to mess around. Can I yank the drive out?"

"No! Don't do that. I'm accessing the computer now."

"You can do that?"

"Yes, I have remote access in order to fix... Sam, someone else is trying to block me. They have access as well. They can see what you're doing."

"Shit, stop them. Kick them off." Then Sam changed her mind. "Wait. Can you find out who it is or where they're located?"

"Yeah, just a minute."

"Work fast."

Sam waited patiently but was tapping her foot as more time passed. Suddenly, a folder appeared on the screen and opened documents, including emails.

"Did you do that?" Sam asked.

"Yes. I think this is what you're looking for."

An email appeared, and Sam couldn't believe her eyes as she read it. "Holy crap."

"Sam, I sent a virus to stop them, but you're compromised. They activated the webcam and saw you. You need to insert the other drive, and it will copy the files. Hurry."

Quickly, she pulled out another flash drive and began copying files. It'd be faster to copy them now and read them later.

"Will the hidden folder be copied?"

"Yes."

"Looks like it's working. Thank you," Sam said.

"Let me stay on with you until it's finished. Just in case."

"Did you get a location of the hacker?"

"I did. They're located in College Station."

"Yeah, I figured. Listen, this is all classified."

"Sam, I would never betray a client or the United States."

"I just had to say it for my own piece of mind. Hey, if you're supposed to be so good, how did the hacker get in?"

"Technology is always changing. It needs to be constantly updated. When you tried to access the hidden folder, it gave them a brief window to hack in. I'm sorry. I should have anticipated that."

"Sounds like it was my fault. It's at ninety-five percent. Thanks again for your help."

"Anytime. Be careful. Goodbye."

Sam looked up every few seconds to make sure no one was approaching. She worked as fast as she could to get as much information as possible. Copying the files seemed to take forever, but it was at ninety-eight percent now.

She almost felt like she was betraying Brooke. Sam was relatively sure Brooke wasn't involved in anything illegal. Even though they had gone back to more of an employer-employee relationship, she still felt close to her. The more time passed, the better their rapport had become.

Suddenly, Sam noticed a young intern standing in the doorway. Sam asked if she could help him, and he replied that he had some mail for Brooke.

"I'll make sure she gets it." Sam stood and walked around the desk to take the mail.

"Her assistant wasn't at her desk."

"That's fine. Thank you," Sam said.

The young man turned and left. Sam let out a brief sigh of relief and went back to check the status of the files. When she thought she had everything she needed, she pulled out the spyware flash drive and the one with all the files she'd copied and put them in her suit jacket pocket. She closed everything out and leaned back in the chair. She closed her eyes and took a few deep breaths.

Why didn't I just copy the files before? Maybe I did, and that was the evidence they took.

"You look good in my chair. Should I be worried?" Brooke said.

Opening her eyes, Sam replied, "Not at all. Just wondering what it felt like." They exchanged smiles, then Sam got up and sat in another chair.

"You know, I've been thinking. How many languages do you speak?"

"Why?"

"Well, if we expand, you could be useful, not only as

head of my security, but a translator, as well. I'd compensate you accordingly."

"Head of your security?"

"I know where I stand with you, Sam. It makes sense to keep you on. Why start over with someone new?"

I think you'll change your tune after I leave here. You'll hate me when you find out what I've done.

"I'll consider it. How was your meeting?"

"Fine. Same old stuff." With that said, Brooke took her seat behind her desk and began to make some calls.

Sam motioned to Brooke that she was going to grab some coffee. Brooke nodded and continued with her work.

Sam walked to the break room and made herself a cup of coffee. She began to reflect on her mission. It was starting to feel like she had been there too long.

Is it normal to feel this way? I made some mistakes, but I've learned a lot as well. This was her first undercover mission, so maybe it was. She needed to get her head straight. Maybe a good workout this evening would help.

Wait. I have the files. It's time to contact Tom and leave.

She'd miss Brooke. *I can't just take off without telling her something. Not after what happened when I went missing. Better to get it over with now. Or should I wait until tonight?*

Sam took a deep breath and let it out. As she left the break room, the intern who had delivered Brooke's mail came out of nowhere and bumped into her. Luckily, she had drunk enough coffee that it didn't spill.

"Excuse me, ma'am. I wasn't paying attention. Are you all right?"

"Yes, no worries," Sam said.

They each apologized and went on their way. Without even realizing, Sam reached for her pocket. It was empty.

The flash drives were gone. She turned and saw the young man moving very quickly down the hall.

Sam set her cup down and followed him as he made his way toward the elevator. She reached him just as he entered, and she got on as well. When he saw her, he started getting nervous. Another woman was also on the elevator but got off on the next floor.

"I suggest you give them back," Sam said, staring straight ahead.

He looked at her and replied, "I'm sorry, what?"

"You've got five seconds." Sam slowly turned her head and shot daggers from her eyes. "Five, four, three..."

Her face and clenched fists made him admit what he'd done. "Okay, okay. Here." He handed her the flash drives. "It's not worth the hundred bucks. Man, you're scary. No wonder she hired you."

Sam asked what he meant.

"You're her bodyguard. We all know it. I'm surprised her father didn't hire someone years ago."

"Not that. I mean the money."

He told her some guy offered him the money if he could get the drives. He said it was a prank and no big deal. The intern described the man to Sam and said he wasn't sure if he worked there. He was wearing a suit, so he thought he might. After he got the drives, he was supposed to leave them at the reception desk downstairs in an envelope marked "Ted."

"Do you know where the supply room is?" Sam asked.

"Yeah."

"Good. Go there, find two blank flash drives, and put them in an envelope, like you were told."

Sam went downstairs and hid around a corner from the reception desk. She couldn't be sure, but from the intern's description, the guy sounded like he could be one of the men in the SUV that Sam had chased away months ago at the bar and again near Brooke's home.

She waited about ten minutes then saw the intern leave the envelope with the receptionist. Five minutes later, a man in a dark suit showed up and collected the envelope. He turned and left out the front door. She discreetly watched as he got into a black SUV and left.

Sam ran to Brooke's car. Luckily, she had the keys with her. She got in and followed the SUV. Her phone synced to the car's system. She called Brooke and told her to stay at the office until she returned from running an errand.

While following the vehicle, Sam reflected on the mission and what she'd just learned. After a forty-minute drive, the SUV pulled up to a small, unmarked office building. The man went inside, carrying the envelope.

Sam had backed off, and she parked out of sight on the side of the building. Without knowing the layout of the interior, she was afraid to go inside in case someone recognized her. She made note of the address and decided to pass it on to Tom. Her curiosity got the better of her though, and she pulled up her map app. Zooming in to her location, this building wasn't labeled. There was a logo on it, but Sam didn't know what it was. It was located off a main road outside of downtown.

Maybe just a peek.

She dismounted the vehicle and quietly made her way toward the very large one-story office building. It was long and had multiple entrances. She walked toward what seemed like the back and saw a row of trailers backed up to the warehouse side of the building. Heading back to the front, she made her way toward the closest awning-covered glass door and walked inside.

There was a directory just inside the second set of glass doors. Scanning it, she gave a slight smile. *Walker Logistics Suite 107. Well, well, that is interesting.*

Walking down the hall, she stopped just before suite 107. She really wanted to get a look inside but hesitated.

Leaving the building, Sam noticed a Goodwill building across the street. Smiling to herself, she went across the street.

Ten minutes later, after shopping in their store and making a donation, Sam went into Walker Logistics. A woman sat behind a desk.

"Welcome to Walker Logistics. May I help you?"

Sam had purchased a T-shirt, jeans, sneakers, and a new ball cap. She pretended to chomp on some gum, and in a deep Southern drawl said, "Yes, ma'am. Hi. I'm uh, looking for a job. Maybe in your warehouse? I'm a hard worker and strong. I can drive a forklift. Got any openings?"

"I'm sorry, we're not hiring right now."

"Are you sure?" Sam glanced around the room and tried to look into an office behind the woman. "Looks like a nice place to work."

"Yes. I'm sorry."

"Oh well, okay." Sam started to turn around but then leaned on the desk and started to slowly fall while placing a hand on her forehead. "Ohh."

"Are you all right?" The woman stood and came around her desk.

"I just... feel a little dizzy."

"I'll get you some water." She helped Sam sit down in her chair. Something Sam had noticed was there were no chairs in this area. As if they didn't expect people to come in and have to wait. "Wait here."

"Uh, yeah."

The woman left to go down a hall, and Sam quickly looked at the desk. There was a sudoku game on the computer and a magazine on the desk. She opened the drawers and found nothing. Odd to say the least. Tom said this company was a front, and it appeared so.

Sam minimized the game and saw an invoice. Pulling it up, she quickly scanned it but didn't get far before she heard the woman returning. Maximizing the game as it was before, Sam slumped in the chair.

"Here's a bottle of water, and I found a protein bar."

"Oh, thank you very much. I guess I got a little dehydrated. Times have been tough." Sam swallowed the water. "Thanks again. You're too kind." Sam slowly stood and walked toward the door.

"Are you sure you don't want to wait a bit?"

"No, you have a job to do, and I need to find one. Thanks for the bar and water." Leaving the building, Sam went to Brooke's vehicle parked around the corner of the building. She wished she had the time to have taken a photo of the invoice, but she'd seen enough.

The invoice was a payment from Walker Logistics to an attorney. Not just any attorney. It was one Sam was familiar with. Sara Caldwell, Esquire. Sara, the woman who Sam gave a shooting lesson to, was in on it.

She sat in the vehicle and searched Sara's name. Her website showed that she graduated from Yale Law School and had once worked for a top law firm in New York City. She now worked for herself and was based in Austin with offices in Dallas and Houston.

What brought you to Texas, Sara?

Sam had stopped looking at the search page when Sara's law firm came up at the top of the page, but she went back to it and scrolled further. Finding a news article with Sara's name in it, she continued reading. Sara had been the victim of a brutal mugging in Manhattan. She had been beaten and spent two weeks in the hospital. Flipping back to her website, Sam noticed it was the same year she founded her law firm.

So, you were mugged and then moved to Texas set up shop. Can't blame you for that.

Sara was probably the one who set up Walker Logistics as the shell corporation. *She was probably sent to just check me out. A woman asking for a shooting lesson would be less imposing than a man.*

Sara's name wasn't the only one on the invoice. Other names were Jordan, Nicolas, and some guy named Ray. *Wonder if he's the one who trailed us to the bar and was outside Brooke's house.*

Needing a visual representation, Sam looked around the car. Brooke kept it clean and neat. Opening the center console, she found what she wanted. A notepad and pen. In the center of the paper she wrote Walker Logistics and drew a circle around it. Then she wrote the names of everyone involved with a line back to Walker Logistics. So far she had Sara, Jordan, and Ray in the States and Nicolas in Paris.

This was great. That invoice linked them all to Walker Logistics. A shell company that owned the SUV that tailed Sam and Brooke to the bar.

Not wanting to have to answer questions about her clothes, Sam changed back into her suit and went back to pick up Brooke.

24

—————

By now, whoever was behind all this knew the flash drives they had were blank. They would most likely be coming for her. She'd kept her guard up since leaving the small building and returning to KenzieCorp. Pissing off these people was not what she wanted, but she might have just done it. She wasn't sure how or if they would react. Attempting to steal the drive from her at the office meant they had eyes on her. The email she found at Brooke's office confirmed her cover was definitely blown. They didn't want those files getting out.

Sam realized she had to act fast and pass the drive off to Tom. She took all precautions to make sure they weren't being followed. Instead of going home, she found an area where she could safely pull over and call Tom.

"What's going on, Sam?" Brooke asked.

"I need to make a phone call. Trust me, okay?"

Brooke nodded, and Sam got out of the car and called Tom. She told him she had the drive with files, but she was compromised.

"You need to come in, now!"

"I'm doing that, but I have to get Brooke to safety."

"What? Is she with you? Why?"

"There's a mole at the company, and I'm not leaving her there alone. Kevin Malone is the one behind this. There's an email in a hidden folder on the drive proving it. I have to get this drive to you, so tell me where to meet you."

They set up a meet in a sports bar in an hour. Sam had been keeping an eye out while speaking to Tom. When she hung up and started to get back into the car, she saw two black SUVs approaching at high speed. The car had been running, so she hopped back in and took off.

"How'd they find us?" It suddenly became obvious. "They must be tracking the car," Sam said. "Shit, they must have hacked the car, the GPS? I didn't find any trackers."

"Sam, what the hell is going on? What are you talking about?" Brooke was holding on for dear life as Sam tried to outrun the vehicles. She stayed on the feeder and side roads to try and avoid interstate traffic.

"A little busy with a car chase, but we'll talk about it later." Sam passed a car by swerving into the oncoming lane.

Brooke had one hand on the door and the other on the center console. Her grip couldn't have gotten any tighter as her knuckles turned white.

One of the SUVs pulled up beside her and tried to force them over. The vehicle then drove in front of Sam. She was boxed in, front and back.

"Crap."

A woman leaned out the window behind the driver, pointing a gun at them. Sam recognized her—it was Sara, the woman she'd given shooting lessons to. She must have been keeping tabs on Sam.

Sara fired a few shots at them with her handgun. A bullet came through the window just missing Sam's left ear.

Either I'm a great teacher, or she didn't need lessons. I wonder if she was the one who shot at me in the park?

Sam caught a sly smile from Sara before she began firing again.

Brooke ducked as another shot hit the window near her.

"Stay down!" Sam yelled.

Sam managed to pull her weapon out and return fire while driving. Being left-handed was an advantage in this case. However, the thought of a cross draw holster came to mind. It'd be easier to cross-draw from her right side while driving.

Live and learn, Sam.

Sara ducked inside the vehicle, and Sam made her move.

"Hang on." Sam swerved to the right onto the shoulder and hit the brakes. The vehicle behind her drove past, and Sam made a U-turn. She wanted to find some traffic to make it harder for these guys. She figured they were tracking the car, so they needed to get rid of it.

Eventually, Sam pulled into a parking lot at a big-box store. She started looking around. She pulled into a spot, got out, and went toward another vehicle. Looking around, she broke the window behind the driver's door. She yelled for Brooke to get in while she hot-wired the truck.

"You can hot-wire a truck? I guess that shouldn't surprise me. Are you going to tell me what's going on now?" Brooke was obviously stressed and wanted answers. But Sam wasn't quite ready to give them to her. Not yet, anyway.

"Soon. Let's get you somewhere safe."

Sam drove to her apartment. They left the truck about a block away and walked the rest of the way. She led Brooke up the stairs to her door. Before she opened it, Sam drew her gun. She told Brooke to stay behind her.

Sam led the way in. After doing a sweep, everything looked fine.

She went to the refrigerator and pulled out two beers. She hadn't been here in a while, but it felt like home.

"Is this your place?" Brooke asked her while opening the beer.

Sam didn't say anything but took a drink.

"I know you lived somewhere before we met."

"Yes." Sam was being very deliberate with her answers. She knew her time on this mission was winding down. Brooke would find out the truth soon enough. She just needed to get the flash drive to Tom. They were already late for her meeting with him. She knew he'd wait for a while, but not too long.

Sam called Tom, briefed him on being chased and shot at, and told him that she was on her way.

Gulping the rest of her beer, she said, "You can stay here. You'll be safe. Lock the door and hide in the bedroom closet, if you feel threatened. Hang on." Sam walked back to her bedroom and came back with a gun, two loaded magazines, and a box of rounds. "Just in case."

Brooke looked at her and opened her suit jacket, revealing her concealed weapon.

"That's my girl," Sam told her, smiling.

"We can bring that along because I'm coming with you. And don't argue with me, because I'm really not in the mood," Brooke told her with the same confidence she used in meetings at work.

Sam didn't say anything. She found a backpack and put the gun, spare ammo, first aid kit, and some other things into it. She went toward the door, turned around, and asked Brooke if she was coming.

Brooke finished her beer and followed her out.

They made their way back to the truck, and Sam drove to her storage unit. Again, she parked about a block away, and they walked in. When Sam opened the storage unit, Brooke saw the motorcycle.

"Nice bike."

"Put this on." Sam handed her a helmet. She did as Sam said. Sam got on the bike and backed it out of the unit. "Would you mind locking it up?"

Brooke pulled the door closed and locked it back up, then she sat on the bike behind Sam.

"You ever been on a bike before?" Sam asked.

"Yes."

"Good. Hang on." Sam gunned it, and Brooke grabbed her around the waist so she wouldn't fall off.

"Very funny," Brooke yelled in her ear.

Sam laughed, and they drove off to the meeting with Tom.

When they arrived, Sam told Brooke to go on in. She locked the helmet away and started toward the door. The bar was busy tonight with the after-work crowd. Once inside, Sam looked for Tom.

As she made her way through the crowd, she felt a pinch in her side. She saw a man reach into her pocket and take the flash drives.

"This is all we wanted." He looked into her eyes then was suddenly gone—lost in the crowd.

Slowly, Sam walked to Tom. She felt a dampness on her side, and her legs felt suddenly weak.

"You look like you need a drink." Tom motioned to the bartender.

"Yeah. How about an Irish car bomb?" The bartender heard her and went to make it.

Brooke saw Sam and made her way over. Upon seeing Tom, she asked him if he worked at the gun range.

"Uh, yeah. Sam used to bring you for practice sessions, right?"

"Yes."

Tom was uncomfortable talking to her. Luckily, the bartender brought Sam's drink, and he didn't have to worry about it. Sam dropped the Irish whiskey and Irish cream into the glass of Guinness and downed it.

Brooke stood on her left side and stared at her.

Sam looked at her and said, "I'm sorry. I never meant to hurt you." She then looked at Tom and collapsed onto the floor. Blood was pooling from her side—where she had been stabbed.

25

Sam opened her eyes and found Tom sitting next to her. A feeling of déjà vu came over her.

"Where am I? What happened?" Sam tried to sit up but groaned in agony.

"Easy. Don't sit up. Just stay there and rest. You're in the hospital. Do you remember anything?"

"I remember the bar. A man. A whiskey and Guinness. Umm. That's it."

Tom chuckled and told her that she had been stabbed, then she'd drunk her car bomb and collapsed. He was apparently extremely impressed with the way she'd downed the drink.

"I'm glad you're impressed."

"You helped solve the case, Sam. Well done," Tom told her.

"You found the real flash drive?"

"Just before you passed out, you said the word backpack. We searched the backpack Brooke had and found the drive. It has everything we need on it. We managed to link Walker

Logistics to Jordan, Nicolas, and some others. Interpol is taking care of Nicolas and his minions. KenzieCorp didn't know about switching the body armor plate inserts for lesser-rated material. It had a high failure rate and wouldn't give soldiers the protection they needed. You saved a lot of lives, Sam."

"I planted an empty drive in my pocket and hid the real one in the backpack. If the files were what we needed, why didn't we go after them first?" Sam asked.

"I think you got the files the day they abducted you. They took the drive from you then. When you disappeared, they thought you were out of the picture. But when you showed back up, they kept an eye on you. Our bosses thought going to Eurosatory might provide a different way of getting information. When you saw Jordan contact Nicolas, it confirmed our suspicions. At that point, the files were more important than ever, but we needed to wait until the time was right, again. Your photos in the warehouse gave us some of the evidence we needed. The drive gave us everything else."

"Any idea how I got to the hospital after I escaped?"

"From what we learned, after you escaped the van, you eventually made your way to the park on your own. You must have lost consciousness there, because a Good Samaritan found you and dropped you off at the hospital."

"That must be when I lost my phone. How did my car get back into my storage unit?"

"Your car?"

"Yeah, my car should have been at the HEB parking lot or towed away on the day they abducted me. I found it in my storage unit. How did it get there?"

"They must have been watching you and followed you to HEB. One of them stole the car from the parking lot and put it in there. They had to get rid of it and then sent the email to Brooke saying you quit."

"I had the key to the storage lock in a biometric lockbox." Then Sam remembered she kept a business card and spare key in her wallet. They took it when they took her license and credit card. All they had to do was go to the storage place, use the code on the card to access the inside area and the spare key to get into the unit. "Damn it! Rookie mistake. How stupid can I be?"

"I don't know. How stupid *can* you be?" Tom asked.

"Just forget it. Let's just say I learned a lesson. Actually, I learned a lot of lessons on this mission." Sam felt like an idiot. "What about the bar? How did they find me at the bar so fast?"

"The intern was the mole. He planted a tracker on you when he took the flash drives."

"Damn. What I can't believe is that a veteran was in charge of all this."

"Yeah."

Sam listened as Tom told her everything they'd found out.

"There's someone here to see you. She's been debriefed and signed a nondisclosure agreement, so you're clear to tell her anything you want." He reached out his hand to shake hers. "Congratulations, Sam. It was a pleasure working with you, even if you did pull a gun on me. They were right about you."

"Right about what?" Sam asked.

"You have the potential to be a great agent. I hope you get the chance, and maybe we'll work together again in the future." Tom turned and left the hospital room.

A few seconds later, the door opened and Sam was stunned to see Brooke enter the room.

"Brooke? What are you doing here?"

"What, an employer can't check up on her employee? Besides, we're friends, aren't we?"

"I don't know. Are we?" Sam asked, thinking Brooke might hate her.

"As far as I'm concerned, we are. You said you'd tell me later what was going on, and I think it's time."

"Have a seat." Sam told Brooke everything. She began with how they set up the incident in Venice and ended with the reason they went to the bar. Sam answered any questions that Brooke had. After all the deception, she was surprised that Brooke still wanted to be around her. But Brooke understood it was her job.

"So, you want to know who it is? Who our Khan Noonien Singh is?" Sam looked at Brooke and thought it should be her to tell her.

"Who? I don't know who that is."

"A bad guy in *Star Trek*. Forget it. Would you believe me if I told you it was Kevin?"

"Kevin? No."

"Yes, I'm sorry," Sam told her.

Brooke looked almost embarrassed. "I guess it shouldn't surprise me. He's still struggling with being injured. He blames everyone, especially the military and the companies that make and supply the armor."

Sam continued, "I found an email in a hidden folder with your files. It was from Kevin to a guy in the shipping department named Mark. He needed an incentive to give Jordan the shipping information. Kevin told him how KenzieCorp made his armor, and because it failed, he was going to make you pay. He lied and told Mark he was gathering evidence of your corruption and was going to turn you into the Feds. He also said he'd pay off Mark's gambling debts if he helped them by giving Jordan the information about when and where your armor was going. Jordan would call Nicolas and inform him. They'd intercept the shipments under the guise of Expédition Rouge and exchange some of the plates before they arrived at their final destinations. Then they'd sell the better plates on the black market. Katrina and I found the warehouse in Paris."

"The night she got shot."

"Yes," Sam confirmed. "I copied your files. I'm sorry."

"Yes, they told me. They said there was information on there that helped prove the link between KenzieCorp and Walker Logistics."

"Kevin was framing you, and it was in those files. Dr. Coventry helped prove those files were faked along with the other files I found."

"She's upgrading our system again, pro bono. But I'm going to keep her on retainer. She's really good."

Sam wanted to smile at the mention of Leia but didn't. "So I've been told. What does this mean for KenzieCorp?"

"Our reputation may take a hit, but I came up with a plan. For every vest sold, one will be donated to police departments nationwide. We're also tightening our security. The good thing is that we won't lose our contract. The switch was made once the military took control of the shipments. So, the military has some things to answer for as well. Sam, I want you to know that our plates are rigorously tested, and we would never sell or use shoddy material."

"I believe you," Sam said as she smiled at her.

"Kevin probably didn't know that we took up the military contract after he was hurt. We were only supplying police departments before that. I guess he just assumed his plate was one of ours. It wasn't."

"Wow."

"Sam, do you know if Kevin's father, Colonel Malone was involved?"

"No, he wasn't."

"Good. That's good."

Sam watched Brooke as she took in all the information. "Are you okay?"

"Yeah. I got over Kevin a long time ago. I'm just sorry he felt he had to go to such extreme measures to deal with his problems. Sam..."

"Go ahead," Sam tried to reassure her.

"Was any of it real?"

"Brooke, my mission started out with a lie. But after I got to know you, the hardest part of it was trying to keep my feelings in check and stay on track with the mission. I never meant to lead you on or wanted to hurt you. Our friendship was very real."

"You may not remember, but you told me that. It was right after your drink and before you hit the floor."

"I meant it... then and now."

"I know. I want to thank you for everything. I hope we can remain friends and keep in touch. Do you know what's next for you?" Brooke asked.

"I would love to keep in touch. As for what's next... I don't know. I guess some time off to let this hole in my side heal. Then it's up to the Air Force. I'm actually still on active duty. Part of my cover was saying I resigned. By the way, did they tell you the name of this operation?"

"Yes. Operation Running Brook. No 'e.' Cute. Did you come up with that?"

"Cute? I thought that was good," Sam said with a little disappointment. "It was a play on your name. You know the water and the mission."

"Yes, Sam, I get it." She rolled her eyes.

They laughed. Sam grimaced a bit, and they stopped.

"Well, I hope you heal quickly and can get back to work soon. If you ever need a job, head of security is yours for the taking. I'd better get going and let you rest. Take care of yourself, Sam." She reached forward gently to give Sam a hug. Sam held in a groan of pain as she returned the hug.

"I'll miss you. Stay safe, Brooke."

Sam watched as she turned and left the room.

SAM WAS in her hospital bed and was bored to death, but they wouldn't let her leave yet. She'd had surgery for the laceration to her kidney. She also hated having them stick her with needles. She hated needles and shots.

Picking up the phone, she called Leia.

"Hello."

"Hi. I thought I'd let you know I'm still in town. At least for a little bit."

"Can I see you? Or are you still working?" Leia asked. "That is if you want to see me."

"No, I'm not working. It's over and yes, I'd like to see you."

Leia let out a sigh of relief that Sam heard. "Great. I think it's my turn to buy dinner."

"Uh, you may have to bring it to me."

"I don't understand."

"I'm in the hospital."

"What? Are you all right? What happened?"

"I can't get into it, but I'm fine. So can we have pizza?"

Leia chuckled. "Sure. Send me the details of what kind of pizza and where you are."

"Okay. Thanks. See you soon." Sam smiled to herself

and sent the text. She was happy and thought back to that first night they spent together. Leia had just held her. That's all. It was as if she knew what Sam needed. Just an emotional connection and to feel safe. Leia had provided that for her. Sam was looking forward to getting to know her.

EPILOGUE

Two months later, Sam had finished her medical leave from the Air Force. She was healing fast and was eager to get back to work. The OSI, Air Force, and other agencies involved with her mission were pleased with what she had done. Her supervisor even wrote her up for the Commendation medal. They gave her a lot of options for what she could do next.

After taking time to consider everything, she opted to stay with the OSI permanently and go through training once she was able. She loved being in the Air Force and had learned so much from that first mission—she knew she'd only get better.

Sam would be working remotely at first, doing background checks for the detachment at Joint Base San Antonio. She would be on desk duty until she was medically cleared to go back to the field. Eventually, she would relocate from Austin to San Antonio. She was just waiting for her orders. She could have gone to headquarters in Washington, DC, but felt she wasn't quite ready. It would be a big step and a great opportunity, but she felt she needed to earn her way—that was something she and Brooke had in common. This operation wasn't enough, in her opinion, so she left the door open for that opportunity in the future. She felt confident she'd get there someday.

SAM STARTED the day like any other—a morning run and a video call with her supervisor. After the call, Sam went to get a glass of orange juice then sat down to check her emails. She was looking forward to this evening when Leia would come over. Things had been going well for them, and they were taking it slow. Getting to know each other.

The doorbell rang, and Sam walked over to answer it. When she opened the door, Katrina was standing there with her son in her arms.

"He let us go."

THE END
Stay tuned for Sam's next mission
Operation: Russian Roulette

ACKNOWLEDGMENTS

I'd like to thank my family and friends. Those who have supported and encouraged me in this journey, I really appreciate it.

To Candace Irvin. Thank you for responding to that first email I sent. After exchanging texts and phone calls, I designated you as my mentor. You took on the role and I am very grateful for your insight and help.

To Ivan Zanchetta. Thank you for a great cover.

ABOUT THE AUTHOR

KA BIGGERSTAFF is a former US Air Force veteran. Ms. Biggerstaff spent most of her military service overseas in Europe to include a deployment to Saudi Arabia in support of Operation Desert Storm. After nearly ten years in law enforcement (security police), she changed careers and taught special education. She currently volunteers with one of the largest Veterans Service Organizations serving on various committees at the local and national level. Ms. Biggerstaff lives in Texas with her husband, children, and dog.

www.KABiggerstaff.com

www.ingramcontent.com/pod-product-compliance
Lightning Source LLC
Chambersburg PA
CBHW020746310726

48969CB00002B/438